DATE DUE			

THE UNQUIET SLEEPER

THE UNQUIET SLEEPER

NORMAN RUSSELL

THORNDIKE
CHIVERS

This Large Print edition is published by Thorndike Press, Waterville, Maine, USA and by BBC Audiobooks Ltd, Bath, England.

Thorndike Press is an imprint of The Gale Group

Thorndike is a trademark and used herein under license.

The text of this Large Print edition is unabridged.

Other aspects of the book may vary from the original edition.

Set in 16 pt. Plantin.

LIBRARY OF CONGRESS CATALOGING-IN-PUBLICATION DATA

Russell, Norman.
  The unquiet sleeper / by Norman Russell.
    p. cm. — (Thorndike Press large print clean reads.)
  ISBN-13: 978-0-7862-9844-0 (alk. paper)
  ISBN-10: 0-7862-9844-8 (alk. paper)
  1. Psychotherapy patients — Fiction. 2. Americans — Crimes against —
Fiction. 3. Large type books. I. Title.
  PR6118.U87U57 2007
  823'.92—dc22   2007023617

BRITISH LIBRARY CATALOGUING-IN-PUBLICATION DATA AVAILABLE

Published in 2007 in the U.S. by arrangement with Robert Hale Limited.
Published in 2007 in the U.K. by arrangement with Robert Hale Limited.

U.K. Hardcover: 978 1 405 64068 8 (Chivers Large Print)
U.K. Softcover: 978 1 405 64069 5 (Camden Large Print)

Printed in the United States of America on permanent paper
10 9 8 7 6 5 4 3 2 1

CONTENTS

1
URSULA'S HOMECOMING

Detective Inspector Saul Jackson of the Warwickshire Constabulary swallowed the last
morsel of his steak and kidney pie, and
washed it down with a mouthful of Sherman's Gladiator mild ale. It was the afternoon of what had proved to be one of those
unexpectedly warm days that could surprise
you in early October – too warm, in fact, to
be travelling in hot, stuffy stopping-trains
halfway across the shire.

He'd been grateful for the hospitality afforded by the Berkeley Arms, where he was
sitting on an oak settle in one of the dining-
room windows of the bustling inn. It wasn't
often that business took him as far east as
Ashborne Hill, where he had caught a train
to Charnley, in order to collect the Special
Licence from Mr Joliffe, his family's solicitor. Of course, the law was the law, but it
seemed ridiculous to have to bother the
Archbishop of Canterbury if you wanted to

marry someone outside your own parish. Well, the licence was now in his pocket, and by late afternoon he would be back at work in Warwick Police Office.

Ashborne Hill, with its steep cobbled streets and its gaunt woollen mill, was a railway town, owing its very existence to the permanent way. The railway had reached it in 1838, providing vital links to Rugby and Coventry towards the north, and to the ancient country town of Charnley to the south. To get from Warwick, where Jackson lived, to Charnley, you had to change first at Coventry, and then at Ashborne, where you caught the stopping-train from Rugby.

The Berkeley Arms backed directly on to the platform of the railway station, and passengers were able to walk directly into the busy and spacious dining-room. It was divided into a number of little booths, each containing a table, and masked from its neighbours by wooden partitions fitted with frosted-glass panels. The dining-room had been quite full when Jackson had settled himself in the window, but then a train had arrived, and a crowd of customers had hastily gathered together their possessions, and left through the rear door.

It was then that Jackson became aware of a young man sitting in one of the booths across the room to his left. For the last half-hour he had been glancing at the clock, and comparing it uneasily with his watch. About twenty-five, Jackson reckoned, a good-looking lad with a fair moustache, and an eager way about him. He was clearly waiting for someone who hadn't turned up, and he looked like the kind of young man who would find waiting for anything beyond a few minutes to be sheer purgatory.

There was something odd about this young man. What was it? Ah, yes; his clothes. His suit was of foreign cut, and its cloth rather lighter than you'd find on the average Englishman. He wasn't Australian, because the accent was wrong. A Canadian, perhaps?

Jackson could not see who was sitting opposite the young man in the booth, because the frosted-glass partition blocked his view, but presently the person spoke, and Jackson heard the quiet tones of an elderly man, which came to him first as an indistinct murmur, to which the younger man eagerly responded.

'Why, sir,' Jackson heard him say, 'you're quite right. I am a bit worried, to tell the truth. I'm a stranger in this country, you see – I only arrived in Liverpool from America last Thursday. Robinson's my name: Elijah Robinson.' The young man extended an arm across the table, and Jackson saw the hand and wrist of the other man in the booth appear briefly as the two men shook hands.

The other man spoke again, and in response to whatever it was that he said, Elijah Robinson burst into speech.

'You see, sir,' he said, 'it's like this. My father, Jacob Robinson, of New York, died earlier this year, and in his will he left a legacy to an old friend of his from his young days, a man who lives in these parts. Father had been preparing to visit this old friend of his before he died, and in his will he left instructions that I was to come over to the old country, and visit this friend. I wrote to him, and he wrote back, saying that I should meet him here, at the Berkeley Arms, today at one o'clock, and it's already twenty to two – say, this is the second of October, isn't it? I haven't got the wrong day?'

Jackson heard the other man in the booth chuckle.

'It's certainly the second, Mr Robinson,' he said. 'But I wonder if your late father's friend has directed you to the wrong inn? The right day, you know, and the right time, but the wrong place? This is the Berkeley Arms. I wonder whether he meant the *Berk-*

shire Arms? What was this gentleman's name?'

'Skeffington. Alexander Skeffington, living at a place called Charnley —'

'Skeffington? Yes, the name's not unfamiliar to me. I think, you know, that your informant must have meant the Berkshire Arms. It's not very far from here. Let me accompany you there, now, and we'll see if my theory is right. If not – well, I suggest you take the next train to Charnley, and ask there.'

Young Mr Robinson was profuse in his thanks. He got to his feet, and retrieved a moss-green carpet bag from under the table. There was a sudden stab of light across the wooden floor, and a welcome burst of cool air, and Jackson realized that there must have been a door leading directly out of the booth on to the street. The door closed, and the two men were gone.

Poor young Mr Robinson! It was unpleasant to be lost at any time, but disagreeable in the extreme when you were lost in a foreign country. Detective Inspector Jackson retrieved a fat notebook from the pocket of his overcoat, untied the faded tape that held its covers closed, and leafed through its crowded pages until he came to the first blank sheet. He took a pencil from an inside

11

pocket, and made a few entries in his neat, copperplate hand.

Elijah Robinson of New York, son of Jacob Robinson, deceased. American, aged about 25. Height: 5 feet 8 ins approx. Fair moustache. Bound for Charnley, to see a man called Alexander Skeffington.

Jackson closed the notebook, secured it with the tape, and returned it to his pocket. Why on earth had he done that? Why record all those useless details? A policeman's habit, he supposed. All was grist to his mill.

The Warwick train would leave at twenty past two. Jackson began to sort through a handful of silver and copper that he had retrieved from his overcoat pocket. Another train had recently entered the station with a hiss of steam followed by the commotion of alighting passengers.

Presently, a young woman came into the dining-room from the station platform. She was a very handsome young lady, with regular features in an oval face crowned by a halo of raven hair. She was dressed neatly and fashionably in dove grey. She sat down at a vacant table, and ordered a cup of cof-fee from a passing waiter. A porter had deposited her hand luggage beside her.

Jackson had called for his bill, and was busy counting out the necessary amount from his handful of coins, but his eyes were surreptitiously fixed on the young woman in grey. There was something tense about her, as though she were attempting to constrain some kind of rising panic. She sipped her coffee when it was brought to her, and occasionally plucked nervously at her white cotton gloves.

As Jackson rose to leave the dining-room, he caught the young lady's eye, and was shocked to see the sudden leap of fear that crossed her face. She had turned pale, and her cup clattered on the saucer. What on earth could have disturbed her so?

At that moment, a well-dressed young man came into the room from another door. The young woman saw him, and her face was transformed with the joy of relief.

'Mr Staunton!' she cried. 'How very kind of you to meet me. You . . . you *are* here to meet me, aren't you?'

'Indeed I am, Miss Holt,' said the man called Staunton. 'Dr Holt's away today, and Kate asked me to meet you here and bring you back to Charnley. The next train's in a quarter of an hour. Never mind a porter: I'll carry these few things to the train.'

More names, thought Jackson. Miss Holt,

Mr Staunton, somebody called Kate. Miss Holt and Mr Staunton were evidently friends, but he had come to meet her at another's behest. Mr Staunton, then, would not be that young lady's confidant. What had been the matter with her? Why should he, Saul Jackson, cause her to go white with fear? Well, it was really none of his business.

Inspector Jackson paid his bill and made his way out on to the platform, where the Warwick train was waiting.

Ursula Holt threw open the window of her upstairs sitting-room at Abbey Lodge, and breathed in the fragrant air of the long walled garden. There was no sign of the riot of colour that had enlivened the sheltered flower beds when she had last seen them in May. Now, everything was tinged with the russet and gold of early October, and the stately beeches were dropping their yellow leaves on to the lawn.

Home at last! Home to her dear cousin Kate, and to her kindly though undemonstrative Uncle Matthew. Her room at Trinity Ford, Dr Meitner's establishment at Inchfield, had been light and well furnished, and its window, too, had looked out on to beautiful tree-fringed grounds. But the window at Trinity Ford had been barred, and at night, after the lamps had been extinguished, she had heard the discreet pushing home of the bolt on the outside of her bedroom door. That was why she had flung open the window now, to savour the delight of being once more a free woman.

She had loved Abbey Lodge ever since she had come to live there with her Uncle Matthew and his family when she was a girl of fourteen. It was a long, low medieval house, set at an angle to its neighbour, Providence House, the substantial Queen Anne residence of Mr Alexander Skeffington, a wealthy gentleman of means. Both houses incorporated a fragment of medieval cloister, all that remained above ground of Charnley Abbey, a Benedictine foundation destroyed at the Reformation.

Mr Skeffington, she knew, would be glad to see her. 'I will never believe that you did those dreadful things, Ursula,' he'd said, when the order for her detention had been confirmed early in May. He had clasped both her hands in his while he was talking, and had fixed her with his eagle glance, as though willing her to believe in her own innocence.

I must stop this reminiscing, thought Ursula. Kate will come upstairs in a moment, and she'll wonder why I haven't started to unpack.

Her valise, securely strapped and labelled, stood on the window seat where John, her uncle's coachman, had placed it. She had been careful to put her locked document case in the top drawer of the dressing-table in the adjoining bedroom.

She stood up, and looked at her image in the mirror over the fireplace. An oval face, regular features, dark-brown eyes to complement her raven hair – nothing there to suggest that she had just returned from incarceration in a lunatic asylum. She glanced at the reflection of her fashionable grey dress, adorned at the neck with white lace, and the Cairngorm brooch that had belonged to her mother. No, there was nothing there to suggest that she had cut a dog's throat, and flung its body down a well. . . .

Footfall on the winding stair told her that her cousin was coming to help her unpack. In a moment the door opened, and Katherine Holt came into the room. She looked as calm and reassuring as ever, and for once her shock of unruly ginger hair had evidently yielded to a vigorous onslaught from the brush! The sun glinted off her little round gold spectacles.

'Your trunk's on its way up from the railway, Polly,' she said. 'Oh, dear! You haven't even started to unpack your valise. Let me do it for you. You look tired out.'

Kate had called her Polly from the day when she'd arrived at the old Warwickshire country town of Charnley, declaring that Ursula was far too solemn a name for a girl of fourteen. At that time, Katherine Holt had been a grown-up young lady of twenty, embarking on what she hoped would be a successful literary career as a novelist. Even at that age, Kate had been able to sense the orphaned girl's insecurity and gaucheness. Being called Polly had made Ursula laugh, and her laughter had begun the intimate friendship of the two girls.

Ursula watched her cousin as she busied herself about the room. Kate's clear, gentle voice never grated on the ear, even on those occasions when she launched excitedly into speech, and seemed in danger of going on for ever! As always, she was wearing a plain black dress and a white apron, as though she silently acquiesced in the general belief that her vocation in life was to wait upon others.

'Father simply couldn't be here to meet you, Polly,' Kate was saying. 'He was detained on business in London, but his train will arrive at five o'clock, and John will be waiting with the carriage at the station. Oh, and Mr Skeffington's away, too, but he'll be back at six, and we're all to dine with him this evening at Providence House.'

'Oh, Kate, isn't that kind of him! He's always believed in me, just as you have. As for Uncle Matthew. . . . Do you think he's embarrassed at having me here again? Is that why he went to London?'

'Of course not,' said Kate indignantly. 'Really, Polly, what silly things you say! Father's delighted – and so is dear Mr Skeffington. I suppose you think *he's* run away to hide from you, too?'

Ursula laughed, and as she did so she was conscious of the fact that it was the first time that she had laughed – *really* laughed – since she had been taken away from Charnley in a closed coach on Friday, 5 May. It was now 2 October. It was high time that she confided some of her recent fears to her cousin.

'Kate,' she began, 'it was a tiresome journey from Inchfield today – nearly three hours in hot trains. When I arrived at Ashborne Hill to catch the train here to Charnley, I saw a man who frightened me so badly that I almost fainted —'

'A man? What man? Was this somebody on the platform?'

'No, no. It was in the Berkeley Arms. You

can walk off the platform directly into its rear dining-room. This man — He was sitting in one of the booths near the front of the room. He was about fifty, and was wearing a brown three-piece suit, with a gold watch chain and medals draped across his waistcoat. He looked like a prosperous farmer, or a well-to-do seed merchant.'

'And he frightened you? What did he say?'

'He didn't say anything. But as he stood up to pay his bill, his eye suddenly caught mine, and I saw that his expression was full of dangerous understanding. He was a stranger to me, Kate, but I felt that he knew all about me. I'd just ordered a cup of coffee, and I almost dropped it in alarm. I saw from his face that he'd seen that I was afraid of him. Who was that man, Kate? And what did he know?'

'Who was he?' said Kate, laughing. 'He was probably nothing more sinister than a stout farmer with a round face. And all he knew was about sowing and planting, and things like that. If you start thinking that every man who looks at you is conspiring against you – well, you can imagine what might happen. You're too sensitive. Try to forget about Trinity Ford.'

Why had Kate's normally humorous face assumed that look of grave concern? And why had there seemed to be a shadow of warning behind her words? They were all telling her to forget. Perhaps they knew, in a way that she did not, that some unutterable catastrophe would occur if she made no effort to follow their advice.

'And then Paul Staunton appeared on the scene to rescue you, as planned,' Kate continued. 'He told me yesterday that he'd be visiting Ashborne Hill on business today, and I told him that he had to make it his business to meet your train.'

'Yes, Kate, it was very thoughtful of you – and very gallant of him! He picked up my luggage and we crossed the track to the other platform. The man who looked like a farmer had gone by then – in the Warwick train, I think. And then. . . .'

Ursula stopped speaking, and swallowed hastily. She mustn't upset dear Kate. But how vile some men were!

'What's the matter now?' cried Kate. 'Don't you dare start weeping all over me, Polly. What's the matter?'

'Oh, it was two men standing on the platform. Two workmen with toolboxes, getting ready to enter the third-class carriage. I heard one of them whisper to the other, "There goes the Madwoman of Charnley, Bob. It's only six months since it happened, and they've let her loose again." And the other man said that they were too lax these days. "They should lock that kind up and throw away the key", he said. "You mark my words, it'll be something more than poor dumb beasts next time. People aren't safe in their beds, these days".'

'Ignorant brutes!' cried Kate stoutly. 'What do oafs like that know about anything? Forget it all, Polly. You're home again, now. Everything's unpacked and stowed away, and tea's nearly ready. I've set it out in Father's study, so that you can still look out at the garden. Come down whenever you're ready.'

Kate bustled out of the room, and Ursula listened to her quick footsteps descending the winding stair to the cool, stone-flagged lobby near the garden door.

Forget? How could she forget? How could she pretend that it had never happened? Ben – that had been the dog's name. Ben, the best of sheepdogs, who would come running to her from Farmer Laidlaw's stable yard, looking at her eagerly in hope of receiving a titbit, and, when it was forthcoming, frisking along at her side as she took him for a walk along the lane.

They had come looking for her at the first light of dawn, and had found her in the bluebell wood, sitting on the grass at the foot of the well, the bloodstained knife still in her hand.

No, it was not a knife. That was the wrong word. It had been a scalpel, one of a set of gleaming instruments kept in a mahogany case in Uncle Matthew's consulting-room. At her trial it had been urged by the defence that she had committed the deed 'whilst in a somnambulistic trance', and independent medical witnesses had been called to prove that 'sleepwalking, with concomitant amnesia', had plagued her all her life.

She had retained no memory of the deed, and that inability to remember had added a new dimension of horror to her predicament. For there had been an outbreak of attacks on sheep in outlying fields around Charnley for three months or so before she had been discovered, scalpel in hand, sitting on the grass near the well in the bluebell wood. Had she, Ursula Holt, been responsible for those hideous mutilations?

After her arrest, all such abominations had ceased. A few loyal friends persisted in their assertion that she was innocent, but neither the local people nor the law had agreed. She had been ordered to be detained for examination at The Trinity Ford Insane Asylum at Inchfield.

Dr Meitner, the superintendent, had conducted a series of rigorous tests over the six-month period of her incarceration, and his conclusion had been much the same as that of the medical witnesses at her trial. 'Somnambular amnesia' had been the root cause of her horrifying acts. Well, armed with that solemn medical opinion, she would try to forgive herself, and forget the whole business.

Ursula Holt heard her cousin calling to her up the winding stair. She left her sitting-room and went downstairs to tea.

When tea was over, Kate insisted on washing up alone, and Ursula went out into the rear garden of Abbey Lodge. The carpet of faded leaves, autumn's golden tribute, lay upon the lawns, and the shrubs in the neat borders still bore purple and yellow blossoms.

Ursula stepped off the lawn and on to the cracked paving stones of their section of the cloister that separated the two adjoining houses. Three decayed arches covered in ivy formed a kind of shelter for garden benches and boxes of tools. At one end there was an old doorway which had originally led into a part of Mr Skeffington's house that had been shut up and forgotten for fifty years or more. The door had always been locked, and as an imaginative fourteen-year-old she had woven fantasies about what lay behind it.

One day, when she had just turned fifteen, she had idly lifted the latch of that door, and, for the first time, it had opened. She'd just had time to tiptoe into a dark, musty vestibule thick with cobwebs when Mr Skeffington had appeared abruptly out of the darkness. Smiling jovially, he had ushered her out again into the cloister, and locked the mysterious door behind them.

'I should never venture through that door again, if I were you, Miss Ursula,' he'd said. 'That old place is the lair of monsters and dragons, which have a nasty habit of devouring inquisitive young ladies and Meddlesome Matties!'

He'd offered her his arm in the old-fashioned way that he had, and they'd walked round the garden, talking about her studies, and what she wanted to do with herself once she'd finished at Miss Liddell's Academy. He'd always been kind to her, and she'd not been frightened at being discovered on the wrong side of the cloister door. But that night she had dreamed of monsters and dragons.

She smiled at her recollection of nigh on

ten years earlier, and began to walk back to the house. Kate appeared at the back door.

'Polly, Father's back!' she cried, and disappeared into the house. Ursula hurried along the path to meet her Uncle Matthew for the first time since Trinity Ford had swallowed her up in May. Would he have changed towards her? Perhaps he had determined to accept her back at Abbey Lodge merely as an act of familial charity. She entered the house through the garden door, and walked timidly through the passage to the front hall.

Uncle Matthew was standing just inside the open door, waiting for John to bring in his luggage. As soon as he saw Ursula he dropped his hat and stick on the floor and opened his arms wide to receive her. There could be no mistaking the genuineness of his gesture, and Ursula submitted willingly to Dr Matthew Holt's bear-hug.

'My dear niece,' cried Ursula's uncle, 'how nice it is to see you again! There, now, I'll let you go. I'm crushing the breath out of you. Kate, what time's dinner? I'm starving. John! Ah, there you are. Be careful when you bring those cardboard boxes in from the carriage. They're flimsy things I bought for Miss Kate and Miss Ursula.'

Ursula stood back and looked at her

elderly uncle. He hadn't changed a bit. He still wore his favourite black frock coat and rusty old suit. His face was as unlined and as pink as ever. He bustled towards his study, followed by Kate, who had perfected the art of helping her father out of his coats while he was still on the move.

He had accepted her immediately and unconditionally, and would carry on as though nothing whatever had happened. She could hear him chattering away to Kate in his study, complaining to her about the press of traffic in Oxford Street, and the lack of facilities on modern trains. As always, he reverted to an ideal era which he called 'the seventies', explaining how wonderful the railways had been in those far-off halcyon days.

He had bought them both beautiful day dresses in subdued floral prints and with the new belts, from Liberty's. It always amazed both girls how unerring this old country physician was in interpreting the tastes of modern young ladies, and choosing presents for them with such good taste. They would wear their new dresses in his honour tomorrow. Meanwhile, it was time for them to change for the forthcoming dinner with Mr Skeffington at Providence House.

■ ■ ■ ■

Soon after six o'clock that evening, Saul Jackson walked up the steep cobbled road climbing up from Barrack Street Police Office in Warwick, and emerged abruptly into the green countryside. The road turned into an unmade winding track, along which a few substantial old dwellings standing in separate gardens formed the hamlet of Meadow Cross.

Jackson opened the door of his seventeenth-century cottage and stooped a little as he entered the dim living-room. He noted that his breakfast things had been washed and returned to the dresser, and knew that Sarah had come to tidy up for him after he had left for Charnley. She had always offered him kindly and unobtrusive help ever since he had come to live in Meadow Cross Lane.

He opened the rear door of the living-room, removed his heavy serge jacket, and sat down in his cane-backed chair near the fire. He had placed the Special Licence on the table for Sarah to see. They'd be married without fuss on 28 October, St Simon and St Jude's Day, by the Reverend Mr Goodheart of Ashgate St Lawrence, whose kindness and cheerful optimism had helped to wrest him from an insidious depression that had gripped him at the time of the Dried-Up Man affair. Could that really have been eighteen months ago?

He looked up as Sarah Brown emerged from the trees of the small orchard that separated his dwelling from Brown's Croft, her cottage further along Meadow Cross Lane. She was wearing her favourite dark-green dress which complemented her rich brown hair and fair skin. She was drying her hands on a kitchen towel.

'I saw you moving about in here, Saul,' she said as she stepped timidly over the back step and into the living-room. Would that timidity, that delicacy about intruding, continue after they were wed?

'Did you get the licence?' she asked.

'It's there on the table, Sarah,' said Jackson. He had risen when Sarah had appeared, but now he resumed his seat at the fireside. 'All we have to do is present it to Mr Goodheart.' He watched her as she sat at the table, and took the legal document from its envelope. He saw her smile as she began reading.

' "Edward, by Divine Providence Lord Archbishop of Canterbury, Primate of All England, and Metropolitan" – goodness me,

Saul, how grand it all sounds!'

'Well, it *is* grand,' said Jackson, stoutly. 'As far as I'm concerned, it's the grandest thing that'll happen this year. Or any other year, for that matter.'

Sarah smiled rather absently. She turned to the end of the document, and said, half to herself, 'Edward Cantuar. I suppose there's some special reason why Dr Benson calls himself that.' She returned the document to its envelope, and glanced round the room. Then she left the table, and sat down opposite Jackson at the fire.

'I've carefully considered what you suggested, Saul,' she said, 'but I've quite made up my mind. I want us to live here, in your house. It's quite large enough for two. Besides, it holds no sad memories for you – Charlotte and the baby never lived here.'

Jackson saw her glance briefly at the ebony-framed photograph standing in the centre of the gnarled black beam that served as a mantelpiece. It showed a woman in her late twenties, with an oval face framed by curling black hair. Her large, frank eyes seemed to look out of the photograph with fearless confidence. No, Charlotte had never lived here.

'But what about Brown's Croft? This place of mine is rented from Lord Brooke, but

your cottage is your own freehold property
—'

'Maybe so, Saul, but it's haunted by the memory of Tom and the children. I want to be here, with you, looking down the lane towards Warwick town from the front step. We can put a tenant into Brown's Croft, and draw rent from it. We'll be quite well-to-do. I'd best be getting back, now. I've a steak and kidney pie finishing nicely in the range oven. I don't want it to burn.'

Saul Jackson looked at Sarah, who had risen from the chair at his fireside, and stood with her hand on the latch of the back door. Would she be able to cope with his devotion to duty?

'We'll talk about the properties later, Sarah,' he said. 'At the moment, though, I'm worried that you'll find it a sore burden being married to a man who's under orders. When I'm assigned to a case, or when I come across something suspicious, I've got to pursue the business to the end. It's a question of duty, you see.'

Sarah put a hand on his arm, as though to stem the flow of words.

'I was wondering when you were going to talk about the call of duty, Saul,' she said. 'Well, I'm marrying Inspector Jackson, the policeman, and the call of duty's part of the marriage settlement. You've got to understand, Saul, that I don't want you to be any different from what you are, and I don't want you to feel constrained by a wife. I must get back now, if that pie's not going to burn. Come across about seven, and we'll have dinner together. There's an apple pie, too.'

Jackson stood at the back door and watched Sarah Brown as she hurried across the grass and into the little orchard. Sarah and he had both lost a family. In 1877, on 5 April, Jackson's twenty-nine-year-old wife, Charlotte, had perished in a fire at Paul's Copse. Their infant daughter, Rebecca, had died in the same fire. Sarah had lost her husband and her three little boys in the terrible outbreak of cholera at Sedley Vale in 1880.

It was almost inevitable that they should have been thrown together, but there was more to their relationship than a commonly shared grief. He and Sarah seemed to complement each other, to understand each other's moods, and to anticipate each other's needs. He had proposed to her a fortnight earlier, and he remembered how offhand he'd seemed in doing so, and the matter-of-fact way in which she had accepted him. Well, on Simon and Jude's Day, they'd become man and wife in a simple ceremony at St Lawrence's, Ashgate. Nothing elaborate or prolonged. Neither of them wanted any fuss.

2
DREAMS OF A SOMNAMBULE

The Holts set off for dinner with Mr Skeffington at half past six, trooping across the front garden of Abbey Lodge and passing through a little wicket gate that brought them to the front of Providence House. The three-storeyed mansion was covered in luxuriant Virginia creeper, which glowed a rich, deep red in the rays of the declining sun. The tall, rectangular windows looked as though they had been freshly painted, and the creeper had been skilfully cut back from the white sashes.

Mr Skeffington had anticipated both his butler and the footman, and had opened the door to his guests himself. He shook hands rather formally with Ursula, and kissed Kate on the cheek. Alexander Skeffington dressed well, and employed a valet to ensure that every detail of his wardrobe was in order. He was wearing an evening suit of old-fashioned cut, with the type of frilled dress shirt that had long gone out of fashion, but the garments were new, the suit cut to his taste and order by a compliant tailor, and the shirts made to echo his preferred style.

Mr Skeffington's house had been built in 1709, with a now closed-up extension added in the 1780s. It was exquisitely furnished, and the painted panels of the graceful rooms were embellished with gilded designs of fruit and musical instruments. Chandeliers covered with dim old brilliants hung from the ceilings of the principal rooms. Providence House revealed itself in every detail as the home of a very wealthy man.

During dinner, which was served to them by the butler, the footman and the house parlour maid, Mr Skeffington made a little speech of welcome to celebrate Ursula's return, and a toast was drunk in her honour. After the servants had left the dining-room, they talked of everyday matters, and the two elderly men became engrossed in a discussion of the wisdom or otherwise of investing in the current issue of Treasury stock. Ursula was relieved the see that she was being treated as though nothing untoward had ever happened to disturb the mundane pleasures of their lives.

Then it was time to adjourn to what Mr Skeffington called the saloon, where coffee had been set out ready for them. A demure little maidservant poured out their coffee, treated her master to a perfunctory bob, and left the room.

'I hope you like Turkish coffee,' said Mr Skeffington. 'What about you, Ursula? If you don't like it, I'll get them to brew some Brazilian.'

His voice was powerful and well articulated, with just a trace of the Australian accent that betrayed his origin.

'Turkish will do very well, thank you, Mr Skeffington,' Ursula replied. What an impressive man he was! His grey hair was thinning, but that seemed only to emphasize the magnificence of his great brow, from beneath which two keen eagle eyes peered out to make their estimate of the world and its inhabitants. He was a kindly man, famous for his charity, but those who had chosen to cross him in his desires had usually rued the day that they had done so.

'Now, Kate,' said Skeffington, 'how is your latest novel progressing? And when are you going to have one published? You've done six, to my knowledge, but so far the publishers haven't succumbed. I was hoping that you'd be the next Mrs Henry Wood.'

'Maybe I will be, sir, one day,' Kate replied, laughing. 'At the moment, though, my heroine is torn between two suitors, one of them being handsome but poor, and the other one ugly but rich. She can't make up her mind which to choose. And neither can I!'

'I know which one I'd choose,' offered Kate's father, chuckling to himself. 'A young lady can never be without too much money.'

'You lack the romantic touch, Holt,' said their host. 'Girls in novels always marry for love, you know. Still, Kate, you keep at it. Determination will pay off in the end. Meanwhile, we'll turn from literature to music. Ursula hasn't heard me playing for months.'

Mr Skeffington rose from his chair, and sat at the keyboard of an old spinet, which had been in the house since it had been built. For such a forceful, intimidating man, it had always surprised Ursula that he should be such a delicately accomplished keyboard artist. He played them an elegant piece by Scarlatti, and the quiet but bell-like tones of the spinet filled the room.

Ursula suddenly realized that he was playing specifically for *her,* and that his performance expressed in sound what, so far, he had forborne to express in words. It was a celebration of the return to normality, and to the possibility of resuming a life free from the pain and burden of guilt.

Ursula was conscious of her Uncle Matthew's gaze fixed on her as she listened to Mr Skeffington's playing. She glanced in his direction, and with a sinking heart she saw in her uncle's speculative gaze his belief that she had indeed committed those awful deeds. He had welcomed her back into his family unconditionally, but she could see that he was quite convinced of her guilt as a shedder of innocent blood. Well, maybe he was right. After all, he was a doctor, and no doubt knew about these things.

Later, as they left the saloon to assemble in the entrance hall prior to returning to Abbey Lodge, Mr Skeffington detained Ursula on the threshold. As of old, he took both her hands in his, and fixed upon her a look that seemed to be compounded of pity and fear. His hands shook slightly, and his whole frame suggested a sudden onset of unease.

'Ursula,' he said in a low voice, 'I want you to remember that you are still only twenty-four, young enough to endure and then survive this horrible business. The nightmare is over! Forget it all, do you hear?

I still maintain that you were completely innocent of those crimes – I think I believe in
your innocence more than you do yourself!
As for your uncle – well, time will tell. But
if you can't forget it all, then you must
pretend that it never happened. That would
be much the better way.'

Still holding her hands in his, he kissed
her lightly on the cheek. A moment later,
she had joined the others, and the party
from Abbey Lodge stepped out into the
chilly air of the October evening.

As soon as his visitors had left, Alexander
Skeffington withdrew to his study, and sat
down in a great carved chair drawn up to a
roll-top desk. The room was lit with candles
placed in silver candelabra, and the gentle
light gave the place a more intimate and
enclosed air than was to be found in the
gas-lit public rooms of the house.

What ghosts haunted this chamber! All
these curios, the glass cases displaying tropi-
cal birds, the mineral specimens in the
cabinets – but above all, the faded framed
photographs of life in Australia, over forty
years ago! There was the picture of Mel-
bourne in 1850, with a crowd of folk wel-
coming a long-forgotten dignitary to the
town. And there, among the figures in the

crowd, was himself, younger, leaner, looking out eagerly at the world of opportunity that was Australia in the '50s. Of course, he never pointed out that figure to visitors, whenever he handed down that photograph as a talking-point. How could he? He was a rich and prosperous Englishman now, twice mayor of Charnley, and with only the faintest lingering trace of his native accent.

Poor Ursula! She had looked well and blooming at dinner, and he had been curiously moved to see her again after her six months' incarceration in the asylum. She had been to all intents and purposes imprisoned in that place for crimes that she had not committed. What was to become of her?

Skeffington stirred as the door opened quietly, and his butler came into the room. He was carrying a tray on which reposed a decanter of whisky and two glasses.

'Ah, Miles, put that down here, will you? I'm expecting Mr Guy Fitzgerald at around ten o'clock. When he arrives, show him straight in here. I wonder. . . . It might be courteous to offer him a bed for the night. Would that be possible?'

'Certainly, sir. I'll see to that straight away. Will there be anything else?'

'I don't think so. The dinner went well, did it not?'

'Yes, sir. It was so nice to see Miss Ursula Holt at liberty once again.'

'Yes, yes, it was. That will do, now, I think.'

When Miles had left the room, Skeffington rummaged through the letters in the pigeon-holes of his desk until he had found one particular letter, which he spread out in front of him. He regarded it with something approaching gloomy distaste.

In God's name, why had old Jacob Robinson decided to renew his acquaintance after nearly half a century? He had sent the letter early in January, proposing himself for a visit to England later in the year. Had Jacob turned sentimental in his own age? He himself had been quite content to live an obscure but worthy life in Charnley, letting the passing years add lustre to his reputation, and further augmentations to his great wealth. Why hadn't Jacob Robinson contented himself with the cosmopolitan pleasures of New York?

Alexander Skeffington shuddered, and the shudder was accompanied by a sigh like that of a soul in pain. What was to become of him? What would happen, now, to poor Ursula Holt? What — ?

'Mr Fitzgerald, sir.'

Miles, silent-footed as ever, had entered the room before Skeffington had had time to collect his wits. He thrust the letter back into its pigeon-hole, stood up, and surveyed his guest. A young man, broad-shouldered, and with a complexion bronzed by work in the open air, Guy Fitzgerald, he thought, was typical of his class. He was a gentleman farmer, and master of 400 acres of land. He dressed plainly but well, and his vigorous step as he advanced into the room spoke of his youthful confidence.

'I hope that you'll forgive this late visit, Mr Skeffington,' Guy Fitzgerald began. The older man brushed the apology aside.

'Not at all, it's my fault for being so confoundedly busy all the time. I was away from Charnley all day, and had guests to entertain this evening. But sit down, won't you? Let me pour you a glass of whisky. Now, let us get down to business. You wrote to say that you were considering making me an offer for Miller's Grange.'

'That is so, sir. As you know, I live within sight of it, and I hope you won't take offence if I say that the old place is getting more and more dilapidated every day.'

Skeffington laughed. He had always liked this young man's naïve directness.

'So you're trying to make me give you a knock-down price? No, there, don't blush, for goodness' sake! I'm only teasing. I expect you know that I was forced to buy that old ruin because it was part and parcel of a single purchase? In order to gain possession of this place – Providence House – I had to take Miller's Grange thrown in, so to speak. What do you want it for?'

'Well, sir, although the farmhouse is big enough for Mother and me, I may want to marry one of these days, and Miller's Grange would make an ideal house to live in with a wife and some children. Of course, it needs a lot doing to it —'

'So you keep telling me. How much will you give me, always supposing that I want to sell it? Do you want to buy the land as well, or just lease that from me?'

'I can give you three hundred pounds cash for the house. Four hundred if I must.'

'Hm. . . . Well, that's not too bad. It's certainly a basis for negotiation. If you want the land, that will cost you nine hundred. I can't go below that price, but I can put you in the way of reputable credit if you wanted to borrow.'

Guy contrived to smile, but his host could see the dejection in the set of the young man's shoulders. He would like to drop the price, but his own reputation as a businessman would suffer if he did. There were other possibilities, though. Fitzgerald could surrender a parcel of his least profitable acreage to make up the price. But half past ten in the evening was not the time to open negotiations.

'I'll tell you what, Mr Fitzgerald,' said Skeffington, 'I can see other ways in which we two could come to an agreement over Miller's Grange, but this is not the time for us to talk. Why not stay the night? You'd be very welcome. And then, tomorrow morning, I'll send for my land agent, and between us we'll look at possibilities. You'll stay? Excellent. Let me ring for Miles. He'll lay you out some night attire and so on. Until the morning!'

When Miles had left the study with Guy Fitzgerald, Skeffington returned to his seat at the desk. He poured himself another glass of whisky, and drank it with a kind of slow deliberation. His hooded grey eyes seemed to be staring into space, but they were in reality seeing images of the events of the past day.

What was to become of Ursula? She had been innocent of the crimes for which she had been shut up in the asylum, of that he was quite certain. But would others ever believe that? Her own uncle was convinced of her guilt, and he was not the only one. Why did these tears come unbidden, and so often? There was nothing that he could do to save her. It seemed as though she had been destined from birth to sacrifice herself to save others. Poor, doomed Ursula Holt.

Once in her bedroom at Abbey Lodge, Ursula lit the oil lamp standing on the bedside table, and extinguished the chamber candle. It had been a long, exhausting day, and this was to be her first night at home. All through the dinner with Mr Skeffington at Providence House, she had been longing for this moment, when she could sleep in her own bed, and in a room where the door was not discreetly bolted on the outside.

But was that necessarily a good thing? She had been a sleepwalker since childhood, awaking cold and frightened in places that she couldn't recognize, and stumbling back guiltily through dark passages inhabited by fearful creatures and chattering voices until she had regained the sanctuary of her bed. Would she walk tonight?

Ursula removed her document case from the top drawer of her dressing-table, where she had placed it earlier in the day. She unlocked it with a key that hung around her neck on a slender chain, and opened it. There were three books in the case, one of which was a slim volume bound in red morocco leather. Dr Meitner had given her this book, urging her to persevere in reading it. Knowledge, he said, would help to cast out fear. What would Uncle Matthew and Kate think of such a volume?

The Somnambule. A Study of Certain Morbid Amnesiac Spasms. By Dr Karl Gustav Altmann, Intendant of the Maria Hospital, Vienna.

She lay on the bed, and turned the pages of the book. Did knowledge really cast out fear? Whenever she read the observations of Dr Karl Gustav Altmann on sleepwalkers, or *somnambules,* as he termed them, she trembled with fright, and would sometimes close the book and throw it from her in something approaching panic.

The involuntary somnambule will frequently exhibit marked changes of character, so that the passive and compliant subject will exhibit all the arrogance of a truculent personality, and frequently resort to acts of unwonted violence. The subject will sometimes recall such intervals of transmuted personality, but on most occasions he will experience the amnesia of substitution, which I characterize by the term cryptamnesia.

Dr Altmann, a young Austrian alienist who was rapidly acquiring a European reputation, wrote of 'acts of unwonted violence'. Well, according to expert witnesses, she, Ursula Holt, had indulged in such violence, wantonly slaughtering the poor sheepdog Ben, and perhaps, too, viciously mutilating sheep in the fields around Charnley.

Everyone told her to forget, but despite her bouts of fear and panic, she wanted to learn more about these frightening mental states, wanted to understand what Dr Altmann had meant by 'cryptamnesia'. Was it the power to suppress, and so forget, all memory of unpalatable deeds? If so, what other enormities may she have committed?

Dr Meitner had told her of his conviction that she would never commit such offences again. Like the others, he had advised her to forget. 'With respect to your own experiences,' he had said on bidding her farewell that very morning, 'I want you to leave Trinity Ford with an unclouded mind. Put these things aside, and start your life afresh.'

Easy enough to give such advice. . . . How

could she forget? How tired she was! It had been a long, exhausting day, bringing with it the delights of release from the asylum and reunion with Kate and Uncle Matthew, and the irrational fear of the man at Ashborne Hill, the man who looked like a farmer. . . . Who was he? And what did he know? Dr Altmann's book slipped off the bed on to the floor. Despite a determination to stay awake for a while, Ursula's eyelids began to flicker and close. . . .

She was in a glittering and gilded ballroom, peopled with men and women in eighteenth-century costume. Chandeliers hung from the high ceiling, and she could smell the aroma of burning candle wax. The people danced to a slow and stately saraband, and behind them she could glimpse the white-wigged members of a chamber orchestra.

One of the dancers, a handsome man in his thirties, saw her, smiled, and beckoned to her. She crossed the ballroom until she stood beside him. He said something, but his words were garbled and indistinct. He beckoned towards an archway at the end of the room, which gave entrance to an alcove containing a finely carved wooden chest. The handsome man pointed to it and, she realized with terror, he was willing her to lift the lid. . . .

Ursula awoke with a start, her heart beating furiously. The dreams, then, had not ceased! She had told Dr Meitner about the phantom ballroom, and how it presented itself to her sleeping mind in subtly different guises. He had seemed noncommittal, and had assured her that the dream would ultimately disappear. Until that moment she had nurtured the hope that he had been right, and that she had left that particular dream behind her at Trinity Ford Insane Asylum. That carved chest. . . . She had told Dr Meitner that if ever she lifted the lid of that chest in one of her recurrent dreams, she would die. Morbid amnesiac spasms. Cryptamnesia. Was it safe for her – safe for others – to live unsupervised and unsecured in unlocked rooms?

It was after twelve, and the lamp was burning low. She undressed, and searched through the drawers of the dressing-table for her nightgown. Kate would have put it away for her when she'd unpacked her things. She arranged everything very neatly, but nothing was in its right place!

Would Uncle Matthew have a bad night? Perhaps he'd stay awake in case she walked again? Perhaps he was secretly afraid of her?

Ah! Here was her nightdress, nestling between sheets of tissue paper in the bottom drawer. As she lifted it up, she bit back a scream. Lying underneath it, half hidden by a piece of torn sheet, was a pair of long white evening gloves, caked in blood that had not yet completely dried.

Guy Fitzgerald left Providence House the next morning, and made his way across the lawns to the public road. Old Skeffington had made a few very positive proposals at breakfast, and had promised to send him copies of the various leases connected with Miller's Grange. His suggestion of an exchange of unprofitable land for dilapidated property had been ingenious, but it needed a certain amount of sober thought. He would talk to Mother about it when he got back to the farm.

It was a bright, warm morning, with plenty of time for a fellow to look about him. A young lady in a patterned frock and a straw boater was walking in the garden of the house next to old Skeffington's, a dark-haired young lady with an oval face. She was carrying a gardening basket, and was making a show of pruning a rose tree. Who on earth could she be? Who lived in that old house adjoining Skeffington's?

'Good morning, miss!' cried Guy, doffing his hat. 'Marvellous weather for the time of year.'

It was a sufficiently trite greeting, but its effect on the young lady was alarming, to say the least. She shied nervously, like a colt, and the basket fell from her hand. What had he said to make her turn so pale? And now she was blushing!

'You have the advantage of me, sir,' said the young lady. 'But you are right: it is splendid weather for the time of the year.'

'My name's Guy Fitzgerald,' said Guy. 'I've been visiting your neighbour, Mr Skeffington. I don't usually come as far as Charnley. I live miles away, deep in the country. To whom have I the pleasure of speaking?'

Whatever made him speak in that fatuous way? It wasn't really like him at all. He had a shrewd suspicion that the nameless young lady would remain in his thoughts for a long time.

'Bolton, Miss Bolton. I'm an Australian relative of Mr Skeffington's. I must go in, now.'

Ursula Holt watched enchanted as Guy Fitzgerald bowed rather stiffly, and continued on his way. What a wonderful young man! His dark hair fell in curls over his forehead, and he looked as though he had the strength of ten, like the man in the poem. . . .

There was something else about him, too. He was a sudden visitant from a world outside the limits of her own confined existence. He had seemed for a brief moment to bring a refreshing breeze to blow away the cobwebs of fear and suspicion that always attempted to entrap her. Guy Fitzgerald. . . . Perhaps Uncle Matthew knew who he was?

Why had she told him that her name was Bolton? It was all part of her embracing fear – fear of exposure to hatred and ridicule for what she was supposed to have done. Mr Skeffington had advised her never to reveal too much of her history to strangers. 'If any stranger asks you your name,' he said, 'you can tell him that you're a Miss Bolton from Australia, and one of my distant relatives. It sounds rather silly and dramatic, but it could be the saving of you, Ursula.'

She supposed that she would never see that young man again, but she would treasure his memory. Guy Fitzgerald had seemed to be beckoning her across the threshold of her mental prison to a freer, saner kind of life.

Silly fantasy! She would never see him

again. Besides, no young man would want to cultivate the company of a girl who found bloodstained gloves in her drawer, and could not remember how they got there.

She found Uncle Matthew in his consulting-room, where he was immersed in *The Times.* When she asked him about Guy Fitzgerald he threw the paper down on the hearth, and sighed with what was evidently embarrassed vexation.

'Guy Fitzgerald? Yes, I know him, or, at least, know of him. So he's been to visit Skeffington? Well, it's none of our business why he did that, is it?'

'But who is he, Uncle Matthew? He passed the time of day to me very civilly. I can't think why you don't like him.'

'Like him? I've nothing against him at all, Ursula. It's just that – well, he's the owner of Laidlaw's Farm, where all the unpleasantness began. Ben the sheepdog, and so forth. Perhaps young Fitzgerald was visiting Skeffington on some farming business. If I were you, my dear, I'd forget this young man. He's bound up with painful memories – memories that we all want you to forget.'

3
MURDER BY SCALPEL

Detective Inspector Saul Jackson of the Warwickshire Constabulary glanced up at the
big railway clock hanging on the wall of the
back room in Barrack Street Police Office.
Ten past eight. Sergeant Bottomley would
be in from his home at Thornton Heath in
a quarter of an hour. He looked once more
at the telegraph message that had come for
him only minutes earlier.

Jackson, Warwick Police Office. Man
ascertained by me to be one Elijah Robinson, a foreigner, found murdered at Ashborne Hill. Immediate help requested. Potter.

Jackson had met old Sergeant Potter once
or twice in connection with the activities of
a persistent gang of poachers plying their
nefarious trade in the Charnley area. Potter
was a dependable man, who ran police af-

fairs in Ashborne Hill with the aid of two young constables. He was accountable to an inspector in Charnley, but the post was vacant, and a new man not expected until December.

Jackson looked out of the window as the echo of a horse's hoofs came to him from the alley leading to the stables. A large, homely-looking man with a flushed red face and a flapping yellow overcoat came into sight, sitting high on a grey pony. Sergeant Bottomley looked clumsy and awkward, but he slid down from his mount with all the skill of an experienced horseman. Presently a clattering of boots in the passage announced the sergeant's arrival in the office.

'Sergeant,' asked Inspector Jackson while Bottomley was still struggling out of his coat, 'do you believe in coincidence? Or are coincidences really acts of Providence?'

The big shambling man smiled vaguely at his superior, and sat down in a Windsor chair placed at the side of the big working table.

'In a word, sir,' he said, 'yes and no, as the case may be.'

'Thank you, Sergeant,' said Jackson. 'That's made the matter very clear to me. Now sit there quietly for a moment and listen while I tell you about my particular coincidence. It's twenty past eight, and you and I are going on a little railway journey at nine. Are you listening?'

'Yes, sir.'

'As you know, I travelled down to Charnley yesterday, to collect the Archbishop's Special Licence from our family solicitor. Everything went according to Cocker, and I'd taken a train from Charnley to Ashborne Hill, where I could catch a connection to Coventry. I was having a bite to eat in the dining-room of the Berkeley Arms, which backs directly on to the platform of the railway station. It had been quite full when I got there, but after a while a train arrived, and a whole crowd of customers gathered their things together and left through the rear door. Are you with me, so far?'

'Yes, sir. And about this coincidence —'

'Wait a bit, Sergeant, I'm coming to that. As I was sitting there, I noticed a restless young man who, for the last half-hour, had been glancing at the clock, and comparing it with his watch. He was clearly waiting impatiently for someone who hadn't turned up.'

'Like waiting for the end of a long story,' muttered Sergeant Bottomley.

'Constrain yourself, will you? There's a point to all this, Sergeant, as you'll see in a minute. I couldn't see who was sitting opposite this young man in the booth, because a frosted-glass partition blocked my view, but whoever it was entered into conversation with the young man, who said that his name was Elijah Robinson, and that he had come all the way from America to visit a friend of his late father. This friend had appointed a meeting there at the Berkeley Arms, but had not arrived. Elijah wondered whether he'd mistaken the date.'

'What happened next, sir?'

'The elderly man – the man I couldn't see because of the glass partition – suggested that Elijah Robinson was right about the date, but that he had mistaken the name of the inn, and that it was the Berkshire Arms, not the Berkeley Arms, where the meeting was to have taken place. The two men got up, and left the dining-room by a door that was out of my line of view.'

'And this friend, sir, the friend of the young man's father: was his name mentioned?'

'It was. Apparently it was Alexander Skeffington, a resident of Charnley. I've never heard of him, but that's not surprising as I don't know Charnley well. And that's the end of the story.'

Sergeant Bottomley moved on his uncomfortable chair, and gave vent to a moist cough.

'A very interesting story, sir,' he said, 'beautifully told. But I don't quite see where "coincidence" comes into it.'

'Read that, Sergeant,' Jackson replied, handing Bottomley the telegram that he had received earlier that morning. 'There's a young man freshly murdered in Ashborne Hill, a young man called Elijah Robinson, according to Sergeant Potter. Something told me to record that conversation between him and the elderly man, and I'm glad that I did. It's the same man, Sergeant, it must be. That's why I told you the whole story, and that's why you and I are going down to Ashborne Hill on the nine o'clock train.'

Saul Jackson stepped down on to the platform at Ashborne Hill Station, followed closely by Sergeant Bottomley. Jackson thought to himself: Sarah will have to get used to this kind of thing, once she stops being Mrs Brown and becomes Mrs Jackson. A policeman couldn't walk away from an investigation just because he had secured a Special Marriage Licence from the Archbishop of Canterbury.

They passed through the ticket barrier, and along a narrow alley that brought them out to the road in front of the Berkeley Arms. An elderly sergeant saluted, and walked ponderously towards them across the cobbled path. He looks relieved to see us, Jackson thought. He'll never have had to cope with murder before.

'Mr Jackson, sir,' said Sergeant Potter without preamble, 'I've left the body lying where I found it, just after seven o'clock this morning. I've a constable standing guard. I removed this pocket book from the man's inner pocket, and found out his name from looking at some of the papers in it. It was also written on a label sewn into the lining of his coat.'

The sergeant handed a leather wallet to Jackson, while glancing quizzically at Bottomley. Inspector Jackson answered the man's unspoken question.

'This is Detective Sergeant Bottomley,' he said. The elderly sergeant nodded in a friendly fashion to Bottomley, and then turned his attention once more to the inspector.

'I'll conduct you to the body now, sir, if you're agreeable.'

They followed Sergeant Potter along a winding street of slate-grey houses interspersed with small shops. There were few people about, though one or two women standing at their front doors eyed them curiously. At the top of the street the sergeant turned abruptly to the left, and the two detectives found themselves walking along a narrow shale path, shaded by a line of oaks rising from behind a wall of rustic brick. Small pools of yellow water pitted the path here and there, relics of a cloudburst some days earlier.

The right-hand side of the path was bounded by the iron railings of a churchyard. There was a wicket gate halfway along the path, which emitted a squeal of rusty protest as Sergeant Potter pushed it open.

'In here, sir,' he said.

In contrast to the shady path, the churchyard was bathed in sunshine. Jackson glanced briefly at the little church adjoining it, noting that it must have predated the railway town of Ashborne by several hundred years. Old, lichen-covered gravestones peered drunkenly above the long grass, which was already strewn with early autumn leaves.

'It's over here, sir!' Sergeant Potter's voice held a hint of reproach. What was Inspector Jackson doing, just standing there, admiring the view? And his sergeant, too. There was a murdered man to examine.

Jackson stood where he was, looking

around the churchyard. Sergeant Potter, he saw, had joined a uniformed constable at a spot some way off, where the railings ended at the wall of a stone shed. He could see their brass buttons gleaming in the sun as they stood uncertainly, waiting for him to join them.

To Jackson's right, another line of oaks arose, and beyond them he could glimpse the glittering windows of what was evidently a woollen mill. Quite a decent sort of place for a murder, Jackson thought. Ahead of him, the churchyard sloped downwards towards a flight of sandstone steps, at the bottom of which stood what was evidently a public house. It was a modern redbrick building, facing an unseen road, and presenting its rear premises to the churchyard. Jackson walked thoughtfully over to where Sergeant Potter was waiting.

'Sergeant,' he asked, 'what's the name of that inn at the bottom of the steps?'

'The *inn?* Aren't you going to look at the *body,* sir? It's just here, in this little hollow.'

Jackson treated the old sergeant to a rather weary smile.

'Oh, yes, Sergeant,' he said, 'I'll be looking at the body, but you see, I'm a detective officer, so the way I work is a bit different from the way *you* work. Well, you know that, because you and I have worked together before. "My ways are not your ways; neither are your ways *my* ways". So before I put your mind at rest by coming to look at the body, answer my question. Just to please me, you know. To humour me, as it were. What's the name of that inn at the bottom of the steps?'

'Sir, it's called The Grapes. It's a free house, sir, not one of Sherman's pubs.'

'Ah! The Grapes. I don't much like the sound of that. . . . Now, let me see the body.'

In a grassy hollow hidden from the path Jackson saw the dead body of Elijah Robinson. He lay on his back, his open eyes reflecting the blue October sky. His face expressed little more than mild surprise. His throat had been neatly cut from ear to ear, and his head and shoulders lay in a pool of rapidly congealing blood. A cloud of bluebottles hovered inquisitively just above the tall churchyard grass.

The two uniformed officers watched as Jackson examined the body. They saw him deftly slip the dead man's watch from his waistcoat pocket, and open the lid. It was still ticking, and showed the present time: 9.42.

Jackson returned the watch, and quickly examined the contents of the other pockets.

He found a notecase, opened it, and silently showed the contents to his colleagues. It contained a considerable number of five-pound notes and American hundred-dollar bills.

'What does that tell us, Sergeant Potter?' he asked.

'Why, sir, it shows us that robbery couldn't have been the motive. But what else could it have been? This man's a complete stranger in Ashborne Hill.'

'Sergeant Bottomley?' said Jackson, and pointed to the pool of congealing blood around the dead man's head. There was a hint of a question in his tone, but there had been no need to tell the sergeant what to do. Bottomley had always been good with blood.

They watched as Bottomley scooped up a mass of blood from the grass, and rubbed it between his palms, his eyes closed in concentration. Then he lifted up the dead man's head, and felt the ground beneath it. Finally, he crouched near the body, nonchalantly wiping his bloody hands on the grass.

'Sir,' he said, 'this man has been dead since about three o'clock yesterday afternoon. Dead for about eighteen hours, that is. Dissolution is just beginning, and I'd advise that the remains be conveyed to a mortuary as soon as possible.'

By one consent the little posse of policemen moved away from the body, and stood together on the shale path of the churchyard. Jackson broke the silence.

'This body, Officers,' he said, 'is that of Elijah Robinson, as you, Sergeant Potter, have already ascertained.' He gave the sergeant a little mock bow. 'He was an American by birth, though of English origin. His age, as you can see, was about twenty-five. He came from New York, in the United States of America. His father —'

'Why, sir,' cried Sergeant Potter in what seemed to be awed amazement, 'how were you able to deduce all that, just from looking at the man?'

Saul Jackson saw the growing expression of respect on the elderly sergeant's face. Sergeant Bottomley contrived to hide a smile behind his hand.

'It's training and experience, Sergeant,' said Jackson, 'and perhaps a touch of genius. This Elijah Robinson was the son of the late Jacob Robinson. He was murdered, I believe, by an elderly man who lured him to this deserted spot from the dining-room of The Berkeley Arms Hotel.'

From somewhere deep in Sergeant Potter's chest a churning, cavernous sound

63

welled up. He was laughing.

'Ah, I see now, sir. You're having your little joke with me! You'd seen this poor young man before ever he was murdered, hadn't you, sir? You'd seen him, here in town?'

'*Of course* I'd seen him before, Sergeant! He was waiting in the Berkeley Arms for someone to turn up, and I noticed him especially, because of the foreign cut of his suit. And I heard him in conversation with the man who I think was his murderer. I'll tell you the whole tale when we've finished here.'

'Are there any further questions you'd like to ask me, Inspector Jackson?' asked Potter. 'As Sergeant Bottomley just said, it's time that this body was removed to the mortuary.'

'I've one other question, Sergeant Potter. How far is it from here to the Berkshire Arms?'

'The Berkshire Arms, sir? There's no place of that name in Ashborne Hill. Only The Berkeley Arms by the station, The Grapes here at St Philip's Steps, and The Armourer in Sheepfold Lane. No, there's no Berkshire Arms, sir.'

Although the sun still shone strongly in the graveyard, Saul Jackson shivered. There was something wrong about this wanton murder. The unseen man in the booth had lured Elijah Robinson to this particular spot because it was well hidden from the public roads. And there, below the graveyard, were the rear premises of a public house. The unseen man would have said, 'There we are, Mr Robinson, the Berkshire Arms,' pointing to The Grapes. And then he would have struck. . . .

The unseen man had local knowledge, but that didn't necessarily mean that he was a local man. Robbery was clearly not the motive – witness the full notecase, and the gold watch. No, this was a private murder of some sort, perpetrated against a young man who had only been days in England.

Elijah Robinson had come to visit a man called Skeffington in Charnley. When he'd finished here in the churchyard, he'd make a few enquiries about this man Skeffington. But not just yet.

'Now, Sergeant Potter,' said Jackson, 'in cases of this sort, the murderer will discard the weapon as soon as he can. More often than not, he simply drops it near his victim. Our man would most likely be covered in blood, so he'd want to leave the scene as unobtrusively as possible. I don't think he'd risk going down those steps over there. He'd more likely return to the secluded path that we came along to get here. We need to conduct an immediate search for the weapon along that path.'

It was the slow-thinking but keen-sighted Sergeant Potter who found the weapon. It had been thrust into a clump of grass further along the railings near to the brick shed, at a point that could only have been reached from the public path. Potter had seen the faint smear of blood on a leaf of a dock plant which was growing half through the railings.

'Mr Jackson, sir,' cried Potter. 'This looks like it!'

Inspector Jackson carefully manoeuvred his fingers through the railings, and withdrew the weapon that had been the death of Elijah Robinson. It was a finely-honed steel scalpel set in an ebony handle. The blade was still wet with blood. An inset brass plate on the handle bore the legend, *W and H Hutchinson, Sheffield 1882.*

'What is it, sir?' asked Sergeant Potter.

'It's a surgeon's knife, Sergeant,' said Jackson, 'what they call a scalpel. It'll have been one of a set. I thought it might be something like this. That wound in the throat – very smooth and workman-like, it was.'

'Very surgeon-like,' added Sergeant Bottomley. Jackson saw the beginning of a perplexed frown etching itself on his sergeant's brow. Sergeant Potter had turned pale, and Jackson was convinced that his pallor was not caused merely by the sight of the bloody instrument of death. Potter knew something – or thought he knew something.

'It looks very much like a post-mortem scalpel, Sergeant Bottomley,' said Jackson. 'Do you remember Dr Venner enjoying himself one day by showing the two of us the tools of his gory trade?'

'Yes, sir. And then he enjoyed himself further by describing how he used them! It certainly looks like an autopsy instrument. There's a thread of white cotton, sir, caught up in the handle. Perhaps our man wore cotton gloves?'

'Perhaps,' Jackson replied. He turned the scalpel over in his hand, and saw a second narrow brass plate inserted in the handle. Engraved upon it was the name *Matthew Holt MD*. He said the name aloud, and Sergeant Potter uttered a strangled sound, which was either a sign of shock or surprise.

'When I was down here yesterday, Sergeant Potter,' said Jackson, 'a young lady came off the station platform and into the dining-room of the Berkeley Arms. This was very soon after the murderer and his victim had left. My train for Warwick was due to leave at twenty past two, and I was just preparing to pay the bill when I caught this young lady's eye. A sudden look of fear leapt into her eyes, and stayed there until she left the room. After a while, a young man came in from the street, and I saw the look of joy and relief that transformed the young lady's face. This man was evidently a friend who had come to meet her at the station. She called him "Mr Staunton", and he called her "Miss Holt." Was that young lady this Dr Holt's daughter?'

'Dr Holt is a respected physician who's lived in Charnley for years, Inspector. He *has* a daughter – Miss Kate, she's called – but the Miss Holt you saw in the Berkeley Arms is his niece, Miss Ursula Holt. The "Mr Staunton" she met is a young accountant with a practice in Charnley.'

'And what can you tell me about Miss Ursula Holt?'

'She – well, sir, I may as well tell you now as later. When you saw Miss Ursula Holt yesterday, she was on her way home from a six months' stay in the lunatic asylum at Inchfield.'

'What was she doing there?'

'She'd been found guilty of cutting a dog's throat, and – well, maybe other things as well. Guilty but unfit to plead, by reason of insanity.'

'Very well, Sergeant. There's a link there, but it would be wrong to draw any kind of conclusion at this stage.'

Jackson turned to Sergeant Bottomley.

'Sergeant,' he said, 'you'd better take charge of this scalpel. Mind you don't cut yourself with it. Wrap it in your handkerchief, if you've got one. That's right. Now, neither of us is known here, yet, so I want you to go down to that inn at the bottom of the steps – The Grapes, it's called – and have a talk to the locals. You know the kind of thing I mean. That scalpel. . . . I don't like the look or feel of this case at all. I think we're going to be in for a long haul.'

4
THE DEAD MAN'S EFFECTS

The landlord of The Grapes looked at the large, homely man with the flushed red face, who had just tossed back his second measure of gin. He looked respectable enough, and surveyed the folk gathered in the public bar with what seemed to be an air of befuddled benevolence. A commercial traveller, perhaps, and a bit of a soak into the bargain. Well, his money seemed good enough.

'Excuse me asking,' said the man in thick tones, 'but is today Tuesday or Wednesday? I know it's the third, or maybe the fourth, but —'

'It's Tuesday, and it's the third of October,' said the landlord curtly. 'Can't you read? There's a calendar there, on the wall beside you.'

'Tuesday,' said the man gravely, 'well, that's very nice. And this is a very nice hotel you've got here, landlord,' he continued, wiping his mouth on the sleeve of his mustard-coloured overcoat. 'Very select. But then, I've heard that Ashborne Hill's a very select place.'

The man reached for the gin bottle across the bar, and poured himself a third glass. His flushed red face regarded the landlord questioningly. The landlord, sour-faced, and balding untidily, shook his head doubtfully.

'Select? I don't know about that, mister. It's a little working town, that's all, with a mill, a few workshops and the railway. We don't get many strangers here.'

There was a murmur of assent from the assembled company, which consisted of four workmen sitting morosely over their beer at a wooden table. Evidently, Ashborne Hill folk liked to keep themselves to themselves. The stranger seemed not to notice the veiled suggestion that he was only there on sufferance.

'Mind you,' continued the man at the bar, 'it's not every day that you have a murder, I expect. A man I've just met in the road outside was telling me that someone was found in the churchyard with his throat cut this morning. A Chinaman, so he said.'

The man picked up a battered brown bowler hat from the bar where he was sitting, and rubbed away with his cuff at some moist beer stains on its brim. He glanced swiftly at his audience, and had they cared to meet his gaze, they would have noticed the shrewdness of his rather fine grey eyes.

'Well, that's where your man was wrong, mister,' volunteered one of the men at the table. 'One of the constables came in here earlier, and told us all about it. That man found dead in the churchyard was an American, and as white as you or me. Somebody'd cut his throat with one of those little knives that surgeons use. Scalpers, or some such word.'

Another workman glanced at the speaker, and the two of them exchanged a knowing smile.

'There's folk here in Ashborne and down the line at Charnley who could put a name to the – the person with the scalpel,' he muttered, and then buried his face in his glass of beer.

'Put a name to him? Well, if you can do that, friend,' said the man at the bar, 'you should tell the police straight away.'

'Now look here, mister!' said the landlord. 'Who are you, anyway, asking all these questions? It's no business of yours what goes on here. Old Sergeant Potter's got the thing in hand, and he's an Ashborne Hill man born and bred, and so are his two constables. We all know each other here. So let's hear no more talk of murder.'

There was a scarcely concealed belligerence in the landlord's voice that made the man in the mustard-coloured overcoat smile, as though he had achieved some hidden object.

'Yes, who are you, mister?' asked another of the workmen, encouraged by the landlord's increasingly hostile tone. 'I've not seen you in these parts before. Whoever killed the American in St Philip's churchyard must have been a stranger, like you. Nobody in Ashborne Hill would kill anyone. So who are you?'

The man at the bar drank the remains of his gin, threw some money on to the bar counter, and stood up. He picked up his battered bowler hat, and settled it firmly on his head. There was something about the man that exuded a kind of menace, a warning that he was not to be driven too far.

Still standing at the bar, he extracted a battered old leather wallet from an inside pocket, rummaged through it for a while, and then presented the surly landlord with a little printed calling card.

'There you are, landlord,' he said, 'that's so you'll know me again when you see me.'

Detective Sergeant H. Bottomley
Warwickshire Constabulary

'H stands for Herbert,' Bottomley added, treating the landlord to a rather dangerous smile. 'I expect that you'll remember the name of Herbert Bottomley after I've been nosing round about your little town for a couple of days or so. Or maybe longer.'

'No offence meant, guvnor,' muttered the landlord, propping the card up against the mirrored shelf behind the bar. 'But you'll understand, Sergeant, that we're all a bit on edge, as it were. We're not used to murders in Ashborne.'

'No offence taken, landlord,' Bottomley replied. 'This is a very nice hotel in a very nice town. I'll bid you good morning.'

Sergeant Bottomley glanced round the bar once more, then turned towards the door leading out to the inn yard, and to the steps up into St Philip's churchyard.

When Herbert Bottomley regained the churchyard he saw that the preparations to remove Elijah Robinson's body had already begun. A canvas screen had been erected at the side of the path, upon which stood an old wheeled hand-hearse. As he watched, a constable emerged from behind the screen.

74

He crossed the churchyard and secured the gates at the top of the steps with a chain and padlock.

Bottomley found Inspector Jackson and Sergeant Potter established more or less comfortably in the stone shed that rose from the long grass where the railings ended. It contained a trestle table, a few chairs, and a pair of well-honed scythes standing in racks against one wall. A moss-green carpet bag, damp and discoloured with rain, stood on the table.

'That, Sergeant,' said Jackson, 'was poor young Mr Robinson's bag. I saw him with it yesterday at the Berkeley Arms. One of Sergeant Potter's constables found it, where it had been thrown into the back garden of a house on the other side of the railings.'

Bottomley opened the bag, and rapidly surveyed its contents. A clean shirt, two changes of underclothing, a razor in a leather case. Here was a toilet bag, and a spare pair of shoes. It was the luggage of a man who had anticipated only a short stay away from wherever he was based.

Sergeant Potter had lit a short pipe, and between those long pulls on the stem with which pipe smokers create the illusion of being thoughtful and intelligent, he was talking to Jackson about his native town.

'It's a railway town, Inspector. It owes its existence to the permanent way. The line came here in 1838, providing links from these parts to Rugby and Coventry towards the north, and down to Charnley to the south.'

'That's how I got to Charnley yesterday, Sergeant,' said Jackson. 'I had to go up to Coventry first to get down here to Ashborne Hill, and from here I caught the stopping-train from Rugby. The two-twenty.'

'That's right, sir. It's the railway that keeps Ashborne Hill alive, so to speak. That, and Halford's Woollen Mill. They employ a good number of Ashborne Hill folk. That Mr Staunton, the accountant, he makes up the books for Halford's.'

'Does he really? Well, it's another link, Sergeant. As to that woollen mill, when I was standing in the churchyard, I could see the rows of windows glinting through the oaks over the far wall. This churchyard's a sheltered spot, but perhaps somebody standing at one of those windows looked down yesterday afternoon, and saw something. You might like to ask around, later today, or tomorrow.'

'Why, sir, I never thought of that. All those windows! It never occurred to me that people might look out of them!'

Herbert Bottomley, who had sat down in a chair near Jackson's, laughed throatily. He knew other rural policemen of Sergeant Potter's type, men who were always smartly turned out, with buttons gleaming, but who were fairly slow on the uptake. They spent their lives out of doors, and were usually afflicted with rheumatics or lung trouble. They had a lot of tenacity, but little imagination.

'Sergeant Potter —' Bottomley began, and then suddenly broke off. 'My name's Herbert, by the way. I expect you've got a Christian name as well?'

'George.'

'Well, George, I've just got back from having a few tots of gin in The Grapes. I was told there that Ashborne Hill folk are all as pure as the driven snow, and it was obvious that they weren't too fond of strangers.'

'Charlie Bennett's a surly kind of man,' observed George Potter, chuckling, 'but he's very law-abiding. Shuts up on the dot at closing time, and won't countenance any roughs.'

'There were a couple of workmen in there, George,' Bottomley continued, 'and they started muttering about folk here in Ashborne and at Charnley who could put a name to what one of them called "the person with the scalpel". What did they mean by that?'

Sergeant Potter snorted impatiently. His pipe had gone out, and he thrust it into the pocket of his uniform frock coat.

'That would have been Pat Lucas and his friend Leslie Arrowsmith. They're partners in a little joinery business. There's no harm in either of them, but they let their tongues run away with them at times.'

'But what did they mean, George? What did they mean by "the person with the scalpel"? If they know something, they must be made to tell us what it is.'

'It's nothing to do with this business, Herbert. It was something that happened down at Charnley earlier this year. That business concerning Miss Ursula Holt.'

'Tell us about it, Sergeant Potter,' said Jackson.

The two detectives listened while Sergeant Potter told them all the details of the story of Ursula Holt, of Ben the slaughtered sheepdog, and of the sheep found mutilated in Charnley's outlying fields.

'Scalpels,' muttered Jackson when Potter had finished his account. 'There are too many knives in this business, and rather too much of a medical flavour for my liking. Either things are exactly what they seem, or somebody's trying to show us things that he'd like us to accept. Take this Miss Ursula Holt, for instance, my little shrinking violet yesterday at the Berkeley Arms. According to local legend, she's a regular knife-wielding maniac, and she was here in Ashborne Hill at the time of the murder —'

'Sir —'

'Yes, yes, I know, Sergeant Bottomley, it's highly unlikely, and the times don't really add up. But there she was, pale and agitated, and there was her uncle's bloody scalpel, hidden in the hedge.'

'Perhaps somebody wants us to think she did it,' said Bottomley.

'Perhaps. And then again, perhaps not. All I'm saying at the moment, Sergeant, is that we need to keep an open mind.

'It's time now for us to look at Elijah Robinson's pocket book. Sergeant Potter and I have already looked at his separate notecase. It contained twenty five-pound notes and five one-hundred dollar bills. There was some small change in his pockets, most of it in American coinage.'

'So, as we agreed before, it couldn't have been robbery,' offered Sergeant Potter. 'He looked a prosperous young fellow from his clothes. It don't seem right for him to have been murdered in a little English churchyard, three thousand miles from home, apparently for no reason.'

'It's been a private murder, Sergeant,' said Jackson. 'Vengeance, perhaps, or maybe something else. I heard him talking about himself while I was in the Berkeley Arms yesterday. He was coming to bring news of a legacy to this Mr Skeffington at Charnley. Now, let's look at this pocket book. It's made of fine black leather, with gilt stamping, and with the initials ER on the front.'

Jackson opened the pocket book, and began to sift through its contents.

'Here's some more money, all dollar bills this time. . . . A few calling cards, showing that he resided in Washington Square, New York. Some train tickets, two hotel bills, one from the Adelphi Hotel in Liverpool, dated last Friday, and – hello! What's *this*?'

Jackson had abstracted a folded letter, comprising a single sheet of pale-blue notepaper. He read it through in silence, and then handed it to Bottomley, who spread it open on his knee, so that Sergeant Potter could read it with him.

Providence House
Charnley
Warks
31 August 1893

My dear Elijah

I was delighted to receive your letter of the tenth, and very much look forward to receiving you here at Charnley in October. I have already heard from your family's solicitor, who told me of the legacy left to me by your late dear father. It was like him to have remembered me with such consideration after the lapse of so many years. He and I shared many perilous adventures together in our youth. We shall talk of all these things when you arrive.

You tell me that you will arrive in Liverpool on the 28 September, and stay for a few days at the Adelphi Hotel, as you need to transact some business in that city. I, too, may be away from Charnley on various dates in early October, so I suggest that you journey to the town of Ashborne Hill on Monday, 9 October, and take luncheon at the Berkeley Arms Hotel. I shall be in the district that day, and will meet you at that hotel at one o'clock in the afternoon. We shall then travel together to Charnley, where a warm welcome will await you!

Ever yours sincerely
Alexander Skeffington

Sergeant Bottomley folded up the letter up and handed it back to Jackson, who returned it to Elijah Robinson's pocket book.

'So that was it, sir!' cried old Sergeant Potter. 'It was the right place, and the right time, but the wrong day. Poor young man. . . . He should have checked the date before he ventured down here from Liverpool.'

Saul Jackson looked speculatively at the old sergeant. He was a good man, and a diligent officer, but he never thought things through.

'Sergeant Potter,' he said quietly, 'how did the murderer know that Elijah Robinson would mistake the day, and turn up at Ashborne Hill a week early? How could he have *known* that, unless he was a mind reader?'

'Why, sir, that's true enough. I never thought of that. But there's the letter from Mr Skeffington for all to see. Poor young Mr Robinson mistook the day, right enough.'

'Well, George, that may not be the case, you know,' said Sergeant Bottomley. 'That letter could have been written beforehand by the murderer, and placed in Elijah Robinson's pocket after he was dead, in order to deceive the police, and to make us believe that he'd come here on the wrong day. That may be a far-fetched idea, but it's a possibility, you see.'

'I actually heard poor Elijah Robinson ask the other man what day it was,' said Jackson. ' "This is the second of October, isn't it? I haven't got the wrong day?" That's what he said, and the other man confirmed that it was indeed the second. So there's something a bit disquieting about that letter, Sergeant Potter.'

Saul Jackson stood up, and slipped Elijah Robinson's pocket book and notecase into his pocket.

'Sergeant Potter,' he said, 'It's gone twelve, so I suggest that the three of us surprise the landlord of The Grapes by taking a spot of luncheon there – a pie and a pint, something of that kind. Then I want you to hold the fort here in Ashborne Hill until tomorrow afternoon. Sergeant Bottomley and I have to catch the one-thirty train to Coventry, and so back to Warwick for the rest of today. There's work waiting there for us on another case, which can't be neglected.'

'And tomorrow, sir?'

'Tomorrow, Sergeant, the two of us are wanted as witnesses in the magistrates' court at Copton Vale. But in the afternoon we'll go down to Charnley and break the news of this murder to Mr Alexander Skef-fington. We'll also call upon this Dr Matthew Holt in order to return his scalpel. Till then, Sergeant, keep this business close to your chest.'

5

THE WITNESS OF THE GLOVES

As Ursula Holt entered the little breakfast-room of Abbey Lodge on Wednesday morning, she saw her cousin Kate hastily hide the morning newspaper behind a cushion. Kate's round, usually cheerful face was flushed, and her eyes looked troubled behind her twinkling glasses.

'Did you sleep well, Polly?' she asked, pouring out a cup of tea for her cousin. 'Father's still asleep. I think he had a bad night, because I could hear him walking about in his room at three in the morning. I lit my candle to peep at the clock.'

'Yes, thank you, Kate,' Ursula replied. 'I slept very well. Not like on that awful Monday night.'

After her discovery of the bloodstained gloves on Monday night, she had sat motionless in the bedside chair for what seemed like hours, until the cold of the autumn night drove her to seek warmth beneath the sheets, but sleep had eluded her. Last night had been different. A whole day had passed since the incident of the gloves, a pleasant day, during which she had contrived to follow Mr Skeffington's advice, and forget unpleasant things. She had, though, allowed pleasing memories of Mr Guy Fitzgerald to float into her consciousness during the day, and the busy daylight hours had been followed by a blissful night of undisturbed sleep.

Ursula sipped her tea gratefully for a while, and then launched into a surprise attack upon her cousin.

'Why did you hide the *Charnley Recorder* just now, Kate?' she asked. 'Is there something there that you think I'm too young to read?'

For reply, Kate felt behind the cushion and produced the local paper.

'There,' she said, pointing to a column on the front page. 'Read it if you must. I thought it might have upset you.'

The column told of a dreadful murder at Ashborne Hill, a young man found in a cemetery with his throat cut. Yes, she could understand Kate's concern. The police had so far declined to reveal the identity of the victim, but he was thought to have been a foreigner. It was widely believed by the residents of Ashborne Hill that the murder weapon had been a scalpel, or surgeon's knife.

Oh, God! Uncle's knives clotted with blood, and the long white gloves – *her* gloves – still wet with the witness to murder. It had taken a whole day for the news to reach Charnley. The gloves! They were still there in the bottom drawer, but now the blood had begun to dry. She couldn't pretend about them any longer. They were her gloves, bought a year earlier to wear with her new evening dress: long, white evening gloves, reaching to the elbow. She would choose her moment later in the day to hide them from the sight of men. She would bury them among the evergreen shrubs in the rear garden.

She had been in Ashborne Hill that very day. *On most occasions the somnambule will experience the amnesia of substitution, which I characterize by the term cryptamnesia.* What had she done?

Kate had sprung up from her chair.

'Polly!' she cried. 'You've turned quite white! I told you that it would upset you. Let me get you a measure of brandy – no, don't refuse, it'll make you right as rain in a jiffy.'

Kate all but ran out of the kitchen, and

Ursula heard her push open the creaking door of the back parlour, where Dr Holt's small store of spirits was kept.

Ashborne Hill. . . . It was there that she had seen the sinister man in brown who had looked at her as though accusing her of some nameless crime. Had she done something wicked between stepping off the train and entering the refreshment room? Surely not! There had been no time. But those gloves. . . . Yes, she'd bury them out of her sight, and banish them from her memory. Do what Mr Skeffington advised: pretend that it had never happened.

When Kate returned with the brandy, Ursula swallowed it gratefully.

'I'm all right, now, Kate,' she said. 'It was kind of you to hide the paper, but I've got to learn how to face up to unpleasant reminders of that sort. I can hear Uncle Matthew getting up. I'll have breakfast now, and then I'll go up and tidy my room.'

The morning passed without incident. Doctor Holt, who still retained a small circle of old patients, left the house at ten, and soon afterwards Paul Staunton paid a call. Paul was a favourite with both girls, a handsome and attractive young man of twenty-six, with abundant fair hair and blue eyes. It was generally assumed that Paul had begun to pay court to Kate.

Paul greeted Kate with an affectionate smile, but when he turned to Ursula she saw the look of concern in his eyes. Kate saw it too, and excused herself. There was, she said, plenty of work waiting for her to do. Paul Staunton followed Ursula into the sheltered rear garden of Abbey Lodge.

'Are you all right, Ursula?' he asked, after they had stepped on to the grass. 'You seemed nervous to me when I met you yesterday at Ashborne Hill. I expect you've heard what happened there?'

'A murder.' Ursula shuddered. This nightmare – would it ever go away? 'Someone was murdered with a scalpel, so the paper says. I'd rather not talk about it, Paul, if you don't mind.'

'Of course, my dear girl. I realize how horrible it must be for you to hear about it so soon after – well, so soon after coming home again. You're all right, aren't you? We're giving a tennis party over at Temperley next week, and we'd all love you to come. You know how fond you are of tennis. You and Kate, you know.'

'Well, it's very kind of you, Paul. Will you give me a couple of days to think about it? Have you called to do Uncle Matthew's books?'

Paul Staunton laughed, and shook his head. 'Quarter day's already gone, and I can assure you that your uncle's books are in an impeccable state. No, I came to see *you,* Ursula. And Kate, of course.'

'Of course.' What a dear fellow he was! His growing affection for Kate seemed to be reciprocated. Perhaps next year there would be a wedding.

'I'm off to Ashborne Hill again, soon,' Paul continued. 'Can't get shut of the beastly place! You know that I do the books for Halford's Mill? Well, there's a supervisor there whom I know quite well to speak to. I got a letter from him this morning, saying that he saw something very odd on Monday that puzzled him. Would I come up the line to see him at the mill?'

Ursula suddenly clutched Paul's wrist, and cried out, 'What did he see? Tell me!'

'Well, I don't know, Ursula. He didn't say. Apparently it's all very hush-hush. But I say, you are all right, aren't you? This fellow's story is probably something quite unimportant. I'll go up to see him as soon as it's convenient, and find out what it was that he saw. I must go now. I've a client due in ten minutes' time.'

Ursula watched Paul Staunton as he returned to the house. That man at Halford's. . . . Had he seen a young woman walking in a trance through the churchyard on Monday, wearing bloodstained white gloves? She must bury them, but not yet. There were too many eyes at all those windows, not just here at the Lodge, but across the cloister in Providence House. Prying eyes. She would have to be careful – no, cunning. That was the word.

Doctor Holt returned from his round at half past twelve. Over luncheon, served in the old panelled dining-room, he shared various choice items of town gossip which had been relayed to him by the patients whom he had visited. He rather pointedly made no reference to the murder at Ashborne Hill.

Kate began to talk about the difficulties of authorship, and Uncle Matthew made sympathetic noises. Ursula smiled to herself. Her uncle never read fiction, and only glanced through the morning paper. His whole reading life was occupied with medical text books, and the eagerly awaited issues of *The Lancet.*

It was a little while after lunch, as Ursula was carrying a basket of freshly ironed linen upstairs, that she glanced out of the landing window, and saw her Nemesis crossing the green and walking purposefully towards the house. Her heart seemed to miss a beat, and the blood pounded in her temples. It was undoubtedly the same man as she had seen in The Berkeley Arms, a man wearing a brown three-piece suit, with a gold watch chain and medals draped across his waistcoat. He was accompanied by a big, shambling fellow in a yellow overcoat. They both looked like farmers, but she knew now in her heart that they were nothing of the kind. They were standing on the public green, in the shadow of the monument to the last prior of Charnley Abbey, talking together. Were they coming to Abbey Lodge?

The gloves! She would have to make a bold attempt as soon as possible to destroy them. Ah! The man from The Berkeley Arms had suddenly turned left, and she saw him walking purposefully along the path that would take him to the front entrance of Providence House. It was his ungainly companion, the man in the yellow overcoat, who presently came up to the door of Abbey Lodge and executed a loud peal on the bell.

'It's a post-mortem scalpel, Sergeant Bottomley,' said Dr Matthew Holt, holding the deadly instrument by its ebony handle, and examining the finely honed steel blade with the keen and concentrated gaze of a connoisseur.

'One of yours, sir?'

'Yes, Sergeant, it's one of mine – as you are well aware, since it has my name engraved on it. It's one of a whole case of such instruments that I bought some time in the eighties from W and H Hutchinson's, of Sheffield.'

Bottomley stood in Dr Holt's study, which doubled as an occasional consulting-room. An examination couch stood against one wall, faced on the other side of the room by a large glazed cupboard containing various instruments, an array of kidney bowls, a chemical balance, and a quantity of neatly arranged medical books.

A door near to the doctor's desk stood half open, and Bottomley gradually became aware of the shifting pattern of shadows falling across the threshold of an unseen room beyond. Forming, dissipating, and then reforming, the shadows must have been cast by someone moving rapidly across the floor. Occasionally, though, the shadows froze, and Bottomley knew that the listener in that other room was eavesdropping on the conversation.

'And this scalpel of mine was used to kill

this poor fellow?' Dr Holt continued. 'The man at Ashborne Hill? There's been something about it in the morning paper.'

'It was indeed, sir,' Bottomley replied. 'The victim's throat was cut very neatly from ear to ear. My guvnor, Detective Inspector Jackson, has gone to talk to your neighbour, Mr Skeffington, because the murdered man was the son of an old friend of his. And I've come, sir, to return this scalpel to you.'

Bottomley watched the elderly physician as he reunited the scalpel with its fellows in a mahogany case with brass fittings, which stood on top of a filing cabinet near the window. Doctor Matthew Holt seemed to be a comfortable kind of man, with a fresh, unlined face, and a frank manner. He wore an old faded suit of black serge, and some of his fingers were stained with tobacco. He came back to sit down behind his cluttered desk, and began to speak without prompting.

'I don't perform autopsies any more, Sergeant Bottomley. It's ten years at least since I was called upon to do so. Those particular instruments are souvenirs – trophies, I suppose. That's why they're displayed on top of that cabinet, in the same way as you might put a canteen of cutlery on show.'

The shadows in the next room, which had been still for a while, resumed their restless dance. There's someone in there listening to everything we say, Bottomley thought. Someone with a light step and a troubled mind. It was probably Miss Ursula. Shadows were dumb, some folk said, but in fact they spoke a language of their own.

Bottomley heard Dr Holt sigh, and watched him join the tips of his fingers together and close his eyes for a moment. He's wondering whether to tell me all about Miss Ursula, thought Bottomley, before I ask him outright. That scalpel didn't get out of its box on its own accord. Best to say nothing. Wait for him to decide.

'I'm only too painfully aware, Sergeant,' said Dr Holt, 'that this is not the first time that a surgical instrument of mine has been used to inflict death upon a living creature. It was an amputation scalpel from a set of antique instruments made in 1800 by Simpson's of London that was used to cut the throat of the poor sheepdog, Ben. Used by my niece, you know, Miss Ursula Holt. You can, if you wish, examine that instrument, which is in a wooden case in that cupboard by the window.'

Bottomley shook his head gently. If he

continued to wait quietly, Dr Holt would tell him all that he wanted to hear without prompting.

'My niece,' Dr Holt continued, 'has suffered all her life from somnambulism – sleepwalking, you know. She's twenty-four now. From the age of twenty she has suffered from persistent dreams, from which she has often awoken to find herself in places quite unknown to her. For the last year or so, she has been able to perform feats of strength during these dreams or trances which would be quite beyond her waking capacity. On one occasion, for instance, she was able to push open a door that had long been nailed up – the door of a room at the back of the house where the floor had been declared unsafe. You can imagine how worried I was.'

The shadows had stopped their endless darting once more, and a shaft of quiet sunlight lay undisturbed across the threshold of the neighbouring room.

'On the fourth of April this year, Sergeant Bottomley, which was a Tuesday, my niece retired to bed at eleven o'clock. She had been sleepwalking sporadically since the last week in March, waking to find herself in various rooms on the ground floor. On two occasions, which took place on the thirty-first of March and the second of April, she had awoken in the garden. I contemplated locking her bedroom door at nights, but decided that this was a harsh and cruel thing to do. I think now that I was mistaken. Grievously so.'

'I see, sir. And what happened on the fourth of April? Miss Ursula had retired to bed at eleven o'clock, you said.'

'Yes, that's right. Well, later that night, or, rather, in the early hours of the morning, my daughter Kate fancied that she heard a noise. She went to find Ursula, and discovered that she was not in her room. It was a little before dawn, and I was horribly alarmed. I sent out John, my coachman, to search for her. My neighbour, Mr Skeffington, was already stirring, and gave us his two footmen to assist in the search.'

Old Dr Holt moistened his lips, and looked away from Bottomley as though ashamed of the tale that he was telling.

'Behind this house, Sergeant,' he continued, 'there is a long plantation of evergreens, beyond which is a very large coppice, known locally as the bluebell wood. There's an old well there, partly sheltered by the trees, where children go to make wishes to what they call the well-fairy. It all sounds so innocent, doesn't it?

'They found Ursula asleep there, her nightdress splashed with blood, and with that amputation scalpel I told you about in her hand. In the well nearby, they found the body of a sheepdog called Ben. His throat had been cut, and he had been thrown down the well. That, Sergeant, was the tragic climax of my dear niece's morbid somnambulism.'

'So she had killed the dog? Killed it herself?'

'She had. They . . . they gain some kind of hidden strength, you see, to do these things. Oh, the grief we all felt! Words cannot convey it. Inspector Collier was still alive then, and he conducted the investigation. Ursula was taken away in a frantic state to the hospital at Copton Vale, where she was held in a secure ward used normally for pregnant felons. Eventually she was brought to trial in the magistrate's court, but was found unfit to plead.'

'And what happened then, sir?'

'She was taken on the fifth of May to the insane asylum at Inchfield, and stayed there, Sergeant, until she was discharged, cured, only yesterday. *Cured,* you understand? She will not offend further, and could not possibly have had anything to do with the murder by scalpel of that young man at Ashborne Hill yesterday. But it was my duty to tell you the whole story, if only to blow away any cobwebs of innuendo in this business. Ursula is quite safe and harmless under my care.'

Sergeant Bottomley got to his feet. He glanced fleetingly towards the half-open door on the adjacent room, and saw that the flitting shadows had disappeared.

'I'm much obliged to you, sir,' said Bottomley, 'for telling me about Miss Ursula. And now I have one question to ask you. How easy is it for strangers to come into your house and help themselves to things that they want? You see, if it wasn't your niece who murdered that young man at Ashborne Hill, it must have been somebody else – somebody who could come into this room and help himself to a handy scalpel.'

'That's a very interesting question, Sergeant. I'd not thought about that kind of thing before. Well, now, there's the front door, which needs a latch key to be opened from the outside. Then there's the door out from the kitchen passage into the rear garden, and a little door in the kitchen, which takes you into the yard, where the middens are. That's all.'

'Very good, sir. And I expect there are open windows from time to time, and I certainly saw a skylight in the roof as I came here today. Oh, and there's a little flight of steps going down into an area, so I expect there's a cellar door at the bottom of it —'

'Steady, Sergeant!' Dr Holt laughed in spite of himself. 'I take your point. So what do you want me to do?'

'I'd like you to put all those instruments — those scalpels and other knives — under lock and key, somewhere, if that's possible. There's no need, sir, to tempt Providence by leaving them lying about. Would you mind if I was to make a little inspection of the house and grounds before I went? I promise you that I won't pry into things that don't concern me. It's just the layout of the place, if you understand me.'

'Go wherever you like, Sergeant. Meanwhile, I'll lock those cases of instruments in my safe.'

Doctor Holt paused as he stood at the filing cabinet, and turned to look at Bottomley.

'I've told you all about my niece, Sergeant, because I don't believe in obfuscation – hiding the truth behind a wall of half-truths and hints. She did those terrible acts, sure enough; but of this murder at Ashborne Hill she is entirely innocent. She is cured, Sergeant Bottomley. It seems to me that someone has tried to use my niece's unhappy history as a cloak to hide his own wicked deed.'

Bottomley retrieved his battered bowler hat from the floor beside his chair, and opened the door of the study.

'I'll bear what you say in mind, sir,' he said, and walked out into the passage.

Quite safe and harmless! That's what her uncle had said about her to that sinister, shambling man in the vulgar yellow overcoat. She had been hovering in the little writing-room adjoining Uncle Matthew's study, pretending to dust and tidy, so that she had heard what the two men had said. Bottomley, Uncle had called him. Sergeant Bottomley.

Quite safe and harmless! Was she a caged beast, to be described like that? Was Abbey Lodge no more than a cage? Uncle had said quite openly that she had killed that poor dog – slit its throat with one of his hideous scalpels. He'd more or less admitted that he was her warder. . . .

Ursula had slipped out of the writing-room and hurried up to her little sitting-room on the first floor. She had locked the door, and collapsed in distress on an armchair. What was she to do? Did Kate really believe in her innocence? One could never be sure with anyone. She was kind and loyal, but was that enough? Perhaps Paul Staunton secretly believed her guilty of the murder at Ashborne Hill. That man at Halford's must have seen something. . . . Only the enigmatic and rather forceful Mr Skeffington believed unconditionally in her innocence.

Him, and one other. Ursula looked fondly at three framed portrait photographs which stood on top of her bamboo bookcase. What wonderful, happy times they recalled! Catherine Stansfield, the subject of all three photographs, had been one of her earliest and dearest friends.

The Stansfields lived in Alderley Hall, an eighteenth-century mansion deep in the Northamptonshire countryside. They were friends of her father, and Ursula had stayed with them for a number of delightful holidays since the age of twelve. It was a beautiful house, with a magnificent ballroom, where the hospitable Stansfields held costume balls, which she and Catherine had attended. They'd had a costumed orchestra playing eighteenth-century music. . . . Was it this ballroom, with its memories of young girlhood, that furnished the setting for her terrifying ballroom dreams?

When had she last stayed at Alderley Hall? It was in 1883, when she had just turned fourteen. Catherine Stansfield was eighteen, and engaged to be married. The first photograph showed Catherine at that age, clad in a ball gown, and standing proudly beside a draped curtain. A pretty, self-assured girl, she would grow into a renowned society beauty.

In that same year, 1883, Ursula's father died, and she had come to live with Uncle Matthew and Kate. She had never returned to Alderley Hall, but she and Catherine had corresponded regularly, and that correspondence had continued even after the dog incident and its terrifying consequences. 'Only a fool or a knave could believe you capable of such acts,' Catherine had written to her. 'One day, the truth of the matter will be known, and the legally sanctioned slanders made against you will be repudiated. When all this nightmare is over, you must come and stay with James and me in London, or at our house in Radley Cross.'

If things became impossible for her at Charnley, she could take up Catherine's invitation. Was Abbey Lodge nothing more than a prison? Was she to be secretly watched by her uncle, with the covert assistance of that frightful policeman? Yes, dear Catherine would provide her with a way of escape.

The second photograph showed Catherine Stansfield after her marriage to the Honourable James Wishart in 1885, and the third captured the quiet pride of the young mother, holding a sleeping baby girl, almost hidden in a long white christening robe. What a beauty Catherine was! She and her husband and baby lived in London, at a house in Bruton Street, Mayfair. The baby, now a little girl of six, had been christened Ursula.

The gloves!

Ursula wrenched open the bottom drawer of the dressing-table and clutched at the soiled evening gloves, still wrapped roughly in tissue paper. She could see the dark stain of the dried blood caked on the cotton fingers. She hastily thrust them into her workbox, placed it under her arm, and slipped out of the room.

All was quiet in the house. Kate, she knew, would be in her little den behind the parlour, struggling with the plot of yet another novel. Her Uncle Matthew would be still sitting in his study, reading, or perhaps dozing over one of his periodicals.

She tiptoed down the stairs, and stood for a moment in the kitchen passage. She could hear the cook singing quietly to herself as she bustled about preparing dinner. Still clutching her workbox, she pushed open the garden door, and slipped out on to the grass. The sun was declining, and long shadows had fallen over the lawns. The garden was completely deserted. Ursula hurried across the grass to the long bed of flowering shrubs, and knelt down.

How could she dig a hole? Ah! Here was a trowel, left sticking in the soil by their gardener, and evidently forgotten. It took her only a minute to scoop out a hole in the well-tended soil. Opening her workbox, she took out the package of bloodstained gloves.

She had just begun to place them in the hole when a strong hand seized her wrist.

'No, miss,' said a rough but not unkind voice, 'hiding evidence is not the way.'

Sergeant Bottomley sat at one end of a garden bench set against the back wall of the cloister. Ursula had moved to the far end, where she held herself as still and wary as a hare in the chase. Between the two of them, captive and captor, lay the blood stained gloves.

Bottomley thought: I can almost hear this girl's heart thumping away in her chest. She's terrified; but not of me. Her uncle declared that she had returned home cured. Could he not see the haunted terror in her face? Perhaps he was short-sighted.

'Why were you trying to bury those gloves, Miss Holt?' asked Bottomley gently.

Ursula threw him a frightened glance. She spoke, but her halting words were not a reply to Bottomley's question.

'I found them in my chest of drawers. I had to hide them, because I saw you coming up to the house with that dreadful man, and I knew that you'd accuse me of the murder of that poor fellow at Ashborne Hill.'

She added, tremulously, 'I don't know why I'm talking so frankly to you. I was afraid of you when your seized my wrist, but I'm not afraid of you now.'

'Well, Miss Ursula, maybe that's because I'm the father of eight daughters, all living. Two are married, two are in service, and the other four are still at home. It helps, you know, when I'm talking to young ladies in distress.'

'Eight daughters,' said Ursula, half to herself. 'How on earth do you cope?'

'Well, miss, it could have been worse. I might have had nine!'

Before Ursula could even frame a smile at this answer, Sergeant Bottomley asked a question.

'And *did* you murder him, miss? The man at Ashborne Hill, you know.'

'No! At least — Maybe I did. I suppose you've found out that I was in Ashborne Hill on Monday? Yes, I might have done it. Sometimes, I wake up from a dream and don't know where I've been before I fell asleep. I don't always remember what I've done. So maybe I *did* murder him, and hid the gloves in my drawer without knowing that I'd done so. And that's why I tried to bury them.'

'Well, miss,' Bottomley continued, 'I don't think you committed that murder at all. I don't think it had anything to do with you. And I think those things because I'm a detective, and I know much more about what happened in Ashborne Hill than you do. So, by burying those gloves, you would have been concealing evidence against the real murderer, you see, thus helping him to put the noose around your own neck, if you'll pardon the coarse language.'

When Ursula had stumbled to her feet in fright from the grass, she had seen such a look of kindly compassion in her big captor's grey eyes that she had bitten back the instinct to scream herself into hysteria. He had put an arm round her shoulders, and led her gently to the garden seat in the shade of the cloister. His voice had been quiet and confiding, with the homely accent of the Warwickshire man. As he spoke of what he called 'the real murderer', Ursula looked at him with intelligent interest for the first time.

'But if I didn't put them in that drawer, who did?'

'They were most probably put there by our killer, Miss Holt, and that suggests a number of interesting little ideas. Whoever put them there is someone who knows all about your recent troubles, and what happened to you last May. And that person must have some familiarity with your house, Abbey Lodge. As for those gloves – well, I shall take them away with me and examine them, because yesterday, I found a thread of cotton stuck to the handle of the scalpel used to murder that poor man. If I find the right kind of tear on one of those gloves, I shall know that the murderer used them. Which also means, miss, that he must have stolen them from your chest of drawers in the first place.'

Bottomley rose to his feet, picked up the bloodstained gloves, and thrust them into one of his capacious overcoat pockets. Ursula plucked up the courage to ask him a question.

'Who was that frightful man who came with you today? The man who went to call on Mr Skeffington? I've seen that man before, and he looked at me as though he knew all about me. He frightens me. I hate him.'

'Well, miss, that frightful man is my guvnor, Detective Inspector Jackson, and when he looked at you, I rather think that he read your fear and anxiety from the way *you* looked. He's trained to read faces, you see; so am I, for that matter. So don't be afraid of Mr Jackson, miss, or of me. When troubles abound, as they say, it's as well to know who your true friends are.'

Herbert Bottomley watched the young woman as she walked slowly back to the house, carrying her workbox under her arm. Once, she turned back to look at him, and managed a shy smile. That girl's peace of mind is so fragile, he thought, that any further shocks could drive her back to the madhouse. Perhaps that was what someone unknown and unseen secretly desired. It was time to look for explanations beyond the confines of Charnley.

6
ALEXANDER SKEFFINGTON'S STORY

'Detective Inspector Jackson? Your name's not unknown to me. Sit down, won't you? This is a terrible and shocking business.'

Saul Jackson looked at Alexander Skeffington as he sat in a great carved chair in his study at Providence House. An impressive, commanding man, very formally dressed in garments that told instantly of great wealth, he still clutched the letter that Jackson had found in Elijah Robinson's pocket book. His grey eyes, half lost beneath the beetling brows, looked troubled.

'I gather, sir,' said Jackson, 'that the news I brought was not unknown to you?'

'That is so. Rumours have been rife since yesterday, and there was a whole column about Elijah Robinson's murder in today's *Charnley Recorder.* What I don't understand is how the poor young man came to be in Ashborne Hill on Monday. He was not due to call there until next Monday —'

'That letter, sir,' Jackson interrupted, 'is it genuine? I mean, did you actually write it?'

'What? Well, of course I wrote it. This is my handwriting. I told him to be at Ashborne Hill on Monday, the ninth of October. For some reason that I cannot fathom he mistook the day, and went there a week too early.'

When Jackson had called at Providence House, a parlour maid had conducted him through a number of elegantly appointed rooms until they came to Mr Alexander Skeffington's study. It seemed to be crammed with curios and framed photographs, and there was a stuffed creature of some kind gazing sharply with bright glass eyes from the confines of an exhibition cabinet. A wallaby, perhaps? Skeffington rose abruptly from his chair, crossed to an open roll-top desk, and picked up a sheet of paper.

'There, Inspector,' he said, with a hint of sardonic humour in his tones, 'that's a genuine specimen of my handwriting. You can compare it with that letter, if you like.'

If this gentleman thinks I'm going to apologize for not taking his every word as gospel truth, thought Jackson, then he's sadly mistaken. Whatever Skeffington may have written in that letter, the fact remained that young Robinson had known that it was the second of October, not the ninth. He, Jackson, had actually heard him ask his murderer whether or not it was the second, and his murderer had assured him that it was.

'It's an odd fact, sir,' he said aloud, 'that the man who murdered Elijah Robinson evidently *knew* that he would be at Ashborne Hill on the second, because he was there lying in wait to entrap him, and lure him to his death. As a matter of fact, I was there myself, and witnessed the very act of entrapment. Unfortunately, I couldn't see the murderer at all, because he was sitting behind a partition.'

Alexander Skeffington started violently.

'You were *there?* You were actually there? What a strange coincidence! Have you considered that it might have been a particularly violent robbery?'

'It was not a robbery, sir. It was premeditated murder, and murder of a ghastly kind. Murder by a surgeon's scalpel —'

Skeffington uttered a sudden cry of distress, and sprang from his chair.

'No, no! It can't be. . . . Not all that business again?'

'You're thinking of the young lady who lives next door to you, aren't you, sir? Miss

Ursula Holt. My colleague, Detective Sergeant Bottomley, is interviewing Dr Holt at this very moment. And yes, the scalpel used was the property of your neighbour, Dr Matthew Holt. But I can assure you, Mr Skeffington, that it is far too early to draw any drastic conclusions from that fact. I gather that you are fond of that young lady?'

'I am. Everybody is. And I can tell you, Inspector, that she never committed any of those vile offences. I've known her since she was a very young girl. Violence of that kind would be entirely alien to her nature. This murder of poor young Elijah must not be laid at her door.'

It was time to change the subject. Skeffington was fast losing his equanimity. Evidently Ursula Holt was something more than simply a neighbour's niece to this elderly unmarried man. Perhaps he saw her as a surrogate daughter?

'What I should like to hear from you, sir,' said Jackson, 'is some account of the late unfortunate Mr Elijah Robinson. He was a stranger in this country – indeed, he arrived here only on Thursday last – and you are the only link to him that we have – the police, I mean.'

'Well, Inspector,' said Skeffington, 'the best way for me to explain about Elijah

Robinson is to take you with me on a long journey back into the past. I'd say that this whole sad and sorry business has its origins over forty years ago, out in my native land of Australia. Gold Fever! That's what they called the mad scramble for instant fortunes, after gold was discovered in Bendigo and Ballarat in '51. You've heard of the Australian gold rush, I expect? Yes, I thought you had.'

Alexander Skeffington sat back in his great carved chair, his keen grey eyes looking back upon the sights of a long-vanished world.

'It was sheer madness, Mr Jackson, though the gold was real enough. Did you know that whole ships' crews deserted, and made their way to the diggings? Farmers, clerks, immigrants in droves from the Old World – they all flocked to the colony of Victoria to make their fortunes.'

'And did they, sir?' asked Jackson. Skeffington's mind seemed to have strayed from its subject for a while. His great eagle brow was drawn down into a frown.

'What? Oh, yes, Inspector. A lot of great fortunes were made, including mine. But many poor fellows lost their all. Others stayed on in Victoria, and did very well as farmers. It was a hard life in the diggings, and there was a lot of lawlessness. We were all better out of it when the fever abated, and the big, steady mining companies were formed.

'There were three of us who embarked on our particular mining adventure – wait, I'll show you a picture of us taken in those far-off days.'

Mr Skeffington rose abruptly, and reached down a framed photograph from the top of a bookcase. He handed it to Jackson, and resumed his seat. Jackson looked at the faded image of three young men, all dressed in rough homespun suits, who stared at the camera in the stern fashion of the time. They were sitting on a bench in front of a rough shack. Jackson recognized Alexander Skeffington immediately. Although a lifetime younger, the features were essentially the same: the beetling brow and aquiline nose, the eagle glitter in the deep-set eyes.

'I see that you've picked me out, Mr Jackson! That photograph was taken in 1851, and shows the three of us who formed a little syndicate to prospect for gold in Bendigo. I'm a native-born Australian, coming from a place called Pinnaroo, in Victoria. Sitting on my right you'll see Jacob Robinson, the father of this poor young man who's been murdered. Doesn't he look a fine fellow?'

'He does, sir,' Jackson replied. 'In fact, he looks uncannily like his unfortunate son. I suppose he was much the same age as you were, in those days?'

'He was. In fact, all three of us were twenty-five. Jacob told me that his family came originally from South Carolina, but moved to New York after the Civil War. As I think you know, he died earlier this year, and in his will he very kindly left me a legacy – the equivalent in dollars of five thousand pounds. It was a generous thought.'

'Had you kept up a correspondence with Mr Jacob Robinson?'

'Oh, no, Inspector. Once our business in Australia was done, I set out for England, where I hoped to set myself up as an English gentleman. Perhaps I succeeded; I don't know! Jacob returned to America, and invested his money in land and manufactories. I had the occasional letter for a year or so, and then we ceased to correspond. It was a very pleasant surprise to hear first from his lawyer, and then from his son, this year. I had never in fact met Elijah Robinson. I would have known him only from a few photographs of him which his father sent to me over the years.'

'So presumably, sir, Elijah would have known *you* only from photographs?'

'What? Yes, yes, I suppose so.'

'And who is this third man in the photograph, sir?' asked Jackson. 'This fair-haired young fellow with the round, mild face? Is that a birth-mark spreading across his forehead? You can't always see things clearly in these old photographs.'

'It's a birth-mark right enough,' said Skeffington. 'What they call a port-wine stain. It wasn't particularly disfiguring, but he was rather sensitive about it, shading his brow with his hand when we met any stranger on the diggings. He was one of the first immigrants we had in 1851. He told us that he'd come from somewhere in Scotland.'

'And aren't you going to tell me his name, sir?' Jackson persisted.

'His name? Yes, I'll tell you. He was called Jim Bolder. And before you ask me what became of him, I'll tell you. The three of us left the diggings in 1855. Jacob and I had both made considerable fortunes. Jacob returned to America, as I told you. I came to England to set up as a gentleman, and Jim Bolder came with me. I'd been negotiating with an estate agent in England to buy this place – Providence House, it's called – for a year before I returned to England, and as soon as I arrived here I took possession of it. It had been shut up for many years, but was sound and in good order. I've lived here ever since.'

'And Jim Bolder?'

'Poor Jim! Well, he'd made what I'd call a competence, enough to give him a modest income of a couple of hundred pounds a year. He stayed with me for a month or two, more or less hiding away here because of the birth-mark. Then he upped sticks and returned to Scotland. I heard very soon after that he'd died of consumption of the lungs.'

Alexander Skeffington stirred in his chair.

'And that, Mr Jackson, is more or less the story of my early life. In the last thirty or more years I have become a pillar of society here in Charnley. Like Josiah, I invested in land, and own a very large acreage in this part of Warwickshire. The days of the diggings are very remote to me, Inspector. Most of my memories are bound up with this charming old town, of which I have twice been mayor. Is there anything else you wish me to tell you?'

'I was wondering, sir, if you would tell me what you were doing between the hours of one o'clock and four on Monday afternoon?'

Alexander Skeffington threw back his head and laughed.

'My goodness, Mr Jackson, you have a nerve! You want me to give you an alibi. Well, I can assure you that I wasn't slaughtering a young man in Ashborne Hill. I was in Coventry on business of one sort or another for most of the day, and I didn't return to Charnley until early evening — here, let me give you this business card. It's from the firm of accountants I was visiting. Thompson and Bulling, of Priory Row, just opposite Holy Trinity Church in Coventry. They'll tell you what I was doing on Monday. I saw them in the late morning, and then I lunched at an hotel. I spent a lot of time walking in the town, visiting St Michael's church, and the art gallery —'

'Please, Mr Skeffington,' said Jackson, smiling, 'there's no need to detail every minute of your day! I hope my question didn't offend you, sir —'

'Of course not, of course not. You must go through the necessary procedures. Well, it was melancholy news that you brought me, but I thank you all the same. If I can be of any further help to you in this business, Inspector, you have only to call on me. The hidden truth about this terrible murder must be brought out to the light of day.'

■ ■ ■ ■

Saul Jackson delicately applied a flaming taper to the oil lamp suspended from the ceiling in its hoop of brass, and the sitting-room of his cottage was flooded with warm light. He replaced the glass globe, and sat down in his old cane chair at the fireside.

'There you are, Sergeant Bottomley,' he said, 'now we can see to talk!'

Sergeant Bottomley, still wearing his yellow overcoat, sat opposite him. His battered brown bowler hat stood crown upward on the floor beside him. Two pewter tankards of mild ale sat on the hearth.

'Mr Alexander Skeffington was a very impressive man,' Jackson said. 'I can understand why he made a fortune out in Australia all those years ago. But the fact remains that he lives next door to the Holts, and is on very friendly terms with them. So it would be fairly easy for him to have helped himself to those scalpels from his neighbour's collection, used them, and then to have left them lying about where people like us could find them. The police, I mean. Likewise with the bloodstained gloves: perhaps he stole them, used them, and then planted them in Miss Ursula's room. I don't feel obligated to take every word of Mr Skeffington's as gospel.'

Sergeant Bottomley swallowed some of his beer, and then placed the tankard back on the hearth.

'Why should he do that, sir? Why should he hide those gloves in Miss Ursula's room, always supposing that he wore them to murder Elijah Robinson? Was it to incriminate her? If murder was laid at her door, you see, she wouldn't hang. They'd send her to a secure asylum for criminal lunatics. Or was it just to create confusion?'

'And then, of course, Sergeant, why should Mr Skeffington want to murder Elijah Robinson in the first place? Why should he want to murder a man whose father, an old friend, had just left him five thousand pounds? He'd gain absolutely nothing from doing that.'

'Not as far as we know, sir. But maybe we don't know far enough.'

Jackson made no reply. He took a deep draught from his tankard, and then retrieved his fat notebook from under his chair. He flicked through the pages for a moment, and then asked Bottomley a question.

'Are we agreed that your Miss Ursula Holt had nothing to do with the murder of Mr Robinson? She couldn't possibly have done it, because the times are all wrong. Ursula Holt left Inchfield Station at eleven in the morning on the day of the murder. She was obliged to catch a slow stopping-train that took three hours to reach Ashborne Hill. The engine broke down, and there was a long wait on the line until a relief locomotive could be brought in from Donnington sidings. She arrived at Ashborne Hill at two o'clock – as you know, I saw her arrive myself.'

'And what about Mr Robinson, sir? When did *he* leave?'

'Poor Mr Robinson and his sinister companion, Sergeant, had left only ten minutes earlier. After that, I had Miss Ursula in full sight until we both left the dining-room of the Berkeley Arms to catch the two-twenty to Charnley. She couldn't have done it.'

Bottomley sighed, and Jackson caught the fleeting look of despair that crossed his face. It was an expression well known to Jackson. It meant that his sergeant was becoming personally involved in the troubles of one of their suspects, in this case of Miss Ursula Holt. Well, he would leave him on a long rein where that young woman was concerned.

'No, sir,' said Bottomley, 'she couldn't have done it, but her mind is so troubled and confused that she's quite prepared to think that she did. "I don't always remember what I've done", she said to me this afternoon. "So maybe I *did* murder him, and hid the gloves in my drawer without knowing that I'd done so". A mind that can indulge in self-deception of that kind, sir, could easily become a prey to someone who wants to make her a scapegoat.'

'How about the people at Abbey Lodge?' asked Jackson. 'That rather quiet and self-effacing physician, Dr Matthew Holt, for instance. Was he really in London that day? After all, we've only his word for it – and they were his scalpels! Oh, and how about Miss Kate? There's a young man calls at the house, a handsome accountant called Paul Staunton. I saw him, too, at Ashborne Hill, so I can vouch for his attractive way with at least one young lady. Maybe Miss Kate's secretly jealous of Ursula, and is looking for ways to get her safely back into the asylum, so that she can have Mr Paul Staunton all to herself.'

Herbert Bottomley permitted himself a throaty laugh. He hauled himself to his feet, and retrieved his hat from beside his chair.

'It's all surmise, sir! You might as well say that Dr Holt's coachman, John, is plotting to wipe out the whole family because he's been left a legacy of five pounds! You might as well —'

'Yes, I know, Sergeant,' said Jackson, laughing in his turn. 'We've had enough of sitting down to theorize. The time's come to advance this investigation beyond the confines of two houses and one obscure churchyard. The first thing I'm going to do is to check up on Alexander Skeffington. He says he's rich. Everybody else says he's rich. And he looks rich. He probably is, but we need to know for sure. It's purely a matter of elimination, Sergeant. I'll walk across the meadows to Sherringham tomorrow, and see whether I can run Banker Barnard to earth.'

'Barnard? He'll be in The Golden Shield, sir, unless his liver's taken him off to the infirmary or the cemetery. He's worse than me, when it comes to the spirits.'

'He is, Sergeant, and I hope you'll take warning by him. The way you're going on, your liver will end up in a jar at medical school, for young medicos to gawp at. But for all that, Banker Barnard knows all there is to know about the wealthy of Warwickshire, so I'll run him to earth tomorrow, and ask him about Mr Skeffington. After that. . . . I'm wondering whether to get in touch with Elijah Robinson's folk in

America. I don't mean by letter. I'd ask Superintendent Mays to arrange a telegraph link with New York, and use that. His father's dead, as we know; but maybe he has a mother, and brothers, and so on. They may know something.'

'And what about me, sir?'

'I'm giving you a free hand, Sergeant. I think you've already planned what you want to do. I'm right, aren't I?'

'Yes, sir. I'm going to re-examine all the evidence against Miss Ursula Holt. I don't like all those scalpels, and I don't like that ugly business with the gloves. I'll start at the well in the bluebell wood, sir, the well where the dog Ben was found with his throat cut. Maybe I'll turn up other villains that we know nothing about.'

'That's a very good idea, Sergeant Bottomley. Whatever you turn up, let it take you as far as you wish. You and I can compare notes later.'

Saul Jackson accompanied his sergeant to the door, and watched him as he walked heavily along Meadow Cross Lane to the paddock where he'd tethered his horse. Woe betide any villains who crossed his path! He looked like a rough country fellow, but he was as cute as a cartload of monkeys.

Presently, Herbert Bottomley emerged

from the paddock, sitting high on a chestnut horse. He raised an arm briefly in greeting, and then cantered away in the direction of Thornton Heath.

Thursday brought warm, bright weather, with a light breeze, and Jackson enjoyed his walk across the meadows beyond Meadow Cross. He emerged on to the road at the foot of Fort Hill, and another hundred yards brought him to the old village of Sherringham. Towering above the huddle of cottages, the medieval church, and the modern redbrick school, was the seat of the Sherringhams, half castle keep, half Tudor mansion house.

The Golden Shield hostelry lay at the far end of the village street, and in the back bar Inspector Jackson found Mr Edwin Barnard, retired manager of an old-established private bank in Stratford-upon-Avon. A stout man wearing a tight black suit, he sat at the table with *The Times* spread out in front of him. A bottle of Sherman's Beefeater Gin stood near to hand, together with a glass. A Cornish pasty reposed in a pile of crumbs on the bare table top. The air was thick with tobacco smoke, and the front of Banker Barnard's black jacket was covered in cigarette ash.

'Ah! Jackson! Now what brings you to my little hide-out this morning? You want to know something, I'll be bound. Well, sit down there, on that bench. Will you take something? No? Well, as you will. What can I do for you?'

'I knew you wouldn't mind me coming here like this, Mr Barnard,' said Jackson. 'You're a man of regular habits, if I may say so, and it's well known that you like to take your morning break here, at The Golden Shield. I want you to tell me about Mr Alexander Skeffington, of Providence House, Charnley. About his financial standing, I mean.'

The retired banker gave Jackson a shrewd, appraising glance. He said nothing for a minute, while he bit into his pasty, and poured himself a small glass of gin.

He knocks it back just like Bottomley does, thought Jackson, and that's the sure sign of a seasoned drinker. But Banker Barnard has a bright red, inflamed nose, whereas Bottomley —

'Skeffington's as sound as a bell,' declared Mr Barnard, spraying pasty crumbs across the table. 'I'll tell you that at once, before I get down to detail. What are you cooking up in that mistrustful mind of yours? Is it something to do with that murder at Ashborne Hill? Or with the murderous young lady – I forget her name – who lives next door to the worthy Skeffington at Charnley? No, you won't tell me. Very well.'

Mr Barnard wiped his lips on a snuff-stained handkerchief, and sat back in his chair. Jackson waited. Banker Barnard, despite his rather disreputable appearance and habits, had lived an impeccable life as a banker, and had made himself master of all kinds of financial knowledge, and not a few financial secrets. He had helped Jackson twice before, and in each instance his expert knowledge had helped the inspector to initiate prosecutions, one for fraud, and the other for murder.

'Alexander Skeffington has lived in that house at Charnley for close on forty years, Mr Jackson,' Barnard said, 'which in banking circles would be a decidedly strong reference if ever he asked for credit – for accommodation, you know. A large entailed loan, something of that sort.'

'And has he ever asked for accommodation?'

'No. Certainly not. He's immensely rich. He keeps his money in three different banks, and it's *real* money, you know, not some paper fantasy. Half a million pounds in gold. There, I knew that'd surprise you!

He's also a great landowner. He has thousands of acres of unsecured land here in Warwickshire, and in Oxfordshire.'

'Unsecured?'

'Meaning that none of that land is mortgaged, or held in tenancy from others. That land of his brings in an income of about twelve thousand a year. So, your Mr Skeffington is, as I say, immensely rich. And to that wealth he allies modesty and taste. He could have bought himself a vast estate, and lived like a duke. Instead, he is content to be seen as a respectable bourgeois, whilst filling his modest mansion with countless treasures. Have I answered your question?'

'You have, Mr Barnard. When this case – I'm conducting a case at the moment – is over, I'm minded to come back here and tell you all about it. If, that is —'

'If, that is, I'm still alive? Fear not, Jackson, I shall be here, waiting, when your case is closed.'

So that's that, thought Jackson, and he retraced his steps to Meadow Cross. Skeffington really is wealthy, and all his money can be quite openly accounted for. It was becoming very clear that any attempt to link Alexander Skeffington with the murder of Elijah Robinson was both futile and vain. Still, it would do no harm to round off the business of Skeffington by visiting his accountants in Coventry. What were they called? Thompson and Bulling, of Priory Row.

The premises of Messrs Thompson and Bulling, chartered accountants, conveyed an air of settled prosperity that no doubt pleased their select clientele. The firm occupied a gloomy, panelled set of chambers in Priory Row, from the bow windows of which one had a clear view of the celebrated spire of Holy Trinity, Coventry.

Mr Bulling, a stout man with thinning hair and hairless pink cheeks, peered at Inspector Jackson's warrant card through gold pince-nez. He pursed his lips, and shook his head, as though deploring the times in which he was obliged to live – times that brought a rural policeman into his discreet and rather exclusive world.

'And in what way can I be of service to you, Inspector Jackson? Mr Thompson and I are accountants, and our business is conducted with clients of the utmost integrity. I cannot imagine what your business with us can be. Eh, Thompson?'

Jackson had noticed another man in the room, a thin, acidulated person who sat half hidden behind a glass partition, a great ledger open in front of him. The man peered round the partition and squinted briefly at the inspector.

'Indeed no, Bulling. It's not our practice to have any kind of commerce with the police.'

'You have a client,' Jackson began, 'a Mr Alexander Skeffington, of Charnley.'

'That is so,' Bulling replied. 'We are very pleased to keep Mr Skeffington's books for him. He is a man of impeccable antecedents. Eh, Thompson?'

'Quite so,' came the voice from behind the glass partition.

If I don't say my piece, Jackson thought, I'll be here all day. I'm in no mood to play cat and mouse with these two wily accountants.

'Gentlemen,' he said, 'Mr Alexander Skeffington has told me that he called upon you this Monday gone, the second of October. I have no reason to doubt his word, but I need to hear from you what time he came into your office here in Priory Row, and what time he left. He was a little vague about times. Perhaps you can be more accurate.'

'Why do you want to know about those times? I fail to see —'

'I am conducting a murder investigation,

Mr Bulling,' said Jackson shortly. 'The slaughter of a young American gentleman in the churchyard of Ashborne Hill. Part of any such investigation consists of the early elimination of various people from the case. Elimination, you understand, dismisses innocent people from the enquiry, leaving the police free to pursue possible suspects.'

Jackson allowed a certain hardness to enter his voice as he added, 'I must now insist that you answer my question. When did Mr Skeffington arrive here, and when did he depart?'

'Murder? Dear me! We read about it in the paper, of course, but Mr Skeffington made no allusion to it. Of course, we're most anxious to assist you, Inspector. Mr Skeffington walked in through that door at – was it before eleven, or after, Thompson? I think it was just before eleven.'

'It was just after,' said the voice from behind the partition. 'The church had just struck the hour. It was about two minutes after eleven.'

'It was about two minutes after eleven, Inspector,' said Mr Bulling. 'We discussed some business matters for an hour, and Mr Skeffington signed a number of documents – enabling instruments, you know. And then we had a glass of sherry. At least, Mr Skeffington and I did. Mr Thompson is teetotal.'

'And when did Mr Skeffington leave, sir?'

'He left – when did he leave, Thompson?'

'Leave? Well, as to that, sir,' said the voice behind the partition, 'I can't swear to an exact time. I was in the cellar for a while, trying to ferret out the Bredwardine papers. But I suppose it was about twelve when Mr Skeffington left.'

'It was about twelve when Mr Skeffington left,' said Mr Bulling. 'He said that he wanted to spend some time in Coventry that day. He never said what it was that he was going to do, and, of course, I never asked him.'

'Well, thank you, gentlemen,' said Jackson, 'you've been very helpful in eliminating Mr Alexander Skeffington from my enquiry. I'll be on my way back to Warwick, now. Let me bid you good day.'

So much, then, for Mr Skeffington's 'alibi'. It had applied only to a morning's interview with his accountants, whom he had left at midday. During the crucial hours of one o'clock to four, he had evidently been wandering around Coventry, enjoying the sights. There could be no credible witnesses to prove that.

Skeffington could have easily caught the 12.30 train from Coventry to Ashborne

Hill, which would have deposited him on the platform there at one o'clock. But why should Skeffington have wanted to murder a young man who was a complete stranger to him? How would he have known him, if he had never seen him? Perhaps there were other, more obscure, explanations.

Had the young American been followed to England by someone bent on destroying him for reasons that could be investigated only in his native city of New York? Or had the mysterious assassin worked in league with someone known to him in Charnley – someone who had access to Dr Holt's house? It was time to leave Skeffington alone, and to look elsewhere.

7
URSULA'S JOURNAL

Friday, 6 October 1893. Last night I dreamt of the haunted ballroom again, but this time my dream was more vivid and protracted than it had been before, and its consequences were terrifying.

You will remember, dear Dr Meitner, that this dream usually finds me present in a glittering and stately ballroom, where a company of ladies and gentlemen are dancing a saraband. One of the dancers, a handsome, smiling young man, speaks to me, but his words are indistinct. He invites me to lift the lid of a carved wooden chest, but the idea fills me with such terror that I invariably awake. Last night's dream, as you will hear, was much worse. Let me give you an account of what I saw.

I found myself in a dark and dusty vestibule, the only light afforded by the candle that I held aloft. It was horribly cold, and I stumbled up a kind of staircase or flight of steps, and came into the ballroom. At first, it was quite dark in that long, sinister chamber, and I saw only as far as my little candle permitted. At my feet I saw a deed box, quite an ordinary affair, with a black and green enamelled lid.

I moved a little to my right, by now quite numb with cold, and saw on the floor something that filled me with an illogical alarm. It was a silvery flute, with a red tassel attached to it. I wanted to pick it up, but some primal instinct forbade me to do so.

All at once the light of many candelabra filled the lofty gilded chamber, and I smelt once more the scent of burning candlewax. I half expected to see the smiling young man, but instead I was accosted by a young Negro boy in livery, and with a fanciful turban on his head. His face carried a fixed smile, not threatening, but decidedly odd, and I noted that he had bright, round blue eyes – a rarity, surely, in members of his race?

The servant spoke to me, but as in my previous dreams, I could not distinguish the words. I wandered further into the room, and saw that it was now filled with its usual company of dancers, all in the costumes of the eighteenth century. I found myself in an area of the room where some tables and chairs had been set out, and saw that a number of figures sat there, with wine glasses before them on the table. I recognized some of these figures as people I knew. One of them was the police inspector who came to Mr Skeffington's house. He fixed his gaze on my face, and once again I felt that this man could read all the stored secrets of my heart.

All these impressions, dear Dr Meitner, were as vivid and as fully realized as any scene of my waking life. I was fearful and apprehensive, all the more so as I felt that this dream – I knew it was a dream – had been experienced once before, many years ago, when I was a young girl.

I progressed further into the room, and saw a small chamber orchestra playing behind a kind of roped-off barrier. Some of the players smiled and nodded at me, and I felt that they were part of the normal world to which I would return once this dream had ended. They were all clad in the old costumes of the last century, with powdered wigs on their heads. Oddly enough, I thought that I knew one or two of those men – that I had, in fact, encountered them at one time in the course of my waking life.

And now the dream faded, to be replaced by a nightmare. There was no young man to beckon me towards the frightful chest this time, but I felt myself impelled to cross the floor of the ballroom and look at it. The dance continued, and the solemn music of the saraband filled the air.

The chest I can see now, as though it had been a real thing. It was about six feet in length, and three feet high, made of stout oak, its coffered lid carved with images of a lion and a fanciful unicorn upholding a five-pointed star. Nothing could have looked more real. I lifted the lid.

For a brief moment – I mean quite literally a fraction of a second – I perceived something clothed and shrunken, something brittle and starved of flesh, a thing that began to strike terror into my soul. And then that image had gone, and lying there in the chest I saw a beautiful wax tableau of 'The Sleeping Beauty', dressed in fairytale clothing.

You are, perhaps, acquainted with the old fairy-tale by Charles Perrault? Condemned to sleep for a hundred years, the Sleeping Beauty will wake up at the behest of a king's son. This recollection of the tale came into my mind while I stood there, in the nightmare, looking down at the wax figure, and vaguely recalling the horrible shrunken thing that had preceded it.

Then, the countenance of the wax image began to shimmer and change, until it had transmuted into the beautiful face of my dear friend Catherine Stansfield. I staggered back from the chest in horror. Why should my friend, a living woman with a noble husband and a dear little girl of her own, appear as a waxen image in this nightmare place?

I was at once conscious again of the intense cold. The music died away, and the dancing figures became dim wraiths. I hurried in the failing light towards the door through which I had entered. I remember seeing the deed box lying on the floor, and then, to my intense relief, I gained the threshold.

Oh, Dr Meitner, how am I to tell you what happened to me then? You were so kind to me, so understanding; and yet, I do not want to be shut up again. Must I tell you? I have sat here for over a minute, watching my chamber candle lose its battle against the bright morning sun besieging the bedroom curtains, and making up my mind to tell you all. I realize that I must.

I woke suddenly to find myself lying on the cloister flags. I was numbed with the cold, and realized that I was wearing only my nightdress, and that my feet were bare. I had been sleepwalking again, and during that fast sleep I had endured the nameless terrors of the haunted ballroom.

Almost immediately I saw the bright light of lanterns bobbing through the dark across the garden, and heard a confusion of voices calling my name. 'Ursula! Ursula! Polly!' Within moments my uncle, John the coachman and dear cousin Kate were around me. They asked me how I was, but none dared ask me how I had got there. Kate who, like Uncle, was wearing a dressing-gown, stooped down and placed a warm blanket across my shoulders. I reached up with my hands to adjust it, and saw that they were cut and bloodied, and that my fingers were running with blood.

'Uncle!' I cried. 'My hands! My hands!' He said nothing, merely glanced at me, and began to search the cloister and its surrounds. After a while I heard him mutter, 'No knives this time', and even in that half whisper I could hear his utter despair. Kate, bless her, had brought a pair of my felt slippers with her. I pulled them on, and rose to my feet.

It was then that I saw another figure standing in the garden. By the light of the lanterns which had been placed on the flags of the cloister, I saw that it was Detective Sergeant Bottomley. While Uncle and the others were preparing to take me back to the warmth and shelter of the house, Mr Bottomley stepped on to the flags, and began to examine the old locked door that had once led into the mysterious dark recesses of Mr Skeffington's house. I saw him look at his hands, and then at me.

'Miss Ursula,' he said, in perfectly normal tones as though nothing untoward had happened, 'would you please come over here? And you, Dr Holt, if you will.'

I saw at once that the door had been wrenched from its frame by main force, and that the old rusted lock hung crookedly from its screws. I saw smears of blood around the lock and the latch, and realized that the blood was my own.

'Unless I'm very much mistaken, Miss Ursula,' said Mr Bottomley gently, 'it was *you* who attempted to wrench this door open. Your hands are cut and torn, and there are traces of skin around that lock.'

Uncle Matthew began a kind of mild protest, but a look from Mr Bottomley silenced him. I made no attempt to deny what the homely-looking detective said. I recalled some words of Dr Karl Gustav Altmann, Intendant of the Maria Hospital at

Vienna, in his book *The Somnambule.* 'The involuntary somnambule frequently resorts to acts of unwonted violence.' I had done that to the door! Why?

I was conscious of the others standing silently, looking at Mr Bottomley. He was still wearing his flapping yellow overcoat, but had wound a red woollen scarf around his neck. I wondered what he had been doing, lurking in the garden at – what time was it? As though in answer, the clock of the nearby church struck three.

'Yes, Mr Bottomley,' I said, 'I expect you're right.'

You see, dear Dr Meitner, I had recalled that incident, ten years ago, when I had ventured through that cloister door, and found myself in a dark vestibule, much like the one in my dream. Had I, in my sleep-walking state, imagined that the haunted ballroom lay behind that door? Had my sleeping self employed manic strength in a vain attempt to force it open?

As though in answer to my question, Sergeant Bottomley seized the latch, and pulled the door wide open. Picking up one of the lanterns he held it aloft. The doorway, we saw, had long ago been bricked up from the inside. Whatever constituted the riddle of my terrifying dream, its solution did not lie behind that solid wall of brick.

There is little more to record. Uncle Matthew bathed and dressed my damaged hands, all the while assuring me that all was going to be well. He looked so violently distressed that I made no attempt to answer him. When he had retired to bed, Kate made us both a cup of tea, making sure that mine was laced with a spoonful of brandy.

I told Kate the main incidents of my dream, and she listened with patience and understanding, asking no questions, expressing no doubts. She sat at the kitchen table, her flaming ginger hair confined to a strong net. The light of our solitary candle glinted off her glasses. What a true and loyal friend she was!

At half past three she accompanied me up to my room. She had filled a stone hot water bottle, and busied herself placing it in my bed. As she left, I took the key out of bedroom door, and silently put it into her hand.

'Will you, Kate?' I asked.

She made no reply, but tears of distress welled up in her eyes, and she nodded her assent before hurrying from the room. I heard the bedroom key turn in the lock. As I closed the curtains, I saw by the feeble moonlight a figure standing motionless in the garden. It was Mr Bottomley. He was staring up at the great bulk of Providence House rising above the old cloister to the right, and I thought that he would become rooted to the spot, so still he seemed.

I determined there and then to record the night's events in my journal for you to see. When the time is ripe, I will post it to you at Inchfield. The brandy, and the soothing hot water bottle, sent me to sleep in minutes, and I awoke from a dreamless and refreshing sleep this morning.

What is to become of me? Where will all this psychic torment lead?

Written by me, Ursula Holt, and completed at 7.30 on the morning of Friday, 6 October 1893.

Herbert Bottomley had stayed the night in a lodging house, one of several in a quiet street near Charnley Station. He had slept fitfully, recalling the stricken girl whom he had seen emerging from the garden door of Abbey Lodge in the dark early hours of the previous night. He had set up a watch at midnight, and his long vigil had been rewarded.

He rose at dawn, drank a cup of tea, and made his way to the evergreen plantation that lay behind the two dwellings, Abbey Lodge and Providence House. The rays of the early sun were seeking a way through the branches of the trees, and a bird was tentatively singing somewhere among the foliage.

Should he have awoken Miss Ursula Holt when she began to cross the lawn barefooted like a wraith, her nightdress glowing a dim white in the light of the moon, her arms stretched out in front of her, as though feeling her way? No. Kindness of that nature could lead often to disaster.

He had watched her walk slowly into the dark cloister, where she had stood motionless for what he estimated to have been ten minutes. Then she had moved towards the door in the cloister wall, and had seized the latch. He had heard the wood rend and snap under the strength of her assault, and for a brief moment he had felt a superstitious fear. How could a young woman perform such a feat of violent strength? But then, he had heard her moan, and she had staggered, still asleep, to the centre of the cloister flags, where she had collapsed. It was then that her family had appeared with lanterns at the garden door.

Bottomley walked out of the plantation, and found himself in a cobbled lane. The bulk of Providence House rose up behind a high wall to his right, and he stood motionless, looking at it. A vast place it seemed, covered entirely in rich red Virginia creeper, which in parts had completely obliterated some of the windows.

Herbert Bottomley sighed, and shook himself like a terrier. Providence House fascinated him, but for the moment it was not apparently prepared to shared its secrets with him. It was time to move on.

To his left, across the lane, rose what Dr Holt had called a coppice. It was, Bottomley reckoned, a fair-sized wood, an integral part of the countryside, whereas the plantation had been a well-ordered piece of town landscaping. This, then, was the bluebell wood, where Miss Ursula had been found, her nightdress splashed with blood.

A short walk brought Bottomley to the wishing well. It was built of old stone, newly pointed, and stood in an arena of trampled grass on the fringe of the wood. An old man was working near the well, piling kindling wood on to a wheelbarrow. He looked up as Bottomley appeared, and regarded him steadily from rheumy eyes.

'You'll be the detective man, I reckon,' said the old man. 'What be you doin' here, master?'

'Yes, gaffer, I'm the detective man. Sergeant Bottomley's my name.'

'Joe Bates. That's who I am. What be you doin' down here?'

Joe Bates had a narrow, white-stubbled, weather-beaten face. He was clad in a moleskin suit, over which he wore a tattered overcoat tied round his middle with string.

'I'm looking at this old well, Joe,' said Bottomley. 'I've heard that Miss Ursula Holt of Abbey Lodge was found here, after she'd cut a dog's throat and thrown it down that well. That's why I'm here. But I expect you knew that already, didn't you?'

The old man grinned, showing a mouthful of stained and broken teeth. He gathered up a dead branch from the grass, and threw it into his barrow. Bottomley reached into one of the pockets of his yellow overcoat, and produced a battered silver flask.

'Come and sit here, on the grass, Joe Bates,' he said, 'and share some of this gin with me. Perhaps you'd like a pipeful of tobacco while you're at it?'

Joe Bates sat down on the grass, and Bottomley joined him. Soon, the two men were availing themselves of the contents of the silver flask and of Bottomley's tobacco pouch. Bottomley had dredged up half a bedraggled cheroot from his pocket, and had carefully lit it with a wax vesta.

'If you don't smoke a pipe, master,' said Joe Bates, 'why do you carry a tobacco pouch with you?'

'I carry it in case anyone I meet fancies a pipeful,' Bottomley replied. 'People like you, out early in the wood, like Proud Maisie in the poem. People who may have been here, by the well, when Miss Ursula Holt was found, after she'd killed that poor dog. What was his name? Ben. Ben the sheepdog. The fifth of April, that was.'

'That's as may be,' said Joe Bates. Bottomley was content to wait.

Joe puffed away quietly at his pipe. His eyes were fixed on the well, but his face told nothing of what he might have been thinking.

'See here, master,' he said at last, 'it's quite true what you say. I was there, you see? But I wasn't called to give evidence. No one wants to listen to a purblind old feller like me. That girl had gone sleepwalking before, so it was no surprise for Dr Holt and his daughter to find her over there, sitting by the well. One or other of them had been up in the night, and had seen her bedroom door open. Something like that, it was. I was already at work, you see, it being just after first light, like it is now.'

'How did they know where she'd gone? She might have gone anywhere.'

'They followed her barefoot trail in the dew. That's what one of Mr Skeffington's men told me. There were two of them. Two lackeys, or footmen, as they call them.'

'Was Mr Skeffington himself there?'

Joe Bates laughed, and shook his head in mock despair.

'You won't let a feller finish his story, will you? No, Mr Skeffington wasn't there. Or if he was, he kept out of sight. There was Dr Holt, looking as pale as ashes, and that red-haired daughter of his, John Forrest, their coachman, and the couple of lackeys from Mr Skeffington's house that I told you about. Miss Ursula was sitting over there, just beyond the well. You could see the blood on her nightgown, and the knife lying in her hand.'

'Lying? What do you mean by that?'

Joe Bates glanced shrewdly at Bottomley. 'I mean just that, master. She weren't clutching it. The knife was lying in her hand, looking for all the world as though someone had put it there. Well, Dr Holt sent one of the lackeys running for old Inspector Collier, and I must say he came pretty sharpish. Did you ever meet him? He had dark shadows under his eyes, and long drooping

149

moustaches, so when he spoke, it looked as though he was talking without moving his lips. I could hear him asking questions and barking out orders to his constable, who'd come with him. Then he looked down the well.'

'What happened to Miss Ursula, Joe, while this Inspector Collier was busy barking?'

'Doctor Holt woke her up. Although her eyes had been open, it seems that she was actually asleep. I saw her look down at the knife lying in her hand, and then she set up a scream – I don't mind telling you, master, that I almost died of fright on the spot. I'm told that them high-class girls are very good at screaming. That one certainly was. And then they took her away.'

'What about Ben the sheepdog?'

'The constable went down the well with one of Farmer Laidlaw's men, and brought him out. Laidlaw himself had waddled up by then. He set up a cry, and wrung his hands, and cast his little piggy eyes up to Heaven, and so on, the hypocrite! That Ben was a good sheepdog, but he was a snapper and a snarler, and met with little kindness at the farm. The only person Ben ever liked was that Miss Ursula. He'd come running to her when he saw her, and she'd give him titbits she'd brought specially from the house. Poor lass, by the looks of things it won't be long before she's back in the madhouse.'

'And that was that?'

'It was. You'll know all about what happened next, you being a policeman yourself, though I must say, master, that you don't look like one. You look more like a farmer or a drover. Inspector Collier, now, he was very smart and gleaming all over with buttons and buckles. He liked shouting and throwing his weight about. Of course, he took no notice of *me.* He died of what they call an apoplexy – a kind of fit, it is.'

Old Joe Bates knocked out his pipe on the stump of a tree, and got slowly to his feet. He turned towards his wheelbarrow, and made as though to move off deeper into the wood. Then he stopped, came up close to Bottomley, and looked at him thoughtfully.

'I reckon you're a different kind of man from Inspector Collier,' he said, 'and that you might listen to what an unlettered old man has to say. No, I'll not appear in any court, and I'll not give evidence, or anything like that, but if you're delving into that business of Miss Ursula Holt, then go and ask that hypocrite Reuben Laidlaw some questions. Find out what happened to his son, Jonah.'

'Thank you kindly, Joe. I'll do as you say. Is there anything else that you can tell me?'

'Well, I'll just say this. That Miss Ursula was sleepwalking, so they say, and in that state she walked out of her home at Abbey Lodge, walked through the plantation and out across the lane into this here wood. It's a long walk in the dark, master, and a cruel drag for a barefoot lass. I just wonder whether someone might have helped her to travel that distance. . . .'

'You mean —'

'I don't rightly know what I mean. I'm just telling you what I think. You see, while they were all fussing round Miss Ursula, I fancied that I saw someone creeping away through the trees towards the lane. I don't know who it was, but he was anxious to get away from the scene. Perhaps it was a poacher going home. I don't know.'

'I wonder what a sheepdog was doing out in the wood at night?' asked Bottomley, half to himself. 'It's too much of a coincidence that he should have chosen that very night when Miss Ursula was walking abroad like a spirit, knife in hand, ready to cut Ben's throat.'

'I know, master. None of it makes sense

to me, but then, I'm just a silly old man. Go and talk to Reuben Laidlaw. His farm's not a hundred yards from here, along the woodland path to Newton Forge. Ask him about his son, Jonah.'

Bottomley stood in the muddy track and looked critically at Laidlaw's Farm. A wide, broken gate lay on its side against a blackthorn hedge, leaving the stable yard open to the road. The yard, like the approaching track, was muddy and untended. Laidlaw's Farm looked as though it was fast running to seed.

I suppose he's got a couple of cows in that shed, Bottomley thought. His sheep will be out in the pasture, or up on one of the hills, or what pass for hills in this part of the shire. That's where Ben would have exercised his canine skills, out there, with the sheep. A snapper and a snarler, according to old Gaffer Bates. Well, somebody had paid him out for his unpleasant ways.

The door of a dilapidated farmhouse opened, and a burly man appeared in the stable yard. He was carrying a spade, and held it in a way that suggested a weapon. The man's face was fat and expressionless, but his small beady eyes viewed Bottomley with open hostility.

'Who are you? What do you want? You get away from here. This is private land.'

For such a big man, thought Bottomley, he has a very high-pitched voice.

'Mr Reuben Laidlaw? I'm Detective Sergeant Bottomley, of the Warwickshire Constabulary. I'd like to ask you a few questions, if you've no objection.'

'What kind of questions? We're law-abiding folk in this house.'

Farmer Laidlaw had thrown down his spade, and squelched through the stable yard, and stood with his arms akimbo, in the open space where the farm gate should have been. There was something ostensibly threatening about his stance, but Bottomley could sense the cringing timidity behind it.

'I just wanted to ask you about your sheepdog, Ben. I've been told that you lost him last April under dreadful circumstances —'

'Poor Ben! He was such a good dog. We were devoted to him, you know, and he to us. There was just my son Jonah and me here to manage this farm, and Ben was like one of the family. I'm sorry I spoke roughly, Mr Bottomley, but we've had quite a few suspicious characters lurking round here lately. No offence, I hope. Has there been more trouble with that madwoman? They

154

should be locked up for life; murdering savages – for that's what it was, murder, dog or no dog.'

'And it was this madwoman who killed poor Ben, was it? This Ursula Holt?'

'That's right. They let her out from the madhouse because she was a doctor's niece – they stick together, those medical men. But she was the one who cut poor Ben's throat with a surgeon's knife, stolen from her uncle's store of such things.'

'Dreadful, Mr Laidlaw. Dear me, you must have been very upset. They found her near here, I've been told.'

'Yes. Just by the old wishing well in the bluebell wood. She was lying on the ground, her eyes wide open, and clutching the knife in her hand. The whole place was soaked with poor Ben's blood. They found him thrown down the well. My son Jonah never recovered from the shock of that day. Quite ill, he was. And the ground landlord, young Squire Fitzgerald, came over from Earl's Green, to find out what all the fuss was about. He agreed that poor Jonah – my son – should be sent off to work as a hired labourer with Mr Pierce at Newton Forge, two miles up the road from here. A change of scene was what he wanted. He's only twenty-four, so I expect he'll get over it all very soon.'

'I expect you miss your Jonah, don't you, Mr Laidlaw?' asked Bottomley.

He watched as two mournful tears ran down the farmer's cheeks. He began to tremble slightly, as though suddenly overcome by some secret grief. Laidlaw's reaction told Bottomley all that he wanted to know. He had framed his apparently simple question to that effect.

'Yes, I miss him, because pastoral farming is cruel hard work for one man without help. Squire Fitzgerald made a few disparaging remarks about the husbandry here, but then, he's got a dozen men to keep things shipshape for him. I expect they'll be taking the madwoman back to the asylum? I hope so, for all our sakes. She won't stop at poor dumb beasts, Mr Bottomley. You mark my words, it'll be people next.'

8
THE MAN AT THE
BEAR AND BILLET

'You sent for me, sir?'

Saul Jackson stood in the doorway of Superintendent Mays' office in Peel House, the imposing headquarters of the County Constabulary on the Parade at Copton Vale. Mr Mays, a greying man with a face like wrinkled parchment, had been absorbed in the study of a long telegraph message when Jackson had knocked and walked in. Although habitually dressed in the imposing uniform of a senior police officer, Mays always looked to Jackson more like a distinguished physician or surgeon than a policeman.

'Ah, Jackson! Sit down, won't you? What I have to tell you is so extraordinary that I'll leave other matters until I've explained it to you. You asked me yesterday to establish telegraphic contact with the police at New York, so that they could assist us in tracing any living relatives of this Elijah Robinson.

A very good idea, that, Jackson. Perhaps the secret of that young man's murder lies in America, rather than in sleepy little Ashborne Hill.'

Superintendent Mays paused, and began to fiddle with some of the papers on his desk. Jackson glanced out of the window, where he could see the sunlit recreation ground stretching up to Hollis Hill, where the tall chimney of Sherman's Brewery belched out heavy black smoke. It was a brewing day, and the whole town centre of Copton Vale would be smelling of hops.

'Yes, a very good idea,' Mays continued. 'Well, before I could do as you asked, this extraordinary cable message was received at the General Telegraph Office in Canal Street, and brought up here to me. Evidently the sender knew nothing of the police protocols, either here or in the States. Most irregular.'

'And what did the cable message say, sir?' It wasn't like Mr Mays to be so obtuse, thought Jackson. There's something embarrassing in that message, otherwise he would have told me straight what it was about.

'It comes from a man called Mr Buchanan Davis, who says that he's Elijah Robinson's uncle on the mother's side. He says that he would like to see the investigating officer

158

personally, as there are questions that he wants to ask. Well, that's you, of course, Jackson. "Tell your officer to come immediately to New York, where he will be met off the boat, and conveyed to my late nephew's house in Washington Square. All expenses paid." What do you think of that, Jackson?'

'Well, sir, under normal circumstances I'd be only too ready to oblige, but it's a difficult time for me, as you'll appreciate. I'm going across to Ashgate St Lawrence tomorrow, to deliver the Special Licence to the rector, and to discuss various other details about the marriage. When did this Mr Buchanan Davis want me to visit him?'

'That's just it, Jackson. He wants you to embark from Liverpool on the *Campania* next Monday, the ninth —'

'*Monday?*' cried Jackson. 'But sir, that's only four days off! And I'll be away for weeks. Sergeant Bottomley went off early this morning to pursue an investigation of his own. There are no detectives at Ashborne Hill or Charnley. And if the wedding is to go off successfully, I need proper time for preparation — Did you say the *Campania*?'

Superintendent Mays caught the change of tone in Jackson's voice, and pressed home his advantage.

'Yes, indeed, Jackson. Just think of it! One of Cunard's latest ships. She won the Blue Riband in June, crossing the Atlantic in five days. She's a floating palace, Jackson, taking nine hundred passengers. And this Mr Davis has pre-booked your passage. All you have to do is make yourself known as you climb the gangway, and you'll be conducted to a single second-class berth. What do you think?'

'I must say, sir, that it sounds very tempting. Five days?'

'Yes. He says here that you'll arrive on Friday, the thirteenth – you're not superstitious, are you? Good, I thought not. Stay three days, and then embark for England on the seventeenth. You'll be back here on the twenty-first, and I'll guarantee you six days paid leave of absence so that you can finish all your arrangements for the wedding. So what do you say? The truth of Elijah Robinson's death may lie in his secret life in New York.'

'Very well, sir. I'll do as you say, and cross to New York. This Mr Buchanan Davis wastes no time – "hustling", that's what they call it in America, I believe.'

Mays handed Jackson the lengthy telegraph message, which he put carefully in the inside pocket of his coat.

'You know how I fret being cooped up in this place, Jackson,' said Mays. 'Quite frankly, I was tempted for a moment to go out to the States in your place! But I'll tell you what I intend to do. While you're away, I'll camp out in your police-office in Warwick, and keep an eye on things. You'd better leave a message for Bottomley, if you can't find him before you leave. Meanwhile, the best of luck. And enjoy your voyage on the SS *Campania*!'

The Reverend Harry Goodheart's study in the eighteenth-century rectory at Ashgate St Lawrence was just as Saul Jackson remembered it from eighteen months earlier. During his investigation of the affair of The Dried-Up Man, the long, sunny room, lit by three windows looking out on to the churchyard, had been a kind of sanctuary to him, a sane and friendly refuge from the demons of terror and superstition that had been walking abroad in the ancient town.

'Mr Jackson,' said Harry Goodheart, 'the fact that you have been suddenly summoned to the New World is no reason for your not eating. Sustain the inner man! Those ham sandwiches are freshly made, or there's hot buttered toast under that china cover on the table.'

Jackson helped himself to a ham sandwich, and poured out a cup of tea from a silver pot standing on a trivet in the hearth. He looked at the tall, athletic man standing by one of the windows, and thought: Mr Goodheart is still the soul of generosity, and probably always will be. Just being in the same room with him lifted one's spirits.

'Thank you for bringing me Dr Benson's licence,' said the rector. 'Everything at this end of things can now proceed smoothly. I'm delighted that Mr Bottomley is to be your best man. He did wonderfull things here during that terrible business. People still talk about him here in Ashgate.'

'There could never have been any other choice, sir;' said Jackson. 'During the years that he's been my sergeant, he's made himself indispensable to me. He's just the man to be at my side when Sarah and I go up to the altar.'

'And Mrs Brown's matron of honour is to be her sister, Miss Hurst,' the rector continued. 'I gather that she, too, has a connection with one of your cases?'

Harry Goodheart sat down in an armchair near the fire. He helped himself to a slice of toast and a cup of tea, and looked at Jackson with interest. An outgoing man, he had a natural love of gossip.

'Ellen – Miss Hurst – is cook to Mr Louis Romanis of Copton Vale,' Jackson replied, 'and she was indirectly concerned in that business of the butchery at Burton Viscount, and its aftermath. So everyone concerned directly with this wedding has been connected with one or other of my cases – including you, sir, if I may say so!'

The Reverend Harry Goodheart laughed, and reached for another slice of toast.

'Well, that's true enough, Mr Jackson. But why aren't you eating? There's some very good seed cake today. Shall I ring for cook to being you some? No? Well, have a buttered scone.'

Jackson replenished his plate, and relaxed. There was no point in trying to evade the rector's hospitality. Still, it was cutting things rather fine. It was Saturday. On Monday morning he would be embarking on the *Campania* for New York.

'How is Dr Ambrose Phillips, sir?' asked Jackson. 'He very much enjoyed conducting that post-mortem examination with Dr Venner. Is he still chairman of the parish council?'

'He is, Mr Jackson. A wonderful help, and a very clever man in his own line, you know. Do you remember how he persuaded me to call in Dr Per Cornelis Brant to mesmerize Miss Deirdre Dovercourt? Well, after that incident, he began corresponding with a number of other distinguished alienists – psychiatrists, they're calling them now.'

Harry Goodheart chuckled. 'He brought me an invitation yesterday to a lecture in London by an up-and-coming foreign specialist in mental trauma. I think he wants me to go up to Town with him, but somehow, I think the calls of my parish are going to prove stronger than any interest of mine in psychiatry!'

Jackson put his empty cup down on its saucer, and looked with interest at his genial host. The case of Ursula Holt revolved around that young woman's mental disturbance, and her personal experience of an insane asylum. Perhaps it would help to describe the affair to Mr Goodheart who, through Dr Ambrose Phillips, could provide Jackson with a link to the world of morbid medicine.

'Talking of psychiatry, sir,' said Jackson, 'this case, which is taking me next Monday across the Atlantic, is much concerned with mental disturbance. I'd like to tell you about it, if I may.'

The Reverend Harry Goodheart sat quietly in his chair, his hands clasped together on his knee, and listened while Jackson gave him an account of the murder of Elijah Robinson, and the troubles of Ursula Holt. The only sounds in the quiet, sunlit room were his own voice, low and confiding, and the ticking of the rector's merry clock on the mantelpiece.

When Jackson's tale was done, the rector sighed, and moved uneasily in his chair.

'There is a hidden evil lurking behind the events that you've described, Mr Jackson,' he said, 'or rather an evil intelligence making use of that unfortunate young woman to mask its own fell deeds. Do you agree? What's that verse in Psalm Ten? "He sitteth lurking in the thievish corners of the streets: and privily in his lurking dens doth he murder the innocent." It was ever thus, and so will it ever be —'

With characteristic abruptness Harry Goodheart sprang from his chair, and began rummaging around on the mantelpiece.

'But come, Mr Jackson, let us see what I can do. You mentioned a Dr Meitner in your account of Miss Holt's incarceration in the asylum. Doctor Phillips mentioned Meitner when he was here the other day. It was he, among others, who arranged for this young Austrian psychiatrist to visit England.

'Wait! Ah! Here it is. This is a combined

invitation card and entrance ticket to his first lecture, to be given at the Royal Institution: "Struggling with the Physical Manifestations of Septic Insanity. By Dr Karl Gustav Altmann, Intendant of the Maria Hospital, Vienna." Septic insanity – ugh! Not really for me, you know!'

'Would you give me that card, sir? One or other of us – the police, I mean – will have to visit Dr Meitner before this case progresses much further. Thank you. And now, Mr Goodheart, I must hurry to catch the coach from The Royal William if I'm to get back to Warwick at a reasonable hour. I shall be away for nearly a fortnight, but Mr Mayes has promised me a week off before the wedding.'

Harry Goodheart shook hands, retaining Jackson's hand for a moment as though unwilling to let him go.

'Goodbye, Mr Jackson,' he said. 'I can sense that you're a little put out by this sudden voyage across the world so soon before your marriage. Try to take a positive view of it – enjoy it, if you can! Providence, you know, works in unexpected and hidden ways. Who knows, something that you hear in America may furnish the ultimate clue to the whole mystery. Meanwhile, let me wish you God speed.'

■ ■ ■ ■

Resplendent in all her youthful pride and glory, the screw steamer *Campania* lay with steam up alongside Liverpool Landing Stage. It was just before eight on the morning of Monday, 9 October. Saul Jackson stood for a moment to admire the great ship, temporarily oblivious to the throng of passengers, their friends and their relatives, surrounding him.

Jackson had not realized that the grand Atlantic liner would be so long – all of 600 feet, he estimated. Her hull was black, her superstructure a gleaming white, and her tall raked funnels were painted in the Cunard livery of black and red. Purposeful plumes of smoke rose from the funnels, and drifted across the River Mersey towards the Wirral shore.

He had returned from Ashgate early on Saturday evening, and had written a long note for Sergeant Bottomley, recording, among other things, the details of his trip to America, and the results of his visit to Harry Goodheart. He had enclosed the invitation to Dr Altmann's lecture, in case Bottomley saw some immediate use for it.

Sarah had risen admirably to the occasion, allaying his fears about the trip, and assuring him that she had plenty to occupy her during his absence. Assured and encouraged by her words and her cheerful demeanour, he had caught the overnight train to Liverpool from Birmingham.

Glancing once again at the magnificent liner, Jackson felt a sudden surge of excitement. The chance of crossing the ocean to America in such a luxurious fashion would not come his way again. He would take Mr Goodheart's advice, and enjoy it.

Herbert Bottomley walked into the remote village of Plemstall, twelve winding miles from Ashborne Hill, on the rainy morning of Tuesday, 10 October. A single-carriage train had taken him to a place called Eastley Platform, a quarter of a mile away from Plemstall, and he had walked into the village from there.

He had visited the village of Newton Forge late on the previous afternoon, where he had sought out Farmer Pierce, and asked after Jonah Laidlaw. No, Jonah was not there any longer. He'd taken him on to oblige Reuben Laidlaw and young Squire Fitzgerald, but he wouldn't tolerate any more mutilation of livestock. Sheep cost money. No, he didn't know where Jonah

Laidlaw had gone. Bottomley had better ask further along the road.

Bottomley's quest had finally brought him to Plemstall, which consisted of a single street of old Cotswold stone houses, a later redbrick settlement which had grown around the old church, and the village's whitewashed public house, The Bear and Billet. The cobbled forecourt of the inn glistened with rain, and there was a smell of wet hay in the air. Bottomley wondered whether it was raining over the Atlantic, where the guvnor had set sail on the previous day for America.

It was dark in the public bar of The Bear and Billet, and the air was thick with tobacco smoke. Half-a-dozen men sat at the rough wooden tables. They were all in the working dress of farm labourers, and they drank their beer quickly, almost furtively, as though the duties of farm and field were already calling them back to work. They glanced up as Bottomley entered the room, and stared at him with a kind of neutral curiosity. No doubt they took him to be a farmer, or a fairly prosperous smallholder.

Bottomley walked over to the bar, and ordered a double measure of gin. When the landlord brought it, the sergeant placed his warrant card open on the counter for the man to read.

'I want to speak to a man called Jonah Laidlaw,' he said without preamble, 'believed to be working for someone here in Plemstall.'

The landlord, an elderly man in shirt sleeves, looked personally affronted. Bottomley realized that the labourers at the tables had stopped talking, and were listening to what he and the landlord were saying.

'Jonah Laidlaw? Yes, he came here to work for Farmer Wilson. He took him on out of charity, I suppose. Well, he don't work for Wilson now, mister. He don't work for no one any more.'

'And can you tell me where I can find him, landlord? This Jonah Laidlaw. I want to question him, you see. Police business.'

The landlord jerked a finger towards the wall behind him.

'He's in there, in the back bar by himself, drinking himself to death. I can't refuse him by law, because this is a public house, and he's done nothing to disturb the peace. He's got a bit of money, and he pays his way, so he can stay there till he dies, for all I care.'

'Does he live here?'

'Of course not. I wouldn't have the likes of him sleeping under my roof. He dosses down in a ruined barn at the village end. Meanwhile, he stays here most of the day, and he can do so, as far as I'm concerned, until his money runs out.'

One of the farm labourers, a tall, stooping man with a glint of anger in his eyes, got up from his bench, and wiped his mouth on his sleeve.

'You're too soft on him, Tom,' he declared, and the other men murmured their assent. 'The likes of him should be sent packing, out of the sight and sound of decent men. If you let him stay here too long, you might find that something unfortunate will happen to him. You know what I mean.'

The big man strode out of the room. Bottomley turned from the bar, and held up his warrant card for the other men to see.

'I don't know for certain what this Laidlaw's done, friends,' he said, 'though I've a shrewd idea what it must have been. But if anyone tries to make something unfortunate happen to him, they'll have to answer to me.'

Bottomley smiled, but there was something so potentially menacing in the smile that the men at the tables dropped their eyes, and concentrated on finishing their beer. Bottomley pushed open a door beside the bar counter, and entered the back room of the inn.

A young man in his early twenties half lay across the table at which he sat, a young man with faded, frightened eyes, and the pinched face of a consumptive, covered in yellow healing bruises. He was dressed carelessly in an old pea jacket and fustian trousers tied at the ankles with string. An empty bottle of spirits stood beside a glass tumbler. Some bottles of ale lay as yet unopened in a wicker basket. Herbert Bottomley came quietly into the small, deserted room, and sat on the bench beside the pale, trembling young man.

'Jonah Laidlaw?' he asked. 'I'm Detective Sergeant Bottomley, from Warwick.'

The young man burst into tears.

'I always hated them,' he said. His voice was tired and feeble, like that of an old man. 'How I hated them! The stupid animals, I mean. I always wanted to work in a factory, but they – the brute beasts – forced me to be tied to the land.'

'A factory? What's so special about a factory, Jonah?'

'I went with a friend up to Birmingham, once,' said the young man. 'He took me to the factory where he worked. It was a huge brick building, warm and dry, and all lit inside by gas. It was a wire works. He was paid a wage every week, and after his work was done, he could go to the music hall, or the pub, or the working men's institute, all clean and dry.'

The young man stopped speaking, and began slowly to wring his hands together. Bottomley noticed how clean they were, and how neatly the nails had been clipped. Jonah Laidlaw's nature had been designed for life in a big city, away from the toil and soil of the countryside.

'I hated them, I tell you,' he continued. 'Stupid demanding brutes, all they could do was make silly, meaningless noises, and go where they were driven. And because I had to order their pointless lives for them, fetching and carrying, mucking out, clearing up after them, rescuing stupid sheep who lost their way in the lanes, and receiving nothing in return but more brute noises and struggles to escape – because I was forced to do all that by them, I was tied forever to the land, to the muck, and the stink, and the hopelessness of it all. How I hated them!'

He talks well for a farmer's lad, thought Bottomley. This Jonah must have received a good schooling, before the demands of work took him away into the fields.

'And then I realized that I could get my

revenge against them through pain – the only emotion they could feel. So I went out at night into the fields with a knife, and I slashed their legs. They'd respond with their usual crude noises, and stand there, the brutes, bleeding, and doing nothing for themselves. They were just waiting for me, their servant, to put things right for them.'

'I expect you did that with a scalpel, didn't you, Jonah?' asked Bottomley gently.

'Scalpel? No. That was the madwoman from Abbey Lodge – or so they said, but I know better. I used a sharp knife from the kitchen. When I got back from the fields, I'd wash it under the pump, and put it back in the kitchen drawer.'

'And what about Ben, the sheepdog —'

'Nasty, yapping brute! Yap! Yap! All it could ever do was yap and snap, like the snarling beast it was. The only person it ever liked was that Miss Ursula. One morning last April I saw her walking about in one of her trances. People aren't safe with her about. Walking in her sleep, she was. She was near the wishing well in the bluebell wood. Ben came running up to her, but when he saw me – saw the man who fed him, and looked after him – he set up his barking and snarling, baring his teeth at me.'

The young man began to tremble again,

and Bottomley saw a pulse beating rapidly in his temple. At the same time, two hectic spots, the sign of the consumptive, glowed red in his pale cheeks.

'I had the madwoman walking towards me, asleep – or pretending to be asleep – and the hellhound jumping up at my arm and savaging my sleeve. I saw red, mister, and picked up a stick. I walloped him with it, and he fell down without a sound. And then I ran away. I didn't mean —'

'But first, you cut his throat, didn't you?'

'Cut his throat? No, I didn't do that, though I might have done if I'd a knife with me. And it wasn't the madwoman, either, even though they say she had the knife in her hand. I saw her sit down on the grass, still asleep, and she had no knife with her. So it must have been someone else. I fancied I heard someone moving among the trees, but I didn't stay to investigate. But whoever it was, he did for the dog, and left him dead in the well. Good riddance!'

'What happened after that, Jonah?'

'Father had found out what I'd been doing, and after that Miss Ursula was discovered at the well, he had a quiet word with Squire Fitzgerald, and sent me up the road to work for Farmer Pierce at Newton Forge. Father was relieved when he heard that Miss

Ursula was found guilty of cutting Ben's throat. Why shouldn't she take the blame for the mutilations at the same time? Nothing was going to save her from the madhouse. That's what Father thought.'

Jonah Laidlaw sighed, and placed his head in his hands. When he spoke next, it was in little more than a whisper.

'And so I went to Newton Forge. Farmer Pierce was a good master, and all went well for a while. And then the animals started to make me their serf again. I knew what to do this time, to show them who was master, the human being or the brute beast. But I was caught, and Farmer Pierce sent me packing.'

'And so you found your way here, to Plemstall?'

'Yes. Farmer Wilson took me on, but the same thing happened again, and I was caught again. They dragged me here, to The Bear and Billet, early in the morning, before the sun had risen. They held a kind of court in the bar, with Tom Peacock, the landlord, as judge. I was found guilty, and the sentence was that I was to be taken into the stable yard and kicked unconscious. And so it was done. I'm naming no names, but some days I sit here among my bottles, and wonder whether they'll come in here and do for me good and proper. Maybe I deserve it.'

The young man suddenly looked up, and clutched Bottomley's sleeve. His eyes shone with an unnerving light, at once fanatical and fearful.

'Do you know, master, that some nights a spirit comes to see me, and tells me to use the knife against myself? Maybe it's a messenger from Heaven, telling me how I can atone. But I don't want to do that. Those brutes deserved it! They came to enslave me when I wanted to be free. So there's my story. No one would ever listen to me before you came. Who did you say you were? I didn't catch your name.'

Bottomley found the parish physician at home in his redbrick house near the church. He was an old man, irascible, and dismissive of miscreants like Jonah Laidlaw.

'Yes, I'm fully aware of that fellow's crimes, Sergeant,' said the doctor. 'I'm also aware of what some of the villagers did to teach him a lesson. Against the law, no doubt, but rough justice, in its own way. I dressed his wounds, and confirmed that he'd come to no grave harm. I don't see what else you expect me to do.'

Bottomley made no reply. He was thinking of Jonah Laidlaw's father, half bullying, half cringing, content to send his mentally ill son away so that no questions would be asked. Reuben Laidlaw was a moral coward, and if he knew as much as his son had just admitted, he was a conniver in the perversion of the cause of justice.

He looked at the old doctor, red-faced and narrow minded, clothed in the certainty of his own righteousness, and he felt a sudden cold anger engulf him. When he spoke, his voice held an edge of menace that had cowed many a guilty man in the past.

'Your patient, Doctor,' he said, 'is quite obviously suffering from mental illness. I'm not a physician, but even I know a madman when I meet one. You know as well as I do that people have sudden brainstorms, and have to live with periods of insanity. So what do you do? You leave a young man of twenty-four to drink himself to death in the back room of a public house, battered soft by your bruiser friends —'

'Now look here, Sergeant!' The old man spluttered in rage, and his pale eyes bulged with the physical effort of dealing with Bottomley's sudden verbal assault. 'This impertinence is insupportable. I'll report you to your superior —'

'What *is* insupportable, sir, is your failure

as a physician to do your duty! That young man needs to be taken from that flea-bitten hovel, The Bear and Billet, and conveyed to the safety of the County Lunatic Asylum at Coventry. I've written a full account of his plight, and I must warn you that if your thuggish friends succeed in murdering him, they will hang, every one of them. Do your duty, Doctor, just as I'm doing mine.'

The old physician had blushed to the roots of his sparse hair. All his anger had dissipated.

'You're right, Sergeant Bottomley,' he said. 'It's taken a layman to recall me to my duty as a doctor. I'll go and see Josiah Laidlaw straight away.'

Bottomley left the doctor's house, and set out to walk the quarter of a mile to Eastley Platform. Jonah Laidlaw's story had shown that Ursula Holt had been entirely innocent of the charges laid against her. She had been incarcerated in Trinity Ford Asylum without just cause. All her fears and fantasies were entirely without foundation. As soon as he got back to Ashborne Hill, he would catch the next train to Charnley, and tell her the good news. Miss Ursula Holt's troubles were over.

9
A Man Dead on
the Line

It was still raining when the small train from Eastley Platform rattled into the marshalling yard of Ashborne Hill Station, and came to an unscheduled halt in mid-track. Bottomley rubbed the sleeve of his coat across the misty carriage window, and peered out through the rivulets of raindrops pouring down the glass. A porter was hurrying along a cinder path between two sets of lines. He was carrying a furled red flag, and it was obvious that he had just stopped the train.

There was no one else in the carriage, and Bottomley lowered the window. The porter looked up at him, blinking the rain out of his eyes.

'You're to get down here, sir, if you will,' he said. 'There's a man dead on the far line. I'll help you down, and lead you into the station.'

Herbert Bottomley did as he was told. He

followed the porter along the cinder path until they emerged into the stretch of marshalling yard just before the platforms rose above the level track. It was then that he saw the scene of the accident. On a line running parallel to a steep embankment over to his right, a precipitous grassy slope capped with a row of tall elms, a cluster of gleaming black umbrellas seemed to be stooping in homage to a gaunt, black engine, which had stopped on the track.

'If you don't mind, friend,' said Bottomley, 'I'd like to go over there, and see what I can do.' He fished into his pocket for his warrant card, which the porter scrutinized suspiciously before handing it back. Bottomley did not look much like the man's conception of what a policeman should look like.

As Bottomley stepped gingerly across the lines, he was hailed by Sergeant Potter, who emerged from the umbrellas to greet him. He looked rather angry and flustered, and was evidently delighted to see Bottomley.

'Herbert!' George Potter managed to produce a kind of subdued cry of pleasure. 'I'm glad you're here. That lot' – he jerked his head to the group of people near the engine – 'that lot don't think much of the police! There's Dr MacPhee, who's by way of being a martinet of the old school, the station master, a few porters, and about ten busybodies from the town. Wouldn't you think they'd —'

'George,' said Bottomley quietly, 'never mind them for the moment. They'll keep. Just tell me what happened. Or what you reckon happened.'

'Well, that train you see standing there is the two fifteen from Sherringham to Copton Vale. The driver told me that when he was about a hundred yards away from here, he saw a body sprawled across the line. He applied the brakes and let off steam, and the result was that the train pushed the body about twenty feet along the track —'

'And is the body mangled, George? Will we be able to identify it?'

It's not mangled, Herbert, and there's no question of having to identify it. It's the body of young Mr Paul Staunton, the accountant from Charnley. I recognized him straight away. I'd have had a closer look, but old MacPhee shooed me away. Look! They're picking the body up from the track.'

The phalanx of umbrellas rose as though animated by a single thought, and as they parted, Bottomley could see that a rough bier fashioned from an unscrewed door had been lifted off the track by three porters and the stationmaster. Their burden had been decently covered with an overcoat.

'Where will they go now, George? Incidentally, you should never let yourself be outfaced by people like this MacPhee. He may be a doctor, but you're a Crown Officer of the Law. So where are they taking him?'

'There's an empty waiting-room on the far platform, Herbert – the line to Charnley. They'll take him there, and old MacPhee will make his examination. I took it upon myself to send for him, and he wasn't best pleased, I can tell you. Look, they've already started out for the waiting-room. Shall we join them?'

'No, George. Leave them be for a moment. Let you and me go and look at that embankment. We'll walk back from the train until we reach the spot where the driver saw the body on the line. You're not afraid of rain, are you?'

The old sergeant grinned, but said nothing. They set off together along the track. The afternoon rain was cold and penetrating, one of those unpleasant and unwanted gifts that October can unexpectedly bestow. They walked on past the silent train, which was waiting to be driven into the station. Presently, they came to a spot where the row of elms high above them ended, and Bottomley stopped abruptly.

'Do you see that flattened grass, George? Do you see where something or someone has slithered down the embankment? Slithered? No, it wasn't that. Just stand back a minute, will you, George? If you look down there, beside the track, you'll see some confused footprints. This rain's making a fine mess of them, but you can see that they're all made by the same kind of boot. They're the tracks of one man. *One* man.'

Herbert Bottomley shaded his eyes and glanced up the steep embankment. There was a fence at the top, and part of it had broken away. He looked up the grassy slope once more, and frowned. No; not slithered. You had to be alive to do that.

'This is murder, George,' he said, and his companion could hear the tone of despair behind his colleague's words. 'Young Mr Staunton was killed – somewhere up there, beyond the elms – and then he was thrown over that fence, smashing the top rail in the process. His body slid down the grass, and came to a stop when it hit the shale path here, beside the line.'

'But he was on the railway line —'

'Yes, he was, because his killer carefully slithered down the slope after him, and dragged his body on to the line. It was meant to look like a railway accident, you see – or possibly a suicide. But the train simply pushed the body further along the line. Murder. Another young man slaughtered in Ashborne Hill.'

Sergeant Bottomley glanced up once more at the line of elms rising above the embankment. There was something teasingly familiar about them.

'George,' he said, 'ought I to know those elm trees?'

'Not those particular trees, Herbert. They're on the far side of Halford's Mill. You're thinking of the row of elms on the other side – the graveyard side, where we found the poor young American's body. But there's no access to the graveyard from Halford's.'

'Halford's. . . . Didn't you tell me that young Mr Staunton kept the books for Halford's? Perhaps that's why he was here in Ashborne Hill today. We'll find out later. Meanwhile, you and I had better go and find that empty waiting-room, and see what this old MacPhee has discovered.'

'Stand back, will you? How do you expect me to see clearly while you're crowding around me like that?'

Dr MacPhee's respectful audience obediently moved back from the body of Paul Staunton, which had been placed on the long table in the centre of the waiting-room. MacPhee was small, and bald, but his sandy moustache bristled with what seemed to be permanent indignation, and his general stance was like that of a little bantam cock. He looked up briefly when the two policemen entered, snorted with some kind of special indignation, and turned once more to the body.

'This young man was clearly dead before the train hit him,' he said. 'Perhaps it was suicide. He could have taken poison, and then lay down on the track —'

'Why should he do that, sir?' asked the stationmaster in a respectful whisper.

'Why? Why? That should be obvious even to a dunderhead. It was to save his family from the stigma of having harboured a suicide in their bosom by making it look like an accident. There's a lot of bruising, caused by the impact of the train, but the train did not cause his death. That's all, I think. I'll be able to tell you more when I've done a post-mortem. Potter, you can take the fellow down now to Canal Street mortuary.'

'Why don't you turn the body over, Dr

MacPhee? You've suggested that the man committed suicide – poisoned himself, and lay down on the line to spare his folks embarrassment. It doesn't sound very likely, sir, if I may say so —'

'And who the devil are you, may I ask? What do you know about dead bodies? Confine yourself to farming, or whatever it is you do for a living. Keep a civil tongue in your head, will you, or get out of the room.'

Doctor MacPhee had straightened up from the body, and was quivering with rage. He danced up and down, his little fists flailing, his face red with anger.

'My name is Detective Sergeant Bottomley, of the Warwickshire Constabulary. I gather that you know my colleague, Sergeant Potter. That's who I am, and I'd advise you, Doctor, to keep a civil tongue in *your* head.'

'What? This is outrageous! I've never been spoken to like this in all my life —'

'Maybe it's time you were,' muttered one of the porters, and a titter of subdued laughter rippled through the doctor's audience. MacPhee realized that if he indulged in one more petulant outburst, he would lose the men's respect for good. He remained silent while Bottomley continued to speak in his quiet, homely voice.

'You see, Doctor, he might have died of a seizure, and fallen on the line. Or he might have been stunned, and *thrown* on the line. Or again, he might have been stabbed in the back. All you have to do, Dr MacPhee, is to ask some of these good folk to turn the body over for you.'

The little doctor said nothing, but motioned to the porters to do what Bottomley had suggested. A patch of congealed blood on the back of Staunton's black serge jacket told them all immediately that Bottomley had been right. Doctor MacPhee bent over the body once again, and parted a rent in the cloth with his finger.

'You're right,' he murmured. 'It's a stab wound, and to judge from the nature of the bleeding, I'd say that stabbing with some sharp, narrow instrument was the cause of death. I'll be able to say for certain once I've opened the body in Canal Street.'

Sergeant Bottomley produced a small round magnifying glass on a handle. He moved towards the body, and the now subdued doctor stood aside. They all watched as the sergeant peered at the wound through his glass, and then delicately inserted the little finger of his right hand into the wound.

'Unless I'm very much mistaken, Doctor,'

said Bottomley, 'that wound was made by a scalpel.'

Old Sergeant Potter seemed to be galvanized by Bottomley's words.

'Constables,' he said, 'go back along the track and search for a scalpel. You know what they look like from the Elijah Robinson business. Report to Sergeant Bottomley and me at Halford's Mill when you've finished your task. Doctor MacPhee, I'm short-handed here in Ashborne Hill. I'd thank you if you'd arrange for the remains to be conveyed to Canal Street yourself.'

The subdued doctor nodded his assent, and the men in the waiting-room moved aside to let the two police officers reach the door.

'Dead? What's happening to Ashborne Hill? Paul Staunton was here at Halford's less than an hour ago.'

Jerome Halford sat behind a desk which was piled high with samples of cloth and yarn. Pattern books filled the shelves lining the walls of his office. The room vibrated to the quiet but pervasive hum of machinery.

'Nevertheless, sir,' said Sergeant Potter, 'he's dead – murdered. I think he was waylaid in the mill grounds as he made his way out to your entrance gates in Sandpit

Lane. He was stabbed in the back, and thrown down the embankment on to the line.'

Mr Halford shook his head, and sighed. A heavily built man with black curly hair, he wore a workman's long brown coat over his black suit. He seemed to be covered with a patina of fine dust.

'You were quite right about him coming here. He does my books every quarter, and is well liked by the hands. He was a gentleman, I suppose, but there was no side on him. He came here today to talk to a man called Derek Moult. I gather that it was Moult's idea that he should call. Dead? But why?'

The glazed door of the office opened, and another man in a brown coat came in.

'Sir,' he said, 'shall we slow down the flyer-leg on number six? At the rate it's going, the frame will be shaken to pieces.'

'Yes, yes. Tell the spinners they needn't ask in future if it has to be done. We'll go over to fixed caps next spring. Is Derek Moult still up on the frames? Good. That'll do, Jones. You'd better come up to the fourth floor, gentlemen, and have a word with Moult yourself. You'll have to climb four flights of iron stairs, because we've no lift here. Everything's moved on hoists.

Come on, I'll take you up there now.'

The fourth floor of Halford's Mill was a vast, many-windowed space, where four long lines of spinning frames, each carrying 200 large spinning bobbins, set up a continuous din which seemed to vibrate the very glass in the windows. Mr Halford beckoned to yet another man in a brown coat, who was busy rejoining some broken threads at one of the frames.

'Moult!' Halford had to shout to make himself heard. 'Here's Mr Potter and another policeman to talk to you. It's about poor Mr Staunton. Take them into the bobbin-room.'

The owner of Halford's Mill hurried away to the winding iron staircase, leaving the two policemen to talk to the man called Derek Moult. He was a slim, pale-faced man of forty or so. Like his master, he was covered in fine dust.

'Come out of the noise, gentlemen,' he said. 'It's quieter in the bobbin-room.'

He led them into a small chamber leading off the spinning floor. Like all the spaces in the mill, it enjoyed a big glazed window. Hundreds of spinning-bobbins stood in racks along the walls.

'I've heard already that poor Mr Staunton has been killed,' he began without preamble.

'It's all my fault. If I hadn't been such an interfering busybody, he'd be alive today.' Tears stood in the workman's eyes. He was clearly very upset.

'What do you mean by that, Mr Moult?' asked Bottomley. 'How could it have been *your* fault?'

'You were here over that business of the young American man, weren't you, sir? Well, it was something I saw on the day poor Mr Elijah Robinson was murdered that worried me. Something odd that I saw in St Philip's churchyard. From up here on the fourth floor, and with all these big windows, you can see almost anything that goes on down there.'

He motioned towards the window, and they looked out. Far down below lay the churchyard where they had discovered the body of Elijah Robinson. Bottomley could just make out the spot where the corpse had lain. He could see the lead roof capping the old church tower. The line of elm trees seemed foreshortened, failing in their task of cloaking the mill from the vulgar view.

'And what was this odd thing that you saw, Mr Moult?' asked Bottomley. 'Saw, I mean, down there in the churchyard, on Monday, the second of October, at about two-thirty in the afternoon?'

'I looked down from one of the windows near number three frame, which I'd been tending, and I saw a very peculiar thing. Two men were walking in the direction of the steps down to The Grapes. They were both gentlemen, as I could see by their clothes, though they were too distant, that far down, for me to see their faces. Well, one was walking behind the other, and this second man – the one walking behind the other – suddenly produced a pair of white gloves, and began to put them on.'

Derek Moult stopped speaking, and glanced down from the window of the bobbin-room. He seemed to be revisiting his memory of the event.

'And what happened then?' Bottomley prompted him.

'He kept pulling the gloves on, and I re-alized that they were a pair of those long, white gloves that ladies wear with formal dress – the type that you pull up the arm, almost as far as the elbow. He was putting on a pair of ladies' gloves.'

Yes, thought Bottomley grimly, he'd done that to keep the splashes of his victim's blood off his own coat sleeves. And later, when all was calm and quiet, he had put those bloodstained gloves back where he had found them – in a drawer of Ursula

Holt's dressing-table. . . .

'Why did you want to tell your story to Mr Staunton?' he asked. 'The proper person to tell would have been Sergeant Potter here, or Mr Halford.'

'I wasn't sure that it was a police matter, and I couldn't bother Master with idle tales of that kind. Besides, he'd think that I was wasting his time looking out of the windows instead of tending the frames.'

'Is he a stern man, your Mr Halford?'

'No, he's not. He's a good master, who does well for himself, because he knows the business. But Mr Staunton was a friendly gentleman, and I often spoke to him when he came up here to look at the machines. He was interested in all that went on, you see, him being the bookkeeper. Well, he came today, as arranged, and I told him what I'd seen. He looked very worried, and I'm not sure that he didn't turn pale. "Keep this to yourself, Moult", he said. "I'll let you know what transpires after I've made a few enquiries". That was less than an hour ago, sir, and now you tell me he's dead – murdered! I think he was murdered for coming here and listening to me. What I told him must have meant something special, something that only he appreciated —'

'Not only Mr Staunton,' said Bottomley.

'There are others who have a very good idea what all this means. Me, for instance. Meanwhile, don't blame yourself, Mr Moult. You've nothing to reproach yourself with. From now on, I'd advise you to keep your own counsel, and leave the matter with the police.'

'That cursed place!' cried Paul Staunton's father. 'Why did my son have to go there, and today of all days, when that murderous villain was on the loose again? Who could have killed him – and *why?*'

'We're very sorry, Mr Staunton,' said Sergeant Potter.

What else was there to say? What else *could* he say? He glanced at Bottomley, who shook his head, but made no reply. Breaking the news of violent death was something that both men had done many times before.

The grey-faced elderly man sitting in his armchair seemed to have shrunken into himself. The two policemen had come straight from Halford's Mill to visit the bereaved father at his modest brick house situated in a lane leading from Charnley's town square.

'It was his birthday, you know,' said Paul Staunton's father. 'He was thirty-two. I never wanted him to accept work in Ashborne Hill. Charnley is more genteel, and there are some very wealthy people living here. But there – what's the use of talking like that? You have to follow your work. I'm only thankful that Paul's mother's not alive. This news would have killed her stone dead.'

'Mr Staunton,' said Bottomley gently, 'I don't suppose you know of anyone who would wish your son Paul any harm? There was nothing on his mind, was there? Nothing that could have suggested that he was worried or afraid?'

'Nothing. Nothing. . . . It must be a madman, like with that other poor young man, the American visitor. It's someone in Ashborne Hill, Sergeant. That's where you should be looking. A madman! Paul was starting to call at Abbey Lodge, you know, by way of paying court to the young lady. But now. . . .'

'The young lady, sir?' asked Bottomley. 'Do you mean Miss Ursula Holt?'

'No, no. Not Ursula. The other one – Kate. He told me that he was very taken with her, and I'd hopes that something would come of it.'

Tears began to roll unheeded down Mr Staunton's cheeks.

'Who could have done such a thing, Mr Potter? It's just like the poor young American all over again. A secret madman lurking in our midst. I suppose we'll never know who did it.'

When the two men regained Charnley town square, Sergeant Potter gingerly retrieved a small brown paper parcel from his pocket, unwrapped it, and showed its contents to Bottomley. It was a wicked-looking scalpel with a brass handle, and they could both see that it was inscribed 'Savigny & Co, 67 James Street, London. 1815.'

'My constables found this, Herbert, just a few feet from where poor Staunton had been dragged on to the line. It had been thrown into the high grass on the embankment.'

'That's an amputation knife,' said Bottomley. 'I've been shown all this type of thing by our police surgeon, Dr Venner, back at Warwick. Perhaps poor Mr Staunton is right, and there's a madman about – a deranged doctor, perhaps. But I doubt it. I doubt it very much. So you're getting the hang of this detection business, are you, George? You'd guessed, hadn't you, that our killer would deliberately throw his weapon away for us to find? That's detective stuff, that is!'

Old Sergeant Potter flushed with pleasure.

'Well, Herbert,' he said, 'I've certainly learnt a lot from you and Mr Jackson over the last couple of weeks. I'm just wondering, you know, about this scalpel.'

He turned the lethal instrument round in his hand, and peered at the inscription on the handle. 'Eighteen-fifteen, Herbert,' he said. 'That's early, isn't it? Getting on for eighty years ago. It's a museum piece, unless I'm very much mistaken.'

'Yes, it's very odd, that. You know, George, that date's given me the ghost of an idea, but for the life of me I can't grasp that idea completely. I think our murderer has just made a slip using that antique to do his wicked work, and if he's done that – made a slip, I mean – then maybe he's getting desperate. I need to have a little cogitation about that scalpel, George, and about that date, too.'

'Well, come back to my house, Herbert, and do your cogitating there. It's nearly five, and time for a bite of dinner. I only live a stone's throw from here. Why don't you stay the night? There's plenty of room now that the boys have married and gone, and it's a cruel slog from this corner of the shire back to Warwick.'

'That's very kind of you, George, and very obliging of your missus to put me up. Thank you very much. It's been a long day, and I'd appreciate something to eat and drink, and a good night's rest. By rights, I should be seeking out young Miss Ursula, to tell her the good news of her innocence in the matter of killing that sheepdog, and mutilating those other animals —'

'That'll keep till tomorrow, Herbert. Poor lass, she'll have heard about Mr Staunton's murder by now, I've no doubt, bad news travelling as swift as wildfire, as the saying goes. That will be enough for her to cope with for one day. You can call on Dr Holt and his family tomorrow.'

10
URSULA'S FLIGHT

'Who could have done it, Polly?' cried Kate Holt, wringing her hands in distress. 'Who'd want to murder such a kind and pleasant man as Paul Staunton? He liked us both so much! Oh, dear!'

Ursula Holt watched her cousin as she dissolved into tears. It was so unlike Kate to give way like that. But then, Paul Staunton had been keen on her. Had she realized that? Paul Staunton had indeed liked them both, but it was Kate whom he'd really come to visit whenever he called at Abbey Lodge.

Uncle Matthew had entered the room while Kate was asking her passionate, unanswerable questions. He put an arm round his daughter's shoulders, and vaguely patted her, as though she were a favourite cat.

'I don't know what's happening to our quiet little corner of the county, girls,' he said. 'First that young man Robinson, and now Paul Staunton. . . . John came in just now to tell me that it was a scalpel again —'

Ursula heard herself scream. She tried to stifle her rising terror, but its expression burst from her unbidden. She could still see that air of uncertainty in Uncle Matthew's eye, his rooted belief that she had done those frightful things in the past. And Kate? Until now, she would have sprung across the room to comfort her. Instead, she sat in her chair near the table, her hands covering her face. Would there be a look of growing suspicion in her cousin's tearful eyes?

'Oh, dash it all!' cried Uncle Matthew, with almost comic remorse. 'I'm sorry, Ursula. I'm an insensitive old curmudgeon. Fancy mentioning scalpels – there, I've done it again. . . .'

Doctor Holt looked helplessly at the two girls, who were both now weeping uncontrollably. He'll go in a minute, thought Ursula. He's good and kind, but he can't cope with this kind of scene. Kate's crying because she's lost Paul, but I'm crying for myself. No one except Mr Skeffington and that man Bottomley believes that I am innocent of hurting those beasts, though maybe that's only kindness on their part.

I'm not entirely convinced of the truth myself, and neither was Dr Meitner.

There, Uncle's apologized his way out of the room. What about Kate? Surely she hasn't lost her faith in me? I can tolerate Uncle's suspicions, but I couldn't bear to lose Kate's regard.

'Well, Polly,' said Kate suddenly, wiping her eyes, and putting back her little round spectacles. 'Crying won't bring Paul back. We've got to move on. I'm going to help cook in the kitchen. Will you be all right here?'

'Yes, I'm quite all right now, thank you, Kate. I'll go to my room, I think, and write some letters. I'll see you at dinner.'

As she turned on the first-floor landing, she glanced through the window, and saw a little knot of men and women loitering on the green. They were pointing at the house, and she could hear one or two of them jeering. She quickly pulled the casement shut, and a sharp-sighted man among them saw her face at the window. He shook a fist at her, and then made a slitting motion across his throat with his hand. At that moment John the coachman erupted angrily from the house, brandishing a horsewhip. Slowly and insolently, the knot of observers dispersed.

Her heart pounding with fright, Ursula hurried up to her room. She would leave the house that very day. Uncle Matthew and Kate mustn't know, because Uncle did not trust her, and the news of Paul's death might have turned Kate against her. Besides, they must be tiring of her madwoman's ways.

Last night she had found herself in the haunted ballroom again. She had looked with uncomprehending horror at the shining silvery flute, with its red tassel, and had half run across the ballroom floor, so it seemed to her, to distance herself from it. The air of the room had been hot and stifling, and she had smelt the scent of burning candlewax from the brilliant crystal candelabra.

The Negro servant boy stood like a statue, his incongruous blue eyes staring ahead of him. She had suddenly wondered, with a stab of fear, whether the boy had died, and whether someone had embalmed him, so that he stood upright against the wall, like a mummy in a museum.

She had found herself standing once more in front of the wooden chest, and this time the carving of a lion and unicorn flanking a five-pointed star was so realistic that she put out her hand to feel the subtle undulations of the carved wood beneath her fingers.

It was then that she heard a voice very near to her saying: 'I have seen this chest before.' Then, she had carefully lifted the lid. There was no wax image this time, only a vague dark shape, from which emerged a thin and shrivelled hand. A gold signet ring hung loosely on its fourth finger, and in looking at the ring, she had realized that the hand was a left hand. Again, a voice very near whispered – or rather, croaked – the words: 'I have seen that hand before.'

She had awoken then, and found herself slumped against the wardrobe door. There was no chance of her escaping and wandering about the house and garden, as Kate now locked her bedroom door on the outside every night.

The dreams were beginning to emerge from the shadow world of fantasy into reality. As she had awoken, she had known that it was her own voice that had spoken the words about the shrivelled hand. This, then, was a new aspect of her inner madness. Once those dreams became indistinguishable from reality, they would send her back to Trinity Ford.

She would go away at once, secretly, to London, and ask her friend Catherine

Stansfield to let her stay. She would pack a few necessities in her travelling-bag. Should she take her journal with her? No. That would look too much like flight, if they came to look through her things. The journal was safe enough, because the key of her locked document case never left her person.

What idyllic times she had spent, years ago, with Catherine, at Alderley Hall! Catherine Stansfield was now Mrs James Wishart, a happy wife and mother, with a beautiful house in Bruton Street, Mayfair. She would be safe from them all there. But first, she would confide her plans to the only person who had ever shown complete and uncompromising faith in her. There was a transparent sincerity about Mr Skeffington that always gave her hope and strength. He was a wise and sane man, and his wisdom would prevail.

Alexander Skeffington sat in his great carved armchair, and listened gravely to Ursula Holt as she told him of her plan to seek sanctuary with her friend Catherine Stansfield. When she had finished speaking, he remained silent for a while, arranging his own ideas before giving her his answer.

'Under normal circumstances, Ursula,' he said at last, 'I would quite simply tell you not to be silly. You're beginning to imagine things about your cousin that are not true. As for your uncle – well, I think you've already learned to live with his rooted suspicions.'

'So you advise me to go home? I tell you, Mr Skeffington, I shall go mad indeed if I have to do that! Even Kate has agreed to lock me in my bedroom at night. Abbey Lodge is becoming as much a prison as Trinity Ford was. I can't —'

Alexander Skeffington held up a hand to quell his young visitor's speech.

'I said "under normal circumstances", Ursula, but these are not normal. I think you are right, and I will be your confidant in this matter. But your friend Mrs Wishart – Catherine Stansfield, as she was – won't she be the first person that your uncle will apply to when he realizes that you have gone?'

'Yes, that's true,' Ursula replied. 'Perhaps she'll let me go to stay at their country place, Alderley Hall, in Northamptonshire. It would be very healing for me there —'

'And that, my dear, is the second place where they will look in their search, and when they find you there, they will bring you back. No, don't begin to cry, there's no need. Didn't I say I'd help you? If you will trust me, I'll arrange to spirit you away to a safe haven this very night. No one but I will know where you are, and you will have direct communication with me here at Providence House.'

'Oh, thank you, dear Mr Skeffington —'

'There's no need for thanks, Ursula. I recognize the need for you to go right away, until the murderer of those two young men is found, and brought to justice. Then you can come home, and if there are any re-criminations, then my back is broad enough to bear them! Come, my dear, let us put this business in train at once.'

Herbert Bottomley walked across the little green fronting Abbey Lodge, and recalled the events of the previous evening. Mrs Potter had proved to be a kindly and cheerful woman, more than willing to feed another man at her table. After dinner, he and George Potter had visited a cosy public house where the old sergeant was well known. They had spent a convivial evening altogether, and after a few gins and a pint of Sherman's Trafalgar Ale, Bottomley had sung a few songs for the assembled company in his pleasant tenor voice. The piano had been a rackety instrument, but the pianist knew its peculiar ways, and the results had been more than satisfactory.

Bottomley pulled the bell handle at the front door of Abbey Lodge, and waited on the doorstep for someone to answer. After yesterday's rain, the morning sunshine was welcome, and the light breeze was beginning to clear his head of the vapours left over from the previous evening.

The front door was suddenly flung open, and Bottomley saw the tearful figure of Katherine Holt, her ginger hair in disarray, and her round face pale and frantic.

'She's gone!' she cried without preamble. 'She's fled, in fear of the whole lot of you, with your torments and persecutions. You'd better come in.'

Kate stood aside, and Herbert Bottomley stepped into the hall. Fled? Why had she done that? He'd failed her. He should have come to see her straight away yesterday afternoon. What was this girl saying to him?

'She went to bed early, just after dinner last night. Of late, I've locked her bedroom door. That was her idea, not mine. But last night she said that she wanted to test herself again – will herself, she said, not to sleep-walk, and to remain in her room. I should have known that something was wrong. I went to call her at half past seven this morning, and when I opened her door, I found that she'd gone.'

'Had her bed been slept in, Miss Kate? Where's Dr Holt? Does he know about this?'

'No, her bed was still made up. Some of her things are missing, and so is a little travelling bag that she has. . . . Yes, my father knows all about it, but he's had to go out on his rounds. He says she'll come back, but that's only wishful thinking on his part. She's gone, I tell you! What are you going to do?'

'I'm going to search her room, miss, if you'll give me permission. I've no search warrant, and you can refuse permission if you want to —'

'No, of course I won't refuse. Come upstairs with me, now.'

This girl's eyes are red from weeping, thought Bottomley. That's not for Miss Ursula, it's for Mr Paul Staunton. Poor girl! She was the strong one, the one who's supposed to be tough and level-headed. Well, he'd keep a judicious eye on poor Miss Kate. That pinny – maybe people regarded her as the missus of the house, the one who did all the work. They had a maid – where was she? – and a cook. It was time that poor Miss Kate struck out for herself.

'Here you are,' said Kate, as they reached the first-floor landing. 'This is her sitting-room, and that's her bedroom beyond. I thought it was going to be a safe haven for her. It's so unfair!'

Kate stood uncertainly on the threshold of her cousin's bedroom, watching Bottomley as he conducted a swift but thorough search of Ursula's effects. How skilled he is, thought Kate. Those big, square hands of his show an unexpected delicacy. Look, he's going through Polly's underclothes now. He leaves nothing untidy. . . . Odd, that a man so careless of his own attire, should take such care of another's things. What's he found, now? Oh, that's Polly's document case. . . .

Herbert Bottomley looked at the young woman hovering at the door, and smiled. He sat on Ursula's dressing-table chair, balancing the leather-covered document case on his knees. He motioned towards an armchair beside the little fireplace.

'Why don't you sit down for a while, Miss Kate?' he asked, and there was something so kindly and unthreatening in the big man's voice that Kate did as she was bidden. Bottomley tried the catch of the document case, which proved to be unyielding. He looked across the room at Kate for a while, as though making up his mind to speak.

'I expect you like keeping house for your father and Miss Ursula, don't you?'

His question was so unexpected that Kate found herself blushing. What an insensitive fellow he was, after all! Keeping house for Ursula?

'What an odd question! What's that got to do with Ursula's disappearance? Of course I look after my father. And I look after Ursula a lot, because she's had a very bad time of it. I can do other things, you know.'

She watched Bottomley as he began to rummage in the pockets of his mustard-coloured overcoat. After a while, he gave a little cry of satisfaction, and produced a bunch of tiny keys tied together with string. She watched fascinated as he fitted one key after another into the lock of Ursula's document case, screwing up his eyes and holding his breath as he gave each one a tentative twist. The fourth key fitted, and in a moment the detective had removed Dr Altmann's monograph and Ursula Holt's journal from their hiding place.

Herbert Bottomley slipped Altmann's book into his pocket. He opened Ursula's journal at a point where its owner had placed a cardboard marker, and began to read.

Last night I dreamt of the haunted ballroom again, but this time my dream was more vivid and protracted than it had been before, and its consequences were terrifying.

He closed the book, still keeping a finger between the pages to mark the place, and turned his attention once more to Kate.

'So you can do other things, Miss Kate. What kind of things?'

'I write novels, if you must know,' Kate replied, flushing a little. In a minute, he'll ask whether any of them had been published. People always do.

'Novels? Well, that's very nice. I'm fond of a novel myself, when I get any time to read. Have you had any of them published?'

'No, I haven't. And I don't suppose I ever shall. But it's no good giving up, is it? Practice makes perfect. And that's what I do when I'm not running this house. Write.'

Bottomley turned back the pages of the journal, letting his eye settle on some of the neat copperplate writing. All the time, though, his attention was fixed on Kate Holt.

I progressed further into the room, and saw a small chamber orchestra playing behind a kind of roped-off barrier.

'And what's your latest book called, Miss Kate? I expect you've given it a title.'

'I have. It's called *Lady Conway's Dilemma*. It's all right, I suppose, but there's something wrong with it. It's about a girl who's wooed by two lovers. One's rich and ugly, and the other's poor but handsome. She doesn't know whether to marry for love or money.'

Tuesday, 10 October 1893. I have had the ballroom dream again, and this time, I saw a skeletal hand. Let me set it down, dear Dr Meitner, in some kind of order.

Herbert Bottomley closed the journal, and sent it to join Dr Altmann's book in one of the capacious pockets of his overcoat.

'Well, now, Miss Kate,' he said, 'why not be original? Let your girl fall in love with the one who's rich and ugly, so that she feels guilty about the one who's poor but handsome. People will think she's marrying for money, you see, and that will hurt her pride. So she pretends to fall for the handsome one, but in fact – yes, how about this? He's so poor that he sees marrying your heroine as a means of achieving his own comfort and security. So he doesn't love her at all, whereas the ugly one does. Is she the Lady Conway in the title? If so, how about all that for a real dilemma?'

Katherine Holt gazed at the big shambling man with awe. What a splendid idea! Why had she not thought of that? She would start revising her manuscript that very afternoon.

'Thank you very much, Sergeant Bottomley,' she said, and the detective noted that the extreme pallor of her face had been replaced by a healthy flush of pink. 'What a marvellous idea! But what about Ursula? Will you —'

'Leave Ursula to me, Miss Kate, and spend a bit of time looking after yourself, for a change. In the meantime, you can tell me who that beautiful young lady is in those photographs that Miss Ursula has put out on display.'

Katherine Holt told Bottomley all about Catherine Wishart, formerly Catherine Stansfield, her town house in Bruton Street, Mayfair, and her family's country seat, Alderley Hall, in Northamptonshire. It was to one or other of those houses, she was convinced, that Ursula Holt was fleeing. She would leave her newfound friend to deduce that obvious fact for himself.

'The more I think of it, Mr Bottomley,' she said, 'the more I'm convinced that Polly – Miss Ursula – has simply taken fright at the recent turn of events, and has sneaked away to hide in Catherine Stansfield's house. Shall I write to her, and find out?'

'It would be far better, Miss Holt, if I were to visit that lady myself. You see, if you wrote, she might write back, and say, "No, Ursula isn't here". But that could well be a fib, you see. But if she said those words to my face, I'd know from her expression whether she was telling me the truth or not. So if you'll give me that lady's address in London, I'll go up there and spy out the lie of the land.'

'And will you let me know what you find out?' asked Kate.

'Yes, I will, miss, I promise you. But for the moment I must get back to Warwick. Mr Jackson's on his way to America at the moment, but my superintendent is planning our course of action personally, and he'll tell me all about it on Friday.'

'Friday the thirteenth,' whispered Kate. She shuddered involuntarily.

'It's just a day, like any other, miss. Don't you worry: it won't take us long to find where Miss Ursula is.'

He smiled kindly at Kate, and left the

room before she could frame an answer.

When Sergeant Bottomley dismounted in the stable yard on Friday morning, he found Alf, the civilian helper, standing disconsolately beside a number of tables and chairs which had been dragged out from the police-office and placed on the cobbles.

'It's been like this ever since he came, Mr Bottomley,' he grumbled. 'He's had me scrub the office floor, and clean the windows inside and out. Now he wants me to scrub these old tables. It's iniquitous, that's what it is. They're covered in grime, these tables. It'll take me all morning. Mr Jackson never makes all this fuss.'

Bottomley handed his horse's bridle to the discomfited Alf, and jerked his head in the direction of the stable.

'Never mind, Alf,' he said. 'Mr Mays could see at once what a splendid worker you are – for ever cleaning up and tidying. Cheer up, it's a nice bright day, with no rain to get you wet while you're working.'

Alf shook his head, and, muttering all the while to himself, led Bottomley's horse into the stable.

'Ah! Sergeant Bottomley! There you are. Sit down, will you, while I tell you what I think we should do. I've arranged a scheme which I think you'll find very helpful.'

The office smelt strongly of carbolic disinfectant. Superintendent Mays, smart as two pins, looked perfectly at home behind Inspector Jackson's desk. Bottomley removed his brown bowler hat and struggled out of his overcoat. He looked round in vain for the hat stand, realized that it was probably out in the yard with Alf, and deposited his things on the floor beside his chair. Superintendent Mays launched into speech.

'The first matter, Sergeant, is the business of Miss Ursula Holt's innocence. You've established that beyond any doubt, and it says much for your skills as a detective. The people at Charnley were gravely at fault. Well done, Sergeant!

'Now, it seems to me that her innocence should remain unannounced until she is found. To make any public statement at this stage could lead to complications. Am I right about that? If you think I'm wrong, then tell me.'

'No, sir, you're right. If the matter got into the papers, and Miss Ursula read it, she could think that it was some sort of trap. She may be innocent, sir, but she's not well in her mind.'

'Good, So we agree on that. The second

point I want to make is this. In your investigation, you're going to have a lot to do with doctors. To start with, there's this madhouse keeper – what was his name? – Meitner.'

Mr Mays leafed through some neatly arranged papers on Inspector Jackson's desk, and produced the invitation to a lecture that had been given to Jackson by the Reverend Harry Goodheart.

'Yes – Dr Meitner,' Mays continued, 'of Trinity Ford Asylum at Inchfield. And then there's this foreign person, Dr Karl Gustav Altmann, Intendant of the Maria Hospital, Vienna. Sounds like a German. Another madhouse keeper. So, in view of your having to question these learned men, I suggest that you take Dr James Venner along with you. He'll be able to understand what these fellows are talking about.'

'Doctor Verner, sir? But will he be available at such short notice?'

'I've already spoken to him, Sergeant, and he's more than willing to comply. He knows something about this chap Altmann, and says he'd like to meet him. So what do you think?'

'I think it's a marvellous idea, sir. Dandy Jim and me have worked closely together before. Thank you very much, sir.'

'Not at all. I suppose "Dandy Jim" is an

affectionate epithet for Dr Venner. However, I'd suggest that it's inappropriate to employ such terms in my presence. Now, can you cope with all this business alone? Or do you want me to get you an inspector?'

'No thank you, sir, I don't need help of that nature. So, if Dr Venner's available, sir, he and I can start on our travels tomorrow.'

That same morning, the SS *Campania* steamed into New York harbour. At twenty-one knots over a distance of 2,864 nautical miles, she had completed the journey in five days, three hours, and twenty minutes.

11
THE HOUSE IN WASHINGTON SQUARE

Gaunt, and ominous, like silent giants pondering a sudden move, the imposing steel and masonry towers of Manhattan loomed out of the morning mist. Saul Jackson stood at the rail of the *Campania* as she passed Sandy Hook, leaving the Atlantic Ocean behind her. As the great liner entered Lower New York Bay, Jackson turned to listen to the man standing beside him.

'Not quite what you expected, I guess, Mr Jackson! "Skyscrapers", we call them, but today, they look more like tottering old men, feeling around for somewhere to rest their weary bones!'

'I must confess, I'd a different image of the skyscrapers, Mr Preston,' said Jackson. 'I'd always imagined them as being bathed in sunlight, with the blue waters of the bay at their feet. Still, I expect I'll be suitably impressed once the fog's lifted.'

It had been a giddying and unique experience for Jackson to cross the Atlantic in the magnificent Cunarder. It was as though a luxurious hotel had suddenly taken to the water. He had eaten his meals in the vast restaurant, where the long tables, covered with lace cloths, had groaned beneath a bewildering variety of fare. There had been a good English breakfast, luncheon, dinner – quite a grand affair, that, with many of the men in evening dress – and a light supper for those who wanted it. The huge room had been lighted by electricity, and all the chairs had been bolted to the floor.

There had been a comfortable and spacious drawing-room, where you could spend the evenings reading, or chatting to the other passengers. After luncheon, you could take a long nap in your well-appointed cabin. No doubt he would never experience such a voyage again. His only regret was that Sarah could not have been with him.

Mr Preston was one of several men whom Jackson had found very congenial. A quietly spoken New Yorker, he was a marine broker by profession, and a frequent visitor to England.

'You know, Mr Jackson,' he was saying, 'there's no single waterfront to New York Harbour. It's one of the most complex harbours in the whole world, a place where three great bodies of water meet. To the south you've got the Atlantic Ocean, and to the east, Long Island Sound. They're both tidal, but their tides don't coincide. And then there's the grand old Hudson River to the north.'

'That's very interesting, Mr Preston. I was wondering, you know, just exactly where this great liner was heading. But I expect the captain knows!'

Mr Preston laughed.

'Why, he knows all right, Mr Jackson. He'll be master of all these cunning tides and currents that do their mysterious work from here at Sandy Hook right up to Albany.'

'The purser said that we'd be docking in half an hour.'

'That's true. Well, it's been a privilege to know you, Mr Jackson. Maybe we'll meet again some time. Look at those tenders! They still go wild when a Blue Riband ship comes into the bay. And you tell me that you're visiting Old Man Davis, the railroad king? Well, when you've passed through Customs, I reckon you'll see a little posse of Buchanan Davis's secretaries waiting for you with a carriage. Davis is a big noise hereabouts, Mr Jackson, and it's his habit to do things in style. You see if I'm not right!' Mr Preston's view of Buchanan Davis had been fully justified. Saul Jackson had just emerged from the Customs shed when he was descended upon by a little gang of four earnest young men in long coats and billycock hats, who hustled him, talking all the time, to a waiting carriage. His modest luggage was also efficiently claimed from officialdom, and strapped on to the roof of the vehicle.

Jackson closed his eyes and listened to the courteous but seemingly unending commentaries of his companions, all of whom had crammed themselves into the carriage with him. Occasionally, he felt bound to ask a question, so as to prevent the whole exercise degenerating into a one-sided conversation.

Had Mr Jackson been to New York before? No? Well, he would find much to interest him. Yes, the traffic was very heavy, and the streetcars made things worse. Where were they bound? Why, they were going to a place called Greenwich Village, where the late Mr Jacob Robinson had lived, in Washington Square. No, Mr Buchanan Davis didn't live there. He had a fine estate up at Albany, the state capital. He sent his apologies to Mr Jackson for not being present in person to greet him, but the calls of business were very pressing that week. He would be back from Westchester early Saturday morning, and would come without fail to Washington Square before midday on that day.

The carriage suddenly left a very busy thoroughfare which one of the young men told him was Fifth Avenue, and entered what appeared to be a public park, on the north side of which lay a row of distinguished old redbrick mansions, their entrances flanked by Doric and Ionic columns. They were partly shaded by pleasant trees. Jackson thought they would have looked quite at home in an English city such as Salisbury or Winchester. But these houses were 3,000 miles away from England. . . .

Yes, thought Jackson, this must be a public park. People were strolling across well-tended lawns in the October sun, and he could hear the cries of children at play, In the distance he could glimpse a mounted policeman moving slowly through the trees. A grand fountain stood in this park, but more impressive than the fountain was a great marble arch, which reminded Jackson of the pictures that he'd seen of the Arc de Triomphe in Paris. He asked one of his young mentors what the arch represented.

'That, sir? Why, it's what we call the Washington Arch, designed by Mr Stanford

White, and put up to celebrate the inauguration of George Washington as President. Mr White is one of the foremost architects of our country.'

'And what is the name of this place? It seems quite different from the rest of New York – at least, from the districts I've seen so far.'

The young secretary laughed.

'Why, sir,' he said, 'this is Washington Square, your destination. Once we've skirted the fountain, we'll drive down The Row, and stop at that house over there.' He pointed from the carriage window at one of the red-brick mansions rising on the north side of the square. 'That, Mr Jackson, was the home of the late lamented Mr Jacob Robinson; likewise of his late lamented son, Elijah.'

Jackson conjured up a vivid memory of the young man, lying dead and butchered in the little churchyard of Ashborne Hill. This was the gracious home from which he had set out on his fatal journey to England. The coachman brought the carriage to a halt in the quiet road known as The Row, and the bevy of young men poured out on to the pavement. As Jackson stepped down from the carriage, the white-painted door of the mansion opened, and a black butler in white tie and tails, accompanied by two footmen, came out on to the doorstep to greet him.

'Oh, it was very sad, sir,' said the old butler, shaking his grizzled head. 'Mr Jacob was a fine, hearty man, never given to a day's illness in his life, but it was a fever that carried him off to Glory. That was in February, sir – eighth February, as I do recall. Is that chicken to your liking, sir? How about the salad? Would you like some more dressing?'

After they were admitted to the house, the four young men had noisily interrogated the butler, whose name appeared to be Hine, to ascertain that he knew exactly what to do for Mr Buchanan Davis's guest from England. Finally satisfied, they had quickly bundled themselves out of the house, clambered into the waiting carriage, and made their exit from the square. Perhaps they were going to join Mr Davis at his business meeting?

Hine had shown Jackson to a pleasant bedroom overlooking a garden at the back of the house, and had helped him to unpack. He was a man well over sixty, obviously used to service in the best houses. To Jackson's surprise, he was shown a bathroom, leading directly from the bedroom, and evidently for his own private use. When he came downstairs again, Hine ushered him into a sumptuously furnished drawing-room, where a meal of chicken salad, lemon pie and a decanter of claret had been set ready on a table.

'This chicken's excellent, thank you, Mr Hine,' said Jackson, 'and so is the salad. And what a splendid house this is! Very elegant, and very well appointed, if I may say so.'

The old servant seemed disinclined to leave Jackson alone. Perhaps it was lonely in this house, Jackson thought, now that both the master and the master's son were dead.

'They *are* nice houses, sir,' Hine agreed. 'Washington Square's been a public park since the 1820s, and rich folk like the Robinsons had these houses built so that they could get away from the disease and crowding of Manhattan. This house was built in 1830.'

The butler laughed, and glanced out of one of the tall sash windows.

' "Propinquity", sir, that's what they used to call it. Having to live too close to the poor and unlettered. So they came out here. I don't know what they think about those tenement houses that they've built on the south side of our square. Full of immigrants, they are, sir, Poles, and Germans, and all sorts. Times are changing.'

'I suppose the Robinsons were a New York family?'

'They came originally from South Carolina, sir, but after the war they came up here. A distant member of the family had purchased this house in 1832, so it was already in the family when we all moved up here from the South.'

'And have you always been employed by the Robinson family, Mr Hine?'

'I've served the Robinsons for over fifty years, sir, thirty of those as an employee, and twenty-two years in servitude. Well, the Robinsons have gone, now, and it's a sore loss for us all to bear – a break with the past, you know. But Mr Buchanan Davis has promised to take me into his household, sir, and when all's settled and agreed, I think his daughter, Miss Sadie, as she was, and her husband, Mr Ellis Crocker, will come to live here, and keep the old place alive. Will there be anything else, sir?'

'Not for the moment, thank you, Mr Hine. I'm very comfortable here.'

'Very good, sir. Mr Hartford Madison will be coming to see you in half an hour's time, if that's convenient.'

'Mr Hartford Madison?'

'Yes, sir. He's Mr Buchanan Davis's

private secretary. He deals with everything to do with the family, as opposed to the business. Please ring, sir, if there's anything else you need.'

When Hine left the room, Saul Jackson finished the last of his claret, left the table, and sat back on a settee. For the moment, his mind was preoccupied by a single comment of the talkative old butler. He had spoken of having worked 'twenty-two years in servitude'. Hine had once been a slave.

The drawing-room was a very comfortable, finely proportioned room, its walls papered in a rich crimson flock. A cheerful fire burned in a marble fireplace set into the wall facing the window, and above the mantelpiece hung a striking three-quarters portrait in oils of a vigorous, clean-shaven man in his forties, a man dressed in the stylish garb of the 1860s. The artist had caught the commanding glitter in his eyes, and the arrogant set of his shoulders.

Jackson rose from the settee, and crossed the room to the fire place. Where had he seen that man before? Of course! It was a likeness of Jacob Robinson, the late owner of the house, and father of the murdered Elijah – the family resemblance was obvious. It was this man, perhaps fifteen years younger than in his portrait, who had stared out at Jackson from the faded photograph of 1851 that Alexander Skeffington had shown him.

On the adjacent wall hung another portrait, a large framed water-colour which Jackson recognized immediately as a copy of one of the other two men in the old photograph. His mind flew back to Providence House, and to the day when Alexander Skeffington had shown him that photograph of three young men in homespun suits, sitting on a bench in front of a rough shack. The younger Skeffington had sat in the middle of the bench, with Jacob Robinson on his right.

The third man in the photograph had been called Jim Bolder, the least successful of the three prospectors, who had accompanied Skeffington back to England, stayed for a while at Providence House, and then returned to Scotland.

The water-colour portrait of Jim Bolder staring down at Jackson from the wall had clearly been copied from a print of the same old photograph. The late Jacob Robinson must have had a fond regard for Jim Bolder, to arrange for a portrait of him to be painted, and placed here, in the elegant drawing-room of his house in Washington Square.

Mr Hartford Madison arrived just as Saul Jackson found himself nodding off in the comfortable drawing-room. He jerked awake as Hine ushered in a fresh-faced young man in his early thirties. He wore a blue serge suit, and carried a white billycock hat.

'Inspector Jackson? Pleased to meet you. Mr Buchanan Davis told me to make myself available to hear the sad tale of our Mr Elijah Robinson. May I prevail upon you to come through into the study? Yes, sir: I'm very pleased to meet you.'

The study was at the back of the house, and the first thing Jackson saw on entering the room was a portrait of young Elijah Robinson. It was standing on an easel, and was draped in black crape. It was an excellent likeness of the man whom Jackson had seen talking to his murderer in the dining-room of the Berkeley Arms at Ashborne Hill. Jackson told the attentive secretary the whole history of Elijah Robinson's death, while the living image of the slaughtered man smiled down at them from the easel.

'Why, sir,' said Hartford Madison when Jackson's tale was done, 'that's a very sad story. If only Mr Elijah Robinson had taken that letter from Alexander Skeffington with him, he wouldn't have mistaken the dates,

231

and he'd be alive today. He was never good at remembering dates.'

'Oh, but he did take the letter with him, Mr Madison. I found it in his pocket. Mr Skeffington himself confirmed that it was genuine. Young Mr Robinson was convinced that he was due to meet Skeffington on the second of October, but the letter stated quite clearly that he was due on Monday, the ninth.'

Young Mr Hartford Madison looked troubled. He shook his head, glanced at the portrait, and then at Jackson.

'You know, sir,' he said, 'that can't be so, because that letter from Mr Alexander Skeffington is in a drawer in that bureau there by the window.'

The secretary sprang from his chair and pulled down the flap of the bureau. He rummaged around among the pigeon holes for a moment, and then returned with a letter, which he handed to Jackson. It was in all respects identical to the letter retrieved from Elijah Robinson's pocket, except for one detail. In this version, Alexander Skeffington suggested that Robinson should journey from Liverpool to Ashborne Hill on Monday, 2 October. In Jackson's version, the date had been given as the ninth.

'What does that suggest to you, Mr

Madison?' asked Jackson, handing the letter back.

'Why, sir,' the secretary replied, 'I guess it suggests to me that somebody's been up to monkey business. If I were you, as soon as I got back to England, I'd invite this Skeffington down to the precinct house for a little talk.'

Hartford Madison left after an hour, promising to return that evening for dinner. Jackson went back to the drawing-room, and stood by the window, looking out across Washington Square. The fountain plashed lazily in the afternoon sun, and the great marble arch glowed white among the green of the trees.

Alexander Skeffington had lied about that letter. It was obvious that he had prepared a second letter with a false date – 9 October – written into it, so that he could claim ignorance of why Elijah had come to Ashborne Hill on the second. But of course it was Skeffington who had planned for the young man to go there on 2 October, as the letter in the bureau had proved.

But why? Why should a demonstrably rich man, about to receive a legacy from an old American friend, brutally murder that man's son? There could be no possible motive. But young Mr Madison was right. Skeffington would have to be questioned again. Motive – that was the stumbling-block.

Madison returned to keep Jackson company at dinner, which proved to be a pleasant meal. The secretary, once freed from the constraints of his daily business, revealed himself as a very agreeable companion. Mr Buchanan Davis, he said, would be back as promised tomorrow. Meanwhile, he hoped that the inspector would enjoy a good night's sleep.

Jackson had just finished his breakfast, which was served to him in the drawing-room, when the noise of a carriage drawing up to the house took him to the window. It was not the same carriage as the one that had brought him to Washington Square, but it was the same bevy of young secretaries who tumbled out on to the pavement. They were followed by a very tall, raw-boned man in a wide-brimmed, tall-crowned white hat. He was wearing a tight-fitting green tweed suit. The front door opened and closed, there was a commotion of raised voices in the hall, and then the new arrivals erupted into the room. The big man seized Jackson's hand in an iron grip, and shook it vigorously.

'Mr Jackson? Buchanan Davis. I'm sorry that I couldn't be here to greet you personally this morning. How are you? Did you have a good crossing? Say, did the boys look after you? Did Madison come up with the goods? Good, good. Well, this is fine. Just fine. Sit down, then you and I can have a little talk. Hine!'

Buchanan Davis suddenly raised his voice to something approaching a bellow, and the old butler came into the room. There were bell pulls beside the fireplace; evidently, the railroad king considered them effete.

'Hine, fetch the bourbon. You'll sample our whiskey, won't you, Jackson? Good. Well, this is just fine. You boys, vamoose!'

The secretaries scuttled from the room. Buchanan Davis chose a settee opposite Jackson's, and sat down. He seemed to be all arms and legs, and the gracious old room appeared to be too small to contain him. His bronzed face sported a neat goatee beard.

Hine entered, deposited a silver tray containing a decanter, two tall glasses, and a jug of iced water on a table between them, and quietly withdrew. Davis poured them both a generous measure of whiskey, and sat back on his settee.

'I was Elijah Robinson's uncle on his

mother's side,' he began without preamble. 'By which I mean, Mr Jackson, that his mother is my sister. This year she has lost her husband to fever, and now her son to murder. That's a terrible burden for poor Jessie to bear. Yes, sir, a terrible burden.'

'And where is the lady now, sir?'

'Jessie is at my estate up in Albany, Mr Jackson, and there she stays with me, my wife and my five sons. I tell you there's room for us all in that mansion of mine. So we'll leave poor Jessie be for the moment. What I want to talk about is my nephew, Elijah. This was his home. He was born in this house. What have you done with his body? What's happened to his effects, his clothes, and so forth?'

'I know that you'll appreciate, Mr Davis,' Jackson began delicately, 'that the poor young man's body could not be left above ground after a few days had passed. After the post-mortem, which was conducted by a qualified police surgeon, his body was buried in a private grave in the village churchyard at Charnley, an ancient township in the county of Warwickshire.'

'Why, that sounds reasonable and decorous, Mr Jackson. And who paid for this private grave?'

'It was paid for, sir, by an old friend of

Mr Jacob Robinson, a gentleman called Alexander Skeffington, who lives in Charnley.'

'Skeffington – oh, yes, I heard a lot about him from Jacob. Jacob was given to reminiscing, usually at great length. Yes, sir. And Skeffington was part of the never-ending story of his wild youth. The family's much obliged to him, and I'll write to tell him so in due course. Will there be any objection to the family erecting a monument over poor young Elijah's grave?'

'None whatever, sir.'

'Good. I'm glad. And his effects?'

'Everything had been cleaned, made tidy, and recorded. His possessions can be forwarded to any address you care to give me.'

The two men sat in silence for a moment, appreciating their whiskey. Jackson's eyes wandered to the portrait of Jim Bolder fixed to the wall adjacent to the fireplace. The artist, he noted, had painted a faint suggestion of Bolder's birthmark across the forehead.

'It looks as though the late Mr Robinson had a high regard for Jim Bolder, one of his two companions at the Australian gold diggings,' he said.

'Jim Bolder? Oh, yes, he was part of Jacob's endless saga of his adventures. I don't know about a high regard, though. He only knew him for a short time at the diggings. I don't think anyone knew what became of him after that.'

'And yet, sir,' said Jackson, 'he had his portrait painted, so he must have had some special regard for him.'

'Had his portrait painted? Did he really? Why, Mr Jackson, I never knew that.'

Saul Jackson found himself rising stiffly from his seat. Something was wrong. *Everything* was wrong. He crossed the room and stood motionless in front of the portrait of Jim Bolder. The image of the mild man with the round face seemed to gaze at him with fine unconcern. The artist had shown his hair trained to hide most of the birthmark on his forehead. Perhaps Jim Bolder had trained it like that?

Buchanan Davis had hauled himself up from his settee and joined Jackson near the fireplace.

'Why, Mr Jackson,' he said, 'you look quite odd! What is it about that portrait that's worrying you?'

'I don't understand what it's doing here, Mr Davis. Why did the late Mr Robinson have this portrait painted? What was so special about Jim Bolder?'

Buchanan Davis laughed, and shook his head.

'I don't quite get your meaning, Mr Jackson. That is a portrait of Mr Alexander Skeffington, as you must know, as you've been talking to the man for the last few weeks! Old Jacob Robinson had a real soft spot for Skeffington – he'd done him some kind of a favour out in Australia – and he had that painting made from an old photograph. They were good friends once, I guess, and that's why he left him a legacy. If you ask me, the friendship was all one-sided, 'cause Skeffington never answered any of his letters.'

Jackson stood in front of the portrait, and tried to rearrange his thoughts. The man in Providence House, the man who had produced the devilry of the fake letter, wasn't Skeffington at all. That was why he feared young Elijah Robinson, and arranged to lure him to his death in Ashborne Hill. Robinson wouldn't have recognized the man who spoke to him in the dining-room of the Berkeley Arms, because he'd never seen him before, and the false 'Skeffington' had known that.

There was an important corollary. Had Elijah Robinson presented himself at Providence House, he would have known at once that the man calling himself Skeffington wasn't Skeffington at all, because he had seen the portrait of the true Skeffington here, in the Washington Square house, every day of his life.

Somehow, the impostor – Jim Bolder? – had made away with Skeffington, and secured his great fortune, living on it in luxury and security for most of his lifetime. Nothing was to stand in the way of the impostor's comfort. And so Elijah Robinson, the innocent bearer of good tidings, had been marked down for death.

12
LONDON EXCURSIONS

While Jackson was talking to Buchanan Davis in New York, Sergeant Bottomley and Dr James Venner were sitting in the consulting-room at Trinity Ford Insane Asylum at Inchfield, listening to the courteous but rather condescending tones of its principal, Dr Meitner. Ursula Holt's journal lay open on the desk in front of him.

Dr Venner had called for Bottomley early that morning at Barrack Street Police Office. His elegant closed carriage with its black gelding between the traces and a man in capes up on the box had attracted some attention from the few residents of the street, who had come out on to their doorsteps to get a closer look. For one anxious moment Bottomley thought that his companion proposed making the whole forty-mile journey by carriage, but his fears were soon allayed.

'If we're to make an excursion into the

countryside today, Bottomley,' Venner had said, 'we may as well start in something approaching style. If we go by carriage to Leamington Spa, we can catch a fast train to Inchfield from there. It will cut an hour at least from our journey.'

And so it had been. Doctor Venner, whom Herbert Bottomley referred to affectionately as Dandy Jim, was a distinguished, grey-haired man in his sixties. For the purposes of their joint investigation, he had arrayed himself in a faultless grey frock coat and black silk stock, in which he had placed an opal pin. He wore pale mauve kid gloves, and sported a gleaming silk hat. Bottomley wondered what old Dr Meitner would make of this elegant figure.

They had arrived at Trinity Ford by mid-morning, and were received very graciously by the elderly alienist. He had listened patiently to Bottomley's story, and then had agreed to read the entries in Ursula's journal, all of which had been addressed personally to him. Now, he was delivering his verdict.

'Most interesting, Dr Venner,' he said. 'When Miss Holt left here, she asked me whether I could give her any advice on coping with the results of her mental disturbance. I proposed that she should keep a journal, recording therein an account of any dreams or hallucinations that she might suffer. It would help, I told her, if she addressed her accounts to me by name. It was not a proposal that she should forward her journal to me. By no means. No, it was to be a form of psychotherapy, a rationalization in verbal form of imagined fears and fantasies. To that end also I gave her a copy of Dr Altmann's book, *The Somnambule.* There, she would encounter a first-rate mind examining her kind of fears in the sober light of reason.'

Dr Meitner smiled, and it was a kind of knowing smile, inviting them to applaud the wisdom of his actions.

'And now,' he continued, 'Mr Bottomley tells me that Miss Holt did not commit those actions – the killing of the dog, and the mutilation of the sheep. I hope that my congratulations are in order, Sergeant! Nevertheless, the fact remains that Miss Holt was the victim of somnambular amnesia. Over the course of six months, I ascertained that there was nothing of more sinister import underlying that condition. These dreams, which she describes in her journal, will fade away in the fullness of time. When Miss Holt left here, Dr Venner, she was cured.'

There was a slight edge to the doctor's voice as he uttered these final words. He carefully closed Ursula's journal, and handed it to Venner across his desk.

'As a physician,' said Venner smoothly, 'I am naturally interested in how you effected that cure, Dr Meitner. Illnesses of Miss Holt's path seldom come to my professional attention.'

'It was done by a process of constant questioning, of facilitating recall of past events in the subject's life, thus forcing her to confront the realities of her own condition. In that confrontation, Dr Venner, lie the seeds of the cure itself. The subject is kept in a state of dependent tranquillity by the regular application of soothing specifics. I have much enjoyed this interview. Perhaps we will meet again, sometime.'

'Well, there you are, Bottomley,' said Dr Venner as they walked down the path leading through the well-tended gardens of the asylum to the main road. 'Meitner chose not to believe you, because your findings don't fit in with his own settled beliefs. She came to him as a slaughterer of livestock, and he cured her. Guilty by reason of temporary insanity. Her journal holds no interest for him.'

'Do you think he's a quack, sir?'

'By no means. He runs a splendid establishment there, very different from the general run of establishments of lunatic constraint, and he follows a regime that has worked well for him in the past. When he speaks of "dependent tranquillity", Bottomley, he means that he kept Miss Holt and the others under his charge in a permanent state of narcosis through the application of laudanum. But he's no help to us now. For him, the matter is closed. What do you think we should do next?'

'Well, sir, the next stage of our enquiry will take us to London. We need to consult this Dr Altmann, and then have a few words with Miss Ursula's friend, Mrs Wishart —'

'Excellent! We could start out for London early on Monday morning. There's a London and North Western Railway express from Warwick on weekdays, leaving at eight minutes past nine. I'll pen a note to Altmann, so that our arrival won't be entirely unexpected. We'd better stay Monday night in Town. Will your good lady be agreeable to that?'

'She will, sir, but —'

'Oh, I know what you're going to say – expense, and so forth. Don't bother about all that, Sergeant. Let me take care of the cost. Doctor Altmann is staying at the Hotel Metropole in Northumberland Avenue You and I will put up at the Arundel, which is not all that far from the Metropole. They do a very decent dinner there for three shillings. I'll meet you in Barrack Street at half past seven on Monday morning.'

Settled comfortably in a first-class compartment of the London train, Dr James Venner turned over the pages of Ursula Holt's journal. He and Bottomley were the only occupants, which meant that they could freely discuss the business that was taking them on the three-hour journey to London. Venner's brows puckered in a frown, and from time to time he uttered little sounds of vexation.

Sergeant Bottomley, sitting opposite him in the unaccustomed luxury of first class, was content to wait until the doctor chose to speak. Dandy Jim had worked with him and the guvnor for years. Although he looked more like a tailor's dummy than a practising doctor, he was, in fact, a first-rate police surgeon. He may be a gentleman, but he was prepared to take the rough with the smooth.

'Sergeant Bottomley,' said Dr Venner at length, 'these accounts of Miss Holt's dreams would seem to suggest that she is far from recovered, despite what Dr Meitner asserted. These are obsessive imaginings. . . . They're leading somewhere, but that mental destination has not yet been attained. What do you think?'

'I've met and spoken to Miss Ursula Holt, sir, and I've read through that journal. Although I've proved that she had no part in those mutilations, that doesn't mean that she's recovered her senses. I think she's still a bit deranged, sir. Fearful, and too ready to be persuaded by what others tell her. I've known young ladies of that kind before, sir. They have fragile minds.'

'Umm. . . . And you took away something else, didn't you, when you searched Miss Holt's room at Abbey Lodge?'

For answer, Bottomley brought down his travelling-bag from the luggage rack, produced the slim book bound in red morocco leather, and handed it to Venner.

'Ah! Dr Karl Gustav Altmann's *The Somnambule.* This is the book that Meitner gave to Miss Holt, no doubt. An excellent study of sleepwalking, Bottomley, from a fresh and original viewpoint. I shall be delighted to meet Dr Altmann when we get to London. In my own modest way I've made a contribution to the subject with a little paper on the physical changes to the brains of amnesiac lunatics. Several such subjects were brought to me for dissection, you know. Yes, only a modest contribution, but Dr Altmann may be interested to hear of it.'

Venner frowned, and put the monograph down beside him on the seat.

'You know, Sergeant,' he said, 'I don't approve of putting works like that into the hands of lay people. They inevitably misinterpret them, and imagine that they've all kinds of diseases, physical or mental. It doesn't do, and I think Meitner was wrong there.'

Bottomley agreed. It couldn't have been healthy for that young woman to frighten herself out of her wits by reading about cryptamnesia by candlelight. No wonder that her journal was a record of so many nameless horrors.

'There's something else I'd like to show you, sir, if I may,' said Bottomley. He rummaged around in his pocket, and produced the scalpel which had been used to murder Paul Staunton. 'What do you think of that, sir?'

Dr Venner held the knife delicately between the thumb and forefinger of his right hand. Bottomley watched as his companion made little cutting motions in the air with the fatal blade.

'Very curious, Sergeant,' he said, handing the scalpel back to Bottomley. 'It's one of a set of amputation knives by Savigny of James Street, and it's dated 1815, as you will have noticed. I say "curious", because this kind of knife is quite out of fashion, and has been for many years. One could describe it without exaggeration as an antique.'

'If I wanted to buy a scalpel like that one, sir, where would I go? I don't suppose that Savigny and Company would be still making them?'

'Well, no: what would be the use of that? Savigny make working blades for modern surgeons to use. You'll often see sets of these old instruments on show in certain consulting-rooms as part of the decor. To create an effect, you know. You can see cases of old surgical instruments for sale at Peterson's in the Burlington Arcade.'

'If you don't mind, Dr Venner, I'd like to pay a call on this Peterson. You see, all the mutilations, and the first murder – the murder of Mr Elijah Robinson – were done with surgical instruments stolen from a similar case in Dr Matthew Holt's consulting-room. Then, I think the murderer realized that he would be caught in the act one day, and decided to buy some instruments of his own —'

'And not being a doctor, he bought an antique set rather than a modern case of knives. And so he slipped up. How very clever of you, Sergeant Bottomley!'

'Thank you, sir. You see, I never suspected Dr Holt from the start, and it didn't take me long to see that poor Miss Ursula Holt was entirely innocent. But our killer is still trying to suggest that she's somehow connected with these murders, even though she couldn't have done either of them. It's a stupid kind of thing to do, sir, and it makes me wonder whether this killer isn't more than a bit mad himself. He's no longer thinking straight.'

'You know who it is, don't you, Sergeant?' said Venner quietly.

'I can't name names without evidence, sir,' said Bottomley, 'and without establishing motive, which neither Mr Jackson nor myself can do for the moment. It doesn't make sense. But yes, sir, I know who did it, well enough.'

At ten minutes past twelve, the express began to slow down, as it approached Euston Station. At the same time, 3,000 miles to the west, Inspector Jackson walked up the gangway of the RMS *Etruria,* another

Cunard liner, which would embark that very day for England.

When Dr Venner and Sergeant Bottomley called upon the famous alienist Karl Gustav Altmann at the Hotel Metropole, they found the door of his first-floor suite standing wide open. From the room beyond, two sounds emerged: the staccato clacking of a typewriter, and the mournful wailing of a violin. Venner glanced at Bottomley and shrugged his shoulders. His action clearly indicated that foreigners had their own peculiar ways of acting, and that it was up to the English to be patient with them.

The room they entered was the sitting-room of the suite. At a round table in the centre of the room a young man dressed in sober black was subjecting a Remington typewriter to a relentless battering. A book was propped up against a coffee pot, and the young man was frowning at it through tinted pince-nez. His narrow face was adorned with a close-cropped jet black beard.

The mournful violin music proceeded from a phonograph. As they entered the room the music came to a stop. The young man sprang from the table, and successfully subdued the instrument before turning to

251

his visitors.

'Dr Venner, and Sergeant Bottomley? Forgive me, gentlemen,' he said, in perfect English, 'I was preparing notes for one of my lectures. The noise of the typewriter jangles my nerves, but at the same time the music soothes them. I received your note, Doctor, and I shall be delighted to examine this poor young woman's journal. Venner, Venner. . . . Were you the author of that paper in *The Lancet,* on physical changes in the brains of amnesiac lunatics? Excellent! I'd like a word with you about that, some time. But come – the journal!'

Dr Altmann took Ursula's journal from Venner, and sat down in an armchair near the fireplace. He motioned to his visitors to do likewise. Bottomley thought: can a bumptious young man like him know as much as Dr Venner? I thought he'd be older. Dr Verner thought: fancy his knowing about that article in *The Lancet!* I wonder where he has his black embroidered waistcoats made?

As Dr Altmann read the pages of Ursula's journal, his visitors saw him frown, and unconsciously gnaw his lower lip. He sat up straight in his chair, muttering to himself. 'A glittering and stately ballroom . . . staircase . . . flight of steps. . . . And what's

252

this? A deed box! A silvery flute!'

The mutterings ceased, to be replaced by a concentrated calm. Bottomley and Venner sat in patient silence for more than ten minutes. Then Altmann spoke.

'This is a sinister, wicked business, gentlemen,' he said, tapping the open pages of the journal sharply with his gold pince-nez. 'There's devil's work here. Upon my word, I wouldn't have missed reading this account for worlds! Meitner's a sound man, but he could not have interpreted this aright.'

'You are able, then, to throw some positive light on Miss Holt's predicament?'

'I am, Dr Venner. These dreams are not mere fantasies, they are what one might call distorted recollections of real places and events. I need some time to draw up a chart, and to separate, as best I can, the facts from the metaphors. . . .

'It's two o'clock now. Can you call upon me at four? I'll be ready then to give you my interpretation of these accounts. One thing I have noticed, that will be of particular relevance to you, Sergeant Bottomley: there was an entry made by this poor young lady on the tenth, in which she speaks of seeing a skeletal hand. She's beginning to remember real things that she has seen in the past, and I very much fear that her memories will prove to be a source of physical danger to her.'

'So this skeletal hand, sir, is a sign of danger?'

'Yes, Sergeant. Because, at some moment in the past, Miss Holt must have seen such a thing – a real skeletal hand, I mean. She may be partly recalling a murder, and the murderer may still be at large. Come back at four. By then, my interpretation will be complete.'

'Ursula? No, Dr Venner, Ursula's not here. Why should she be?'

There was no hostility in Catherine Wishart's voice, simply curiosity. She stood near the white marble mantelpiece of the Wishart's elegant town house in Bruton Street, Mayfair, and Dr Venner, who was an expert in such things, noted that she stood in such a way as to be able to glance from time to time at her own profile in the fireplace mirror. Catherine Wishart, formerly Catherine Stansfield, was fully aware of her own standing as a noted Society beauty of the day.

'We thought she might be here, Mrs Wishart,' said Venner, 'because you have always been her staunch friend. When she left home without telling anyone where she was going, her family naturally thought of you.'

'You are acting for her family? It seems a curious occupation for a physician.'

Herbert Bottomley saw Venner blush, either with vexation or embarrassment. So far, he had said nothing, choosing to sit silently on an upright chair near the door, listening to the smooth tones of his companion. It was now time for him to speak.

'Asking your pardon, ma'am,' said Bottomley, and his loud voice came so unexpectedly that Catherine Wishart uttered a little shriek of alarm, 'but this is police business of a very serious nature. Doctor Venner is a police surgeon.' He added, after a fleeting moment's thought, 'Dr Venner doesn't carry messages for anyone, ma'am.'

It was Mrs Wishart's turn to blush. Why had she been so rude to this elegant and distinguished doctor?

'I stand corrected, Sergeant Bottomley,' she said, 'and if an apology is in order, Dr Venner, then I give it to you freely. But the truth is, I'm always on tenterhooks whenever strangers ask me questions about Ursula. She has been gravely wronged, slandered, and imprisoned in an asylum without reason – no, sir, don't tell me all about sheep and sheepdogs, because I won't listen! Only a fool or a knave could possibly believe that dear girl capable of such acts.'

Catherine Wishart left the mantelpiece, and sat down in a damask-covered chair. She moved with unconscious grace, but there was artifice in her choice of a chair in the sunlit window bay, which would enhance the dramatic effect of her mauve silk afternoon dress. She began to speak, and her voice was quieter and more thoughtful now that she was no longer on the defensive.

'Ursula Holt became my friend when she was twelve years old, and I was sixteen. I hadn't done the season then, of course, and we two girls were able to enjoy ourselves in the free and easy way of country houses in those days. All this was in the early eighties, at Alderley Hall, our family's place in Northamptonshire. We forged bonds of friendship there, Dr Venner, that have never been broken.'

'And she has not been here this last week?' Dr Venner persisted. 'Has she not written to you, proposing a visit?'

'No. She has done neither of those things. She is not here, and she is not at our house in Radley Cross. I don't know where she is.'

Catherine's dark eyes flashed with sudden anger.

'It's all this persecution that's driving her frantic, I've no doubt, and all because she's a sleepwalker! What's the cure for that? Lock her bedroom door! That's what we did when Ursula visited at Alderley Hall. My little girl – another Ursula – was a bedwetter until she was four, but neither my husband nor myself contemplated having her confined to an asylum. Her nurse simply changed the sheets.'

'Could Miss Ursula have gone down to Alderley Hall, ma'am? Pining for old times, as it were?'

'I hardly think so, Sergeant,' said Catherine, smiling. 'Alderley Hall belongs to my brother, who inherited it from my father. Ursula was *my* friend, not his. In any case, had she wanted to go down there, she would certainly have applied to me first.'

Catherine Wishart's features softened into an expression that betokened a mood of wistful recollection. Her instinctive animosity to her visitors was fading.

'You know, Dr Venner,' she said. 'those were idyllic days! Alderley Hall's a beautiful house, built entirely as one piece in the last century. My parents were very hospitable people, and they gave splendid costume balls several times a year, in the magnificent ballroom. Everybody came – at least, everybody who was anybody in the county. Ursula and I loved those dances. . . . Things are so innocent, aren't they, when one is young?'

Venner smiled to himself. This beautiful young lady, he could see, was not yet thirty.

'You mention costume balls, Mrs Wishart,' he said. 'I attended one of those once, in my own youth. I went garbed as a Roman emperor.'

'Ours were all in the costumes of the eighteenth century, with powdered wigs, and wonderfully embroidered suits for the men. We – the girls, I mean – had to wear great billowing dresses and little tricorne hats, and we stuck little black patches to our cheeks. Mama allowed us both to use cosmetic make-up, which was great fun, you know, as ladies of any rank or station just don't use stuff like that.'

Catherine had relaxed fully now, and the rather haughty beauty had been replaced by a young woman enjoying memories of her girlhood.

'And did you have old-fashioned music, ma'am?' asked Bottomley, 'with bassoons, and the viola da gamba, and so forth?'

'Yes, we did. We used to hire a little chamber orchestra, and the men came decked out in livery, with those peculiar tie-wigs. Yes, that's right. And they played eighteenth-century music in a little enclosure in the ballroom, especially made for them.'

'Any flutes, ma'am?'

'Flutes? What an odd question! There may have been. I can't remember.'

'This ballroom at Alderley Hall interests us immensely, Mrs Wishart,' said Venner. He glanced briefly at Bottomley, who nodded his agreement. 'I wonder whether you would pen us an introductory note, so that we could pay a visit?'

'Certainly, if that's what you wish. Are you going to tell me what's happening to Ursula? No, I can see it's a secret. Well, I'll write you a note. My brother won't mind. Actually, his wife and he are abroad at the moment, so Alderley Hall's in the charge of the housekeeper. You've chosen your time well.'

Later, as they waited in the hall to be let out of the house, Catherine Wishart appeared at the top of the stairs.

'Doctor Venner,' she said, 'if Ursula Holt turns up on my doorstep after you've gone, I'll take her in without question. And I shan't tell anyone, you understand, unless she gives me permission.'

Doctor Venner said nothing, and the two men left the house. A little maid in cap and apron was busy mopping the area steps. Herbert Bottomley stopped to look at her.

'You've done a good job there, miss,' he said. 'You could eat your dinner off them steps.'

The maid glanced briefly at Bottomley, smiled, and then dropped her eyes.

'I don't suppose you've a young lady staying here, have you?' asked Bottomley. 'Miss Ursula Holt, she's called. Ever so beautiful, I'm told, just like your missus. But neither of them could hold a candle to you, Mary.'

'It's Susan,' said the girl, laughing in spite of herself. 'And Miss Holt's not here. We've not seen her for ever so long. Missus is ever so fond of her. She's had a lot of trouble, you see, and missus has a kind heart – oh! Thank you, sir!'

Bottomley had given the maid a shilling. As he and Venner stepped into Bruton Street she gave them a little curtsy, and disappeared down the area steps.

'No, Doctor,' said Bottomley, 'Miss Ursula's not there. But this ballroom – it ties in with the ballroom of Ursula's dreams, and we need to tell Dr Altmann about that. But there's still time for us to visit that man you mentioned in Burlington Arcade. The one who sells antique medical instruments.'

'We can walk it from here, Sergeant. It's

straight down Bond Street, and then right, into Piccadilly. Peterson's. That's the name of the shop. After we've visited him, we'd better take a cab back to the Hotel Metropole, so as to be in plenty of time.'

Doctor Venner set out with something of a spring in his normally sedate step.

'You know, Sergeant Bottomley,' he said, 'I'm rather enjoying all this detection business!'

Bottomley treated his companion to a lopsided smile.

'I rather thought you were, sir!' he replied. 'I think I'll leave you to do the detecting when we get to Piccadilly.'

Burlington Arcade, a covered thoroughfare 200 yards in length, had been built as a bazaar in 1819 by Lord George Cavendish, later Earl of Burlington. Mr Peterson's place of business was little more than a kiosk wedged between two grander shops in the left-hand row of the arcade.

Peterson, a lanky, dark-featured man wearing a tasselled silk cap, sat behind a small mahogany counter. His wares, mainly cases of surgical instruments and white ivory phrenology heads, were displayed on shelves that rose to the dim ceiling. Bottomley handed him the scalpel that had killed

Paul Staunton, and Peterson greeted it as though it were an old friend.

'Yes, gentlemen,' he said, 'I remember it well. It was one of a set made for Savigny of James Street in 1815. There were nine amputation instruments in a wooden case lined with red velvet, together with a tourniquet, various threads, three needles and a spare hacksaw blade. A very fine set altogether.'

'I don't suppose you remember who bought that set from you?' asked Venner. He glanced briefly at Bottomley, and added, 'This is a matter of police business, you understand. My colleague here is a police detective.'

'Police? Well, well. . . . Are you going to tell me what it's all about? No, I thought you wouldn't. Now, as a matter of fact, I keep a record of all purchasers, with their addresses. Let me see.'

Mr Peterson produced a ledger from beneath the counter, and quickly leafed through it.

'Yes, here we are. It was on 20 September this year, which was a Wednesday, and the purchaser was a Dr Matthew Holt, giving his address as Abbey Lodge, Charnley, Warwickshire.'

Doctor Venner's eyes met Bottomley's,

and the sergeant saw their glint of triumph.

'Thank you very much, Mr Peterson,' said Venner, 'you have been of great help to us in our investigation. Do you send out catalogues?'

'Indeed I do, sir. Just leave me your calling card, and I'll see you have the latest copy by tomorrow's post.'

As they turned from the counter to leave the shop, Herbert Bottomley addressed a few well-chosen words to Mr Peterson.

'This Dr Holt, sir,' he said, 'I seem to know the name. Isn't he a short, hunchbacked man with ginger hair? A man who speaks with a strong Scots accent?'

'Well, no, Mr Bottomley; Dr Holt was a tall, eagle-eyed man with beetling brows – a very commanding person. And as for his accent, I thought he spoke very well, though there was a faint suggestion of the colonial about his vowels.'

'Dear me, Sergeant,' said Venner as they turned into Piccadilly, 'you showed yourself to be the winner, there! I'd not thought to elicit a description of Dr Holt from Peterson. I take it, then, that the description doesn't fit the real Dr Holt?'

'It doesn't, sir, but then, I never thought it would. Our murderer was too clever for his own good, because that description tells me quite clearly who he is. There's a lot of work to do still, Doctor, and I wish Mr Jackson were here to advise and supervise. But it's only a matter of time, now. Although he doesn't know it, our murderer has already condemned himself to death.'

13
Seeking the
Haunted Ballroom

When Venner and Bottomley returned to
Dr Altmann's suite at the Metropole, they
found him poring over a carefully drawn
plan of the ballroom which had been described so vividly by Ursula Holt in her
journal. He motioned to them both to draw
up chairs to the table, and without giving
either man the chance to recount his own
adventures, he launched into speech.

'This, gentlemen,' he said, 'is a plan of the
haunted ballroom that Miss Holt sees in
her dreams. Let me say at once that although this young woman is a somnambule,
her dreams are true dreams: they are not
recollections of nocturnal wanderings *rationalized* as dreams, on returning to bed.'

'But she could have had those dreams
while sleepwalking, couldn't she, sir?' asked
Bottomley. 'She could dream of being in
the ballroom while walking in a trance
around the garden?'

'Oh, yes, Sergeant. I know what you are thinking about, and I'll return to the point later. In these painful dreams, the young woman – I shall call her Ursula rather than Miss Holt, for convenience – finds herself present in this ballroom, where she makes a kind of progress to an ultimate goal. I have marked the stages of that progress in red ink, with little explanatory drawings in black along the route. Her progress starts here' – he pointed to a spot at the bottom left-hand corner of the plan – 'at an entrance, which she first describes in her account written on Friday, 6 October. It is "a dark and dusty vestibule", from which she mounted what she called "a kind of staircase or flight of steps". There's a realism about those words, gentlemen, that make me think that the ballroom is no fantasy of imagination, but a real place, at one time known to Ursula, but now, perhaps, forgotten.'

Doctor Venner looked as though he was about to speak. Bottomley shook his head very slightly, and Venner held his peace. Bottomley was right. This was not the time to talk about Catherine Stansfield and Alderley Hall.

'I want now to talk very briefly about one of the chief characteristics of these fantasy journeys of the mind, which I have studied

266

extensively in my examination of various inmates of the Maria Hospital at Vienna. These "journey" dreams are often confused recollections of dangerous or life-threatening incidents in real life, which have been totally forgotten in patients who, like Ursula, are subject to hysterical spasm.'

Altmann was evidently unaware that he had adopted the tone and stance of a lecturer. In any case, thought Venner, his expository method of talking was extremely effective.

'In the course of such dreams,' Altmann continued, 'the subject may encounter images of objects or even people associated with the original life-threatening incident. If those images produce fear, then the subject will try to substitute harmless images in their place. For instance, a hammer, used in a fatal assault, could be seen in a dream as a walking-stick.'

'So a bad object will often be replaced by a good one, in order to allay fear?'

'Yes, Dr Venner, though there are cases where a bad object is still perceived, apparently as an urgent warning of immediate danger. But not in this case. The presence of these "substitutes", as I call them, in the somnambule's dreams, intermingled with the shadows of real objects, often renders the subject's dream meaningless to him. People like me exist to render those night-fantasies meaningful.'

Doctor Altmann picked up the copy of Ursula's journal, and held it open in his left hand. His right hand held a pencil, which he used as a pointer to guide his visitors' way along his depiction of Ursula's sleeping journey through the haunted ballroom.

'Imagine, gentlemen,' he began, 'that you are Ursula, and that you have just stepped out of that dark, chilly vestibule, stumbled up the steps and so into the ballroom. What is the first thing that you see?'

'I don't suppose I see anything, Doctor,' said Bottomley, 'because it's too dark. I only have a little candle with me.'

'Excellent! A dark vestibule, a candle, a dark, sinister chamber. And then, as though thrown down at her feet, Ursula sees – a deed box. You see that I've drawn such a box there, on the plan. "Quite an ordinary affair, with a black and green enamelled lid", Ursula writes. What do you make of that deed box, Dr Venner?'

'The deed box? It can't be a substitute, can it? Her description sounds too mundane to me. After all, there's not much very threatening about a deed box.'

'I agree. It's not a substitute, which means

that at one time in the past, in a cold, dark chamber reached by steps from a darkened vestibule, Ursula saw an open deed box lying on the floor at her feet.'

Doctor Altmann moved away from the table for a moment, removed his pince-nez, and screwed up his eyes. Venner and Bottomley watched him, fascinated. What would this interpreter of dreams say next?

'An open deed box. . . . Perhaps a rifled deed box? Rifled, and thrown hastily down on to the floor. It's a possibility. And all that, gentlemen, occurred, I think, at a real time, and in a real place. But now what happens? What did Ursula do next? "I moved a little to my right, by now quite numb with cold, and saw on the floor something that filled me with an illogical alarm".'

Altmann returned to the table, and pointed with his pencil at another drawing, a rough representation of a flute. He had drawn it in black, with a tassel attached, depicted in vivid red ink. Sergeant Bottomley stirred in his chair.

'Yes, Sergeant,' cried Altmann excitedly, 'what does that suggest to you?'

'It's one of those substitutes, sir. Miss Ursula was alarmed, and so she substituted a flute with a red tassel for whatever it was that alarmed her. It might have been. . . . It might have been an iron bar, or a jemmy, something metallic, and long, like a flute.'

'And the red tassel? A patch of blood?'

'No, sir – more likely a bloodstained handkerchief, or cloth.'

'I think you're right, Sergeant. It's certainly a substitute, and your suggestion tallies with my own as yet unformed idea. When Ursula endured the original happening upon which her dreams are based, I believe that she was present at a scene of murder.'

'Well done, Altmann!' murmured Dr Venner.

'Yes, sir,' echoed Bottomley, 'well done. I've read that journal three times over, but until now I never knew the key to open its secrets.'

'Thank you, gentlemen,' said the alienist, blushing with pleasure. 'You are very kind. But there's more here for us to examine – far more. I suggest that we adjourn downstairs for tea, during which perhaps you'll tell me something of Miss Ursula Holt's background and history. Half an hour's relaxed converse, and then, if you are willing, back up here.'

'By all means,' said Dr Venner. 'And over tea, Sergeant Bottomley and I will tell you of the important discoveries that we have made this afternoon.'

'Certainly, but come, gentlemen, I'm famished. Let us descend at once to the lounge.'

Superintendent Mays carefully unfolded the long telegraph-form, and laid it on Inspector Jackson's desk. He had enjoyed running the Warwick Police Office during Jackson's absence in America, but now the task was beginning to pall. There was a limit to one's interest in the daily run of surly, inarticulate poachers and the like who had crossed his path during the last week. The maturing criminal fraternity of Copton Vale exhibited a much higher level of sophistication. Still, Jackson would be back on Friday.

The telegraph message was from the police records department at Sydney, New South Wales, with a copy to Lieutenant Connor of the New York Police Department.

Your description fits that of James Bolder, known as Gentleman Jim, alias Hawkeye Jim Bolder, born 1826 at Port Jackson, New South Wales. Bolder was a convicted confidence trickster and petty thief. Came originally from Scotland with parents, but lived at Port Jackson since infancy. Was in the Gold Fever of 1851, after which he was said to have returned to the United Kingdom. Will send a certified photograph in the post.

Gentleman Jim? What was Jackson up to, now? He must have contacted Sydney from New York for some reason, and this is their reply. Jackson must have told them to send it here to us in England, as he would have embarked before their reply could reach him in New York.

Should he leave it locked up in a drawer until Jackson returned on Friday? No, that wasn't the way. Whoever Jim Bolder was, his identity was of sufficient interest to Jackson to make him send a long-distance cable to Australia. Bottomley had sent him a postcard from London telling him that he and Venner were staying at the Arundel Hotel. He would send the Australian cable there by special messenger. Sergeant Bottomley could take the matter from there.

Altmann, Venner and Bottomley had re-assembled around the table in Altmann's suite. The Viennese alienist took up his pencil, and placed it on his drawing of the tasselled flute. Once again, he was holding Ursula's journal open in his left hand.

'She would not pick it up, because she knew it signalled danger. And at the same time, the ballroom filled with light: it became "a lofty, gilded chamber". Her journal tells us that she has had these ballroom dreams before, and that in them she had been accosted by "a smiling young man". This time, as the room lightens, she sees a young Negro servant, with blue eyes, and wearing a turban. That, surely, is a recollection of someone real?

'When we had tea together, you told me of this ballroom at a country house in Northamptonshire, a house at which Ursula was a frequent guest. Is it too fantastic if I suggest that these dreams have that ballroom for their setting? Let us move further into the haunted room.

'Ursula passes the mysterious servant, and finds herself in an area where tables and chairs have been set out. People are drinking there, while a stately dance continues around them. Memories, gentlemen – Ursula's confused but authentic memories of those costume balls that you tell me were held there, years ago!'

'Sir,' said Bottomley, 'Miss Ursula said that one of those figures sitting at the table was my guvnor, Inspector Jackson. What was he doing there?'

Doctor Altmann was quiet for a moment. He reread the relevant passage of Ursula's journal, his lips moving silently as he did so.

'Could there have been an occasion in her waking moments, Sergeant, when she saw this Mr Jackson sitting in an area of tables, drinking, or perhaps eating? This could be an instance of double memory – one pictured recollection superimposed upon another. You see, Ursula remarks that "once again I felt that this man could read all the stored secrets of my heart". "Once again" – she had seen him before, and evidently feared him for that reason.'

'I know what it is, sir,' said Bottomley. 'On the day that Miss Ursula travelled home from the asylum, she stopped in the dining-room of a hotel, where Mr Jackson was finishing a meal. She saw him then, and he told me that he read alarm in her glance.'

'Excellent! As you see, gentlemen, we are making sound progress. What happens next? She leaves the people at the tables, and moves further into the room until she comes to a little roped-off area devoted to a small chamber orchestra. All the players are in costume, and one or two of them recognize her – and she them. At this stage in her dream, Ursula is clearly recollecting accurate details of one of those costume balls at – what did you call it? – Alderley Hall.'

'Don't you think we should go there, Altmann?' asked Venner. 'I've secured an introduction to the people there, and it could be very instructive.'

'A very good idea, Dr Venner. I myself would be very willing to accompany you. There is just one aspect of the case that causes me a certain amount of disquiet. Ursula's recollections of the ballroom at Alderley Hall are very vivid. She sees the brilliantly lighted chandeliers, smells the candlewax, hears the music of the saraband. She sees the little chamber orchestra, and recognizes some of the players.

'But. . . . At the beginning of her dream, she finds herself in a dark, cold vestibule, from which lead a flight of steps, up which she "stumbles". The only light is that of her candle. The ballroom, when she steps into it, is in total darkness. It is only after she had been frightened by the red-tasselled flute that the chamber suddenly floods with light. What does that suggest to you? Well, you see, it suggests that she is dreaming about *two distinct ballrooms* —'

'Oh, come, now, Altmann! Isn't that going a bit too far?'

'Well, Venner, maybe. But it's worth bearing in mind. There, you see, Sergeant Bottomley's nodding in agreement. But come, let us finish our journey through the haunted ballroom.

'At the end of the room, Ursula sees a chest. There is nothing vague about her recollection here. She describes its dimensions, six feet in length and three feet high, its lid carved with a lion and unicorn upholding a five-pointed star. That, gentleman, is surely a real chest? Perhaps we shall find it at Alderley Hall.'

Dr Altmann leaned closer to the plan, and drew in a sharp breath, as though anticipating something spectacular or exciting.

'The chest is no threat to her, and she sees it as it is. But then she opens it. . . . Immediately, she glimpses the truth – the awful reality that her mind attempts at all times to shut out of her consciousness. It is "something clothed and shrunken, something brittle and starved of flesh". Surely it is the body of someone long dead?'

'The victim of a murder!' cried Venner. 'A murdered man, hidden in a chest and left to the mercy of time. And on some occasion in the past, young Ursula Holt saw it in the flesh!'

'Well done, Doctor. Yes, the truth must be something of that nature, though the surrounding facts lie quite beyond our knowledge. So what does Ursula do, as soon as she glimpses that terrible sight?'

'Sir,' said Bottomley, 'her mind supplies one of those substitutes you told us about. I can work that one out for myself – she replaces the dead body by a wax tableau, and then distances herself further from the reality by making that tableau an image of the Sleeping Beauty —'

'And finally, Sergeant,' said Altmann, 'and finally, she caps the substitution by giving the wax image the face of her friend, the beautiful Catherine Wishart. A good image is substituted for a bad – beauty for ugliness. But let me assure you both, gentlemen, that in that transient image of a skeletal man still clothed, Miss Ursula Holt saw the victim of a murder.'

Bottomley and Venner quite spontaneously burst into applause. The Austrian specialist, delighted, bowed gravely to both of them.

'Thank you, gentlemen,' he said, 'that sign of your approbation alone was worth my making the journey to England! But please, let us accompany poor Miss Holt back from the chest to what I may term freedom. Listen to what she says.

' "I was at once conscious again of the

intense cold. The music died away, and the dancing figures became dim wraiths. I hurried in the failing light towards the door. . . . I remember seeing the deed box lying on the floor, and then, to my intense relief, I gained the threshold." You see? The light fades, and that other ballroom, dark and cold, returns. I still wonder whether there were not *two* ballrooms!'

Herbert Bottomley had listened in silence to these words, and his face had assumed an expression halfway between sternness and despair.

'She said that she felt intense cold, sir,' he said, glancing at Altmann. 'I reckon that was because she was coming to, like a patient after an operation, and was realizing that she was lying outside in the cold, on the cloister flags.'

'Yes, Sergeant,' said Altmann, 'I know that point was troubling you when we started out on this psychological investigation. You saw, didn't you, that Ursula had wrenched a long-sealed door off its hinges, damaging her hands in the process. That is typical of involuntary somnambules – sleepwalkers, you know. They can summon up great strength, and perform deeds that would be impossible for them in the waking state.'

'Why do you think she did that to the

door, sir?'

'I think that she was, by then, partly awake, and saw that door as an element of the original setting of her ballroom dream. She tried to break that door down, Sergeant, because she thought it was barring her exit. She did not realize that she was, as it were, on the wrong side of the door! Once fully awake, she rationalized her action as an attempt to break *into* the ballroom.'

Bottomley shook his head, as though unconvinced, but said nothing. Altmann carefully closed Ursula's journal, and rolled up his plan.

'This Northampton,' he asked, 'is it very far from London? I begin my course of lectures at the Royal Institution on Thursday, and I'm sorely tempted to see this ballroom at Alderley Hall.'

'It's sixty-six miles from London,' said Dr Venner. 'There are frequent trains from St Pancras. I'd certainly like to make a visit, after what we have heard today. What about you, Bottomley? Will you come?'

'Yes, sir. I think it's a sensible thing to do, in the circumstances.'

'Tomorrow, then!' cried Altmann. 'Let us hope, gentlemen, that the ultimate truth about Miss Ursula Holt's neurosis will be uncovered in Alderley Hall.'

279

■ ■ ■ ■

'Oh, sir,' said Mrs Meade, housekeeper to Mr and Mrs Stansfield of Alderley Hall, 'they were precious days, when Miss Catherine was young! I often think of those times, when Miss Ursula would visit. Of course, the old master and mistress were alive in those days. Things have moved on since then.'

Mrs Meade, a pleasant-featured woman in her fifties, addressed herself to the elegant Dr Venner, virtually ignoring the fearsome foreigner with the black beard, and the rather rough but amiable fellow who accompanied them. Doctor Venner would have fitted in perfectly as someone invited to dine and sleep at Alderley Hall.

The three investigators had been conveyed by dogcart from Alderley Station, and now stood in a cool hallway, floored with black and white tiles. A grandfather clock ticked somnolently behind the front door. Facing them was a magnificent carved mahogany staircase leading to upstairs galleries, all lit by tall windows.

'If you would follow me, Dr Venner,' said Mrs Meade, 'I will take you upstairs to the ballroom. It's a famous feature of the house, you know, and is in constant use for comings-out, anniversaries, and so forth.'

They followed the housekeeper up the wide staircase and on to the first-floor landing. Directly facing the head of the stairs was a pair of double doors set in a Classical pediment. The panels of the doors were carved with representations of various musical instruments, which had been lightly gilded. Mrs Meade threw open the doors.

'The ballroom, Dr Venner,' she said, and stood aside for the visitors to enter. It was, perhaps, fortunate for the visitors that Mrs Meade was a supremely incurious woman. They had brought a letter of introduction with them, and that was enough for her. Why they should want to see the ballroom was a matter of serene indifference to her.

Venner and Altmann immediately advanced into the room, looking about them curiously, but Sergeant Bottomley stood at the door for a while, in an attempt to sense the overall atmosphere of the long, sunlit chamber.

There was nothing here of the dark ballroom of Miss Ursula's dreams, nothing to suggest coldness or fear. The room had fine, arched windows along both walls, showing that this ballroom at Alderley Hall had been built to stand independently of the rest of the structure, though integrated into the main house by the great staircase leading up to its impressive double doors. There was a good deal of gilded carving, and the high ceiling boasted a mock hammer-beam roof in painted plaster. Eight many-branched chandeliers hung from the ceiling, and Bottomley saw that they still held candles. Had the house been in a large town, he mused, those chandeliers would long ago have been converted to gas. Miss Ursula mentioned in her dream that she smelt the scent of burning wax in her haunted ballroom.

'Over here, Bottomley!' cried Dr Venner. 'Come and look at this.'

The sergeant joined his two companions, who stood at a spot along the right-hand wall where a number of small round tables, covered in green baize, clustered together with a dozen small, gilded chairs.

'It was here, Bottomley,' said Venner, pointing to the chairs, 'that Ursula imagined that she saw Inspector Jackson. It would seem that we have indeed discovered the place where her terrible dreams have their origin. What is the purpose of these tables and chairs, Mrs Meade?'

'Well, sir, they're used for people to sit out a particular dance, or to rest when the fancy takes them. Of course, the tables are covered with cloths when there's a function going on in here.'

'And is that often?'

'Oh, yes, sir. There are frequent jollifications here at the Hall.'

'Jollifications?'

'Yes, Altmann. Celebrations, you know. Happy gatherings.'

They moved further into the room, and paused at the corner where Ursula had seen the orchestra playing. The space was occupied by a closed grand piano.

'Mrs Meade,' asked Venner, 'is there ever a kind of orchestra stationed in this corner, where you see the piano?'

'Why, sir, how clever of you! Yes, that's where the chamber orchestra is stationed when we have the dances. They sit behind a roped-off barrier, and when all's done, the footmen put the grand piano back in its place.'

Doctor Venner's face assumed an expression of aloof satisfaction. He smiled graciously at his companions, as much as to say, 'There, you see what a clever fellow I am?' Doctor Altmann seemed unimpressed.

'It's all very well, Venner, but it's not the whole truth of the matter, of that I'm sure. I didn't expect to be greeted by a costumed Negro servant, and I didn't expect to trip over a deed box or a bloodstained iron bar as I crossed the threshold. But that entrance – that grand portico – what has that got to do with Ursula's gloomy vestibule, and dismal flight of steps?'

'But the chairs, and the roped-off area —'

'These chairs and tables – yes, I grant you that they could have formed part of the background to the dream, because, of course, this ballroom and its contents were familiar and friendly to Ursula. But it's only part of the story. Where, for instance, is the carved chest, in which she found what I believe to be a dead and murdered body? Where is *that*?'

The far corner of the room contained no mysterious chest, or any other item of furniture. Instead, a glazed door led out on to a little balcony overlooking the extensive rear lawns of the mansion.

'Gentlemen,' said Altmann, 'it has been an interesting and instructive visit, and I'm glad that we came. But this is not the right ballroom! No – please, Venner, don't try to find reasons to contradict me. This is not the gloomy and frightening chamber through which our somnambule moves in fear and trembling to a terrifying goal. We must look elsewhere.'

As he said these words, Altmann glanced

briefly at Bottomley, and saw the detective give a brief nod of assent. It was what he had expected.

The two doctors moved towards the door, talking quietly together. Altmann seemed quite unperturbed. Doctor Venner looked dejected. Herbert Bottomley and the house keeper followed them.

'This has always been a happy room, hasn't it, ma'am?' asked Bottomley. 'It's got its own cheerful spirit, if I may put it like that.'

Mrs Meade looked with sudden interest at the big, shambling countryman who had accompanied the two gentlemen.

'Why, yes, Mr Bottomley, that's very true. The master calls it the happy genius of the place – *genius loci,* or some such Latin phrase. Of course, it was built as a place of entertainment by the master's great grandparents, who were celebrated for their hospitality. Indeed, the whole Stansfield family are kindly, hospitable folk. So yes, Mr Bottomley, it's a happy room.'

The two doctors were silent on the journey by trap back to the railway station. Bottomley thought to himself: Dr Altmann's thinking things out, and Dandy Jim's nursing his disappointment. 'We must look elsewhere', Dr Altmann had said. Well, he, Bottomley, knew well enough where to look for the haunted ballroom when the time was ripe. That would be as soon as the guvnor set foot on English soil once more, that coming Friday.

Later on the evening of the same day, when the three men had arrived back in London, Sergeant Bottomley found the Australian cable awaiting him. When he had read it in the privacy of his own room, he folded it, and carefully slipped it into his pocket book.

14
THE GUEST AT
MILLER'S GRANGE

Guy Fitzgerald, sitting high in the saddle of
a great shire horse, progressed slowly along
the bridle path that ran parallel to the
boundary fence of Miller's Grange. It had
been a profitable morning, and he could
still see in his mind's eye the long, freshly
turned furrows of the upper field. He had
let it lie fallow for as long as he dared, but
now the dark soil was refreshed, ready for
the new planting. He'd left the farm-hands
to make all good, and secure the ploughs,
while he went home to Church End Farm
for a while on patient old Wellington.

As he neared the narrow public road that
would take him into the hamlet of Earl's
Green, he saw young Miss Bolton, the girl
to whom he'd talked after his visit to old
Skeffington at Charnley. She was walking
rather mournfully in the neglected garden
of the Grange. (Taming that garden would
be one of his first tasks if he was successful

in purchasing the tottering old house.)

Miss Bolton was wearing an elegant cotton dress, decorated with a subdued floral print, and had tied a patterned scarf around her head. Once again, she was carrying a garden basket. How vulnerable she looked! He'd always imagined that Australian girls were robust and independent.

'Good morning, Miss Bolton!' he called, bringing the horse to a stand on the path. He watched as the young woman started in alarm, and was pleased when a rather uncertain smile brightened her face.

'Mr Fitzgerald, isn't it?' Miss Bolton replied. 'What are you doing out here?'

'I live here, Miss Bolton,' said Guy, 'at Church End Farm yonder. Perhaps I should ask the same question of you!'

The young lady smiled again, but shook her head. Evidently she wanted to preserve her little secret! Guy watched as she put her basket down carefully on the unmown grass, and picked her way through banks of dock and nettle to reach the fence.

'We've met before,' said Guy, 'and we're more or less neighbours. You must come to tea some time, and meet Mother. She'd welcome a young lady visitor.'

'I'd like that very much, Mr Fitzgerald,' the young lady replied. 'Although I've been here nearly a week, I've had no time to leave cards. Does your mother like young ladies?'

Guy laughed loud, and Wellington moved restlessly until his master patted his neck.

'I was the only boy among four children,' he replied. 'My three sisters have all fled the nest long since. That's why Mother would welcome a young lady visitor. So, for that matter, would I.'

He had the satisfaction of seeing the young lady blush, noting that it was a blush of pleasure, not embarrassment. Perhaps Miss Bolton was becoming lonely living in that tumbledown ruin of a house, with only Susan Partridge for company.

'I'll not detain you further, Miss Bolton,' said Guy, raising his hat. 'That was an open invitation, by the way. When you feel ready to accept, send Susan round with a note.'

As he rode away down the bridle path, he saw the young lady standing in the grass, looking after him, her hand shading her eyes against the strong October sun.

'I saw Miss Bolton just now, Mother,' said Guy Fitzgerald, pouring himself a cup of tea from a large brown teapot. He had eaten a hearty meal of boiled ham, cabbage and potatoes, served to him by their maid-of-all-work, Effie, and already his eye was glancing nervously at the grandfather clock beside the fireplace.

'Did you really?' Guy's mother replied. He glanced at her as she spoke, and saw the familiar look of amused indulgence that she reserved for moments of this kind. His mother, small, grey-haired and still handsome, had always been a past mistress of mind reading when it came to her only son's apparently ingenuous statements.

'Yes. I saw her once before, you know, at Charnley. She's very pretty – in fact, Ma, she's a regular corker! Far too nice a person to be living at Miller's Grange. She's very refined for an Australian girl.'

'Are Australian girls unrefined, then, Guy? How many have you met?'

'Oh, you know what I mean, Ma. As for the Grange – well, I think old Skeffington's going to sell. I can meet his price, though I wasn't going to tell *him* that! Still, we'll talk about that tonight. Is that the time? I'd better get back to the farm.'

He rose from the table, and made towards the farmhouse door. Mrs Fitzgerald put a gently restraining hand on his arm.

'You don't know who she is, do you?' she asked. Her voice was very quiet.

'Miss Bolton? She's a distant relative of Mr Alexander Skeffington of Charnley.

She's staying at the Grange for a few days – possibly a week. That's what Susan told me.'

'It was Mr Skeffington's silly fancy to make her call herself Bolton. She's Ursula Holt, the poor mad girl who came out of the asylum a couple of weeks ago. That's who your Miss Bolton is.'

Guy sat down again at the table. He looked at his mother's calm face, and saw the concern in her eyes.

'Who told you that?' he asked, and his voice sounded unnaturally harsh.

'Mr Amlett, the knife-grinder,' his mother replied. 'You know what Amlett's like. He travels all over the shire, and while he sharpens knives, people talk to him. He's like a local telegraph when it comes to relaying gossip. Ursula Holt was the girl who they said mutilated sheep, and killed that sheepdog. Then people said that she murdered a young man at Ashborne Hill, and goodness knows what else. And now she's here, at the Grange, living under an assumed name. I think that Mr Skeffington, who's a kindly man, is hiding her away for a while. Mr Amlett said that Charnley was getting too uncomfortable for her.'

'I more or less gave her an invitation to come here to tea.'

'Did you? And are you going to withdraw

that invitation, now that you've heard what Mr Amlett said?'

'No! Damn it all, Ma, I don't believe a word of it. I'll make up my own mind about her. Anyway, I've only just seen her for the second time this morning. So will you let her come to the house or not?'

'Of course I will. You're a good lad, Guy, to keep an open mind. Meanwhile, I suppose you'd better go on calling her Miss Bolton.'

Ursula Holt stood in the garden of Miller's Grange, looking after the retreating figure of Guy Fitzgerald. What a fine young man he was! Those black curls, and that bronzed complexion, his easy, arrogant carriage in the saddle of the great shire horse. She had held his image constantly in her mind since she had first seen him, striding confidently from Mr Skeffington's house. Why had she never seen young men of his stamp before?

If Susan saw her, she'd wonder why she was standing by the boundary fence in the stiff breeze, apparently fixed to the spot. There he was again, reappearing beyond the trees at the bottom of the lane! He lived with his mother, and had invited her to tea, so he wasn't married. Oh! He was looking back. . . . He was waving to her! Now he was gone. Awaking from her reverie, Ursula picked up her gardening basket and walked thoughtfully towards the house.

Miller's Grange was neglected, and parts of it were in urgent need of repair, but there seemed to be nothing at all sinister about it. It was an ancient place, dating from Tudor times, and it boasted a great number of cheerful, diamond-paned windows that kept all its rooms well lighted and inviting during the hours of daylight. Its furnishings were old and faded, but no less comfortable for that.

As Ursula entered the old parlour of the house, she was greeted by a cheerful, friendly woman in her forties, who had set a meal of braised chicken ready on the table, and was engaged in manoeuvring a quantity of mashed potato from a copper pan on to the plate.

'There you are, miss,' said the woman, 'I think you've got everything there. There's the carafe of water, an apple pudding under that cover, and the coffee pot for afterwards.'

'Thank you, Susan,' Ursula replied, and sat down at the table. Susan Partridge stood near the door, the copper pan cradled in her arms, but she showed no inclination to leave. Ursula was glad. She had been at the

Grange for nearly a week – ever since Mr Skeffington had brought her there secretly, driving his own carriage, so that no one in Providence House would see him leave. She had been attracted to the old house and its grounds immediately, and her pleasure in this secret hideaway had been enhanced by the reassuring presence of Susan Partridge.

'I saw you talking to Mr Guy Fitzgerald over the paling, miss,' said Susan. She may have seen young Miss Bolton blush over her plate of chicken, but if so, she said nothing about it. 'Mr Guy's by way of being the local squire. This corner of the shire's all pure farming country, and Mr Guy owns hundreds of acres round here.'

'He's not married, is he?'

'No, miss. He *was* very fond of a young lady at one time, but she died. Well, she was drowned in the River Best, poor soul. So we're all waiting to see what he'll do next.'

'This house – Mr Skeffington doesn't seem very fond of it, does he? I wonder why he bought it? Providence House, where he lives at Charnley, is very well maintained.'

'Well, you see, miss,' said Susan, carefully depositing the copper pan on a window sill, 'this house, Miller's Grange, and Providence House, in Charnley, used to belong to a family called Lemprière. They came from

France, originally. Huggernauts, or some such name.'

'Huguenots.'

'That's right, miss. Well, these Lemprières inherited a huge estate in France, which came their way after the old French kings were restored, so they put the two properties out for sale. It was a parcel of property, you see, and you couldn't buy one without the other. So when Mr Skeffington came to England from Australia, all those years ago, he bought Providence House to live in, and had to buy this place into the bargain. But he only rarely comes here.'

'Has anyone ever lived here since those days, Susan?'

'Not *lived* here, Miss Bolton, no. But people stay from time to time, visitors from overseas, like yourself. Mr Skeffington pays me a little wage to keep an eye on the place, and air it, and my husband does a bit around the gardens. But it's a wild place, with some dangerous spots, and you'll need to watch your footing, miss, if you go exploring in the grounds.'

Susan Partridge rather reluctantly picked up the pan from the window sill, and went out of the parlour, leaving Ursula alone with her thoughts.

Mr Skeffington had stayed the night when

he had brought her secretly to the Grange. The house, lit by a few candles, had seemed gloomy and forbidding, and she had retired almost immediately to bed in a dark old room with twisted panelling. Next morning, though, the sun had shone cheerfully through the east facing windows of the parlour, and Susan Partridge had appeared from her cottage in the hamlet to cook the master and his guest a hot breakfast. It was while she was fortifying herself for the coming day with eggs and bacon that Ursula had realized something of great import. She had slept soundly, and without sleepwalking, for the first time in many a sad day.

'What you need, Ursula,' Alexander Skeffington had told her, 'is a complete rest and change of scene, for at least two weeks or more. That's why I've suggested that you take an assumed name – Bolton will do. You see, if your uncle starts fussing, and sends somebody out in search of you, well, nobody's going to be interested in a young Miss Bolton, staying at Miller's Grange! And again, nobody's going to carry tales back to Charnley. But in fact, I'll keep your uncle sweet, by telling him you've gone to visit friends. What do you think?'

'It's a good idea, Mr Skeffington,' she'd said. 'How kind of you to arrange all this!'

'No, no. . . .' He had turned away abruptly, and she had seen tears springing up in his eyes. Then he had recovered himself, and added, 'I am concerned only for your future, Ursula. I want all that vile business of asylums and so on put behind you. Here, I hope, you will be able to forget.'

He had risen from the breakfast table, and she saw that he had been ready booted and spurred for his ride back to Charnley. He intended to send a man over for his carriage later in the day.

'This is not a prison, Ursula,' he'd said. 'Go out into the hamlet if the fancy takes you. And remember, if you want to communicate with me, let Susan know, and she'll send a man up to Charnley to see me. I'll return here in a fortnight, on the twenty-fourth, and Susan will cook us a fine country dinner. I'll bring one of those bottles of old crusted port that I keep in my cellar for special occasions, and you and I will drink a toast to your future!'

It had been a cheerful farewell, Ursula mused, but his eyes had been red-rimmed, as though he had spent some part of the night weeping at some secret sorrow in his chamber.

What was today? Tuesday, 17 October. Did she want to go back to Charnley? This old neglected house in its open aspect of rough garden and tangled overgrowth of dock and fern, held for her an exhilarating sense of freedom. Recollections of Abbey Lodge seemed now to stifle her. She missed her old uncle, and dear Kate, but the Grange held out other, different, possibilities of intimacy.

She was thinking of Guy Fitzgerald.

Ursula had found that Miller's Grange stood at the centre of a five-acre demesne, most of which had fallen into ruin. The garden had more or less reverted to rough pasture, though someone – Susan's husband? – had cleared some of it by liberal use of a scythe. Beyond the garden, nettle and dock, bindweed and briar had reduced the five acres of pasture and arable land to a wilderness.

Ursula decided that she would make a foray into the wild and untended reaches of the estate after lunch. But first, she would explore the back attics of the house, where, so Susan had assured her, 'all kinds of curious things' were stored. She would peep into those unvisited rooms, and then make an excursion into the demesne.

As she mounted the winding stair leading to the upper storey, Ursula recalled how all her nights at the Grange had been free of dreams, and that she had not once walked in her sleep. Perhaps it was something in the air of the place?

The two small attics, both with dim little windows, were filled with ancient wooden furniture, most of it dating from the seventeenth century. Standing against the walls were various old oil-paintings, some falling from their frames. There were massive wardrobes, a number of chests, and against the wall of one room a dismantled four-poster bed.

What were these curious brass stands? Ah, she remembered! They were elaborate floor-standing supports for oil lamps, a discarded relic of the last century. Everything was covered in dust, and there were many untenanted cobwebs festooned across the furnishings.

What was this? Ursula shuddered as she examined the headboard of the dismantled four-poster. Carved deep in to the ancient oak was the five-pointed star, flanked by a lion and a unicorn – the device that she had seen carved on the phantom chest of her ballroom dreams. Instantly, she recalled the shrivelled hand, a left hand with a gold signet ring hanging loosely on the fourth finger. And now, she recollected something that had eluded her before. There was a wrist, a brown wrist, surrounded by a yellowing shirt cuff. . . . Yes, she had seen that hand before, not in a dream, but in real life. One day, soon, she would remember where.

There was a soft footfall in the passage, and for a moment it seemed to Ursula that her heart stopped beating. A shadow fell across the door, and Susan entered. She was carrying a wicked-looking carving knife in one hand, and a polishing-cloth in the other.

'Why, Miss Bolton,' she said, 'whatever are you doing up here? I thought you'd gone out into the garden. These old stairs creak a lot, and I wondered who it could be upstairs in the attics. So you're looking at all the old furniture? I know what I'd do with it, miss, if this were *my* house.'

'And what's that, Susan?'

'I'd have it all carried out into the wilderness and burnt! Something could be made of this old place, if only Master would take an interest. But he's never liked it.'

'Susan, what is the meaning of this carving on the bed-head? A star, a lion, and a unicorn?'

'That? That was the coat-of-arms of the Lemprière family that I told you about. The Huggernauts. I believe that Mr Skeffington had all the old furniture moved down here from Providence House when he came to live there, all those years ago. He kept one or two pieces, like the old spinet, but he was a very wealthy gentleman, and wanted all new furniture brought from London. So that's where it all came from, miss. Providence House, over at Charnley.'

It was quiet and peaceful wandering at will through the strange ruined landscape of the demesne. The Grange, with its crooked roof of lichen-covered tiles, soon disappeared from view, and so did the boundary fence separating the demesne from the public road to Earl's Green. Unseen birds chattered in the tangled undergrowth, and once, a lithe and furtive fox dashed across her path. There were no familiar scents of garden flowers here, just the not unpleasant balsamic perfume of unseen branches and stumps of trees, rotting beneath the carpet of weeds.

Ursula had glimpsed a squat tower on an earlier foray into the wilderness. It came into view again now, and she made her way towards it along the narrow, barely discernible path through the stunted bushes. Presently she came into a clearing, its floor covered in beech mast, and the debris of fallen masonry.

She saw now that the tower belonged to a ruined chapel, a little Gothic folly of a place, long fallen into decay. Susan had told her that the Lemprière family had used it as a burial place. One of them, early in the eighteenth century, had built the chapel over an earlier vault.

'It's all fallen down now, miss, and dangerous underfoot. Don't you go anywhere near that chapel.'

The arched entrance to the ruin had long ago been bricked up, but halfway along the south side of the chapel a flight of steps led down to a yawning, doorless opening. Ursula stood on the path, and looked down at what she knew must be the entrance to a vault. Here, presumably, the Lemprières of old lay in their silent tombs. Should she go down and explore? Part of her mind cried out for her to run back to the comfort of the Grange, and the cheerful company of Susan Partridge. A mere month ago, she would have yielded to that instinct. But she was stronger, now, no longer inclined to start at shadows. The bracing air and exhilarating freedom of the Grange had wrought that welcome change in her. She put her foot upon the first of the slippery steps that descended to the vault.

The dark chamber smelt of damp earth,

and was chillingly cold. A dim light filtered into the vault from a gaping hole in the chapel floor above. There was little to see: a few old tomb chests hidden beneath a tangle of ivy. She was turning to climb the steps up to the sunlit wilderness above, when she glimpsed a ray of light reflecting from something metallic. It was the polished handle of a spade, which had been set upright in a mound of earth. Beside the mound was a freshly dug grave.

Herbert Bottomley gathered up a pile of tinder-dry kindling, slung it across his knees, and tied it deftly with string. He threw the resultant bundle into Joe Bates's wheelbarrow. The old woodsman looked up from his own task, and nodded his thanks. The two men were working near the wishing well on the fringes of the bluebell wood, where Miss Ursula Holt had been discovered, bloodstained and bewildered, in the previous April. It was the morning of Wednesday, 18 October.

'This boy,' said Bottomley, pausing in his work to look at the old man, 'can he hold his tongue? If not, his life could be in danger. We're dealing with the worst kind of killer here, gaffer – the kind that's only half insane at the moment, but is heading straight for the madhouse.'

'He's a good lad, this Arthur Jones,' said Joe Bates. 'If you tell him not to blab, he won't. And he can climb any tree in Christendom.'

The two men worked in silence for a while, and then by common consent they sat down on a fallen tree, and Bottomley produced his tobacco pouch.

'Do you remember that day in April, Joe?' asked Bottomley, when the old man's pipe was burning nicely. 'That day when you saw Miss Ursula sitting by the well, her dress all smeared with blood, and a knife lying in her hand? Well, you told me to talk to Reuben Laidlaw about it, and I did.'

Joe Bates puffed away at his pipe. He glanced briefly at Bottomley, but said nothing.

'After that,' Bottomley continued, 'I tracked down Laidlaw's son, Jonah, at Plemstall.'

Joe removed his pipe long enough to remark, 'That's a good way out', before clamping it carefully once more between his tobacco-stained teeth.

'It is,' Bottomley agreed. 'Well, the upshot of it was, that Jonah confessed to all those mutilations, and told me that he'd hit Ben the sheepdog with a stick, to stop him snarling. But he didn't cut Ben's throat. That's what he told me, and I believed him. He said that there was someone lurking among the trees. Maybe *he* did it.'

'Maybe.'

'You saw him, too, didn't you, Joe?' said Bottomley. 'You told me that you saw someone slinking away through the trees. And you suggested that someone may have carried Miss Ursula part of the way from her home to the wishing well. Helped her on her way to the madhouse, so to speak.'

Old Joe Bates sighed, and shook his head. He knocked his pipe out on the bole of a tree, blew through it, and put it into his pocket.

'Now, wild horses are not going to drag any names from me, master,' he said. 'I'm an unlettered old man who scratches a living by collecting brushwood. So, you'll get no names from me. But yes, I'm quite sure that a man carried that lass in his arms from some point beyond the cobbled lane, before leaving her to stumble the rest of the way, and all this time her being fast asleep!'

'You saw him?'

'Yes. And maybe Jonah Laidlaw is right, and that man placed a bloody knife in the girl's hand, and smeared her dress with blood. Maybe all that's true. I don't know about Ben, and what happened to him, but maybe everything that Jonah told you is true. So that lass was innocent, and that's why I'll help you all I can. But I'll not name names, because a man who's half on the road to the madhouse himself might take his vengeance on me if he knew I'd spoken out.'

'All right, Joe,' said Bottomley. 'That's fair enough by me. You've told me – or hinted to me – all that I need to know for the moment. Is this your boy coming, now?'

A sturdy lad of fourteen or so had appeared on one of the paths leading through the wood. Lithe and dark-haired, he had greeted Joe Bates with a cheerful grin, but when he saw Sergeant Bottomley, his face assumed the neutral, almost surly expression of a typical boy's shyness in the presence of a stranger.

'This is Arthur Jones,' said Joe Bates. 'Arthur, pay attention to this gentleman, and do what he tells you to do.'

Herbert Bottomley put his hands on the boy's shoulders, and surveyed him at arm's length. He was impressed by the frank expression in the boy's eyes, and by his general air of responsibility.

'Now, Arthur,' said Bottomley, 'Mr Bates there will have told you what I want you to do for me. Is it true that you can shin up trees like a squirrel?'

'Yes, sir.' The boy's face relaxed, and he treated Bottomley to a cheerful smile.

'And do you think you could climb up the wall of a house covered in creeper, and look for something that I'll tell you about in a minute?'

'Yes, sir.'

'You know who I am, don't you?'

'Yes, sir. You're Sergeant Bottomley, and you're a detective.'

'That's right, so you know that anything I ask you to do is to help the police. Well, we'd best be getting along, then. And you're not to tell anyone about what you've done when you've done it. You're not to tell your best friend, or your worst enemy, or anyone else. Is that understood, Arthur?'

'Yes, sir.'

Herbert Bottomley led the way out of the clearing on the skirts of the bluebell wood, until he came to the cobbled lane separating the woodland from the evergreen plantation. Ahead of him, the vast bulk of Providence House rose majestically in the October sun. Its whole surface, covered in Virginia creeper, looked to him as though it had been soaked in blood.

'The man who owns this house, Arthur,'

said Bottomley, 'is away from Charnley today. I know that, because I saw him leave in his carriage earlier this morning. Come with me now, and I will tell you what I want you to do.'

Bottomley led his two companions round to that side of Providence House that faced away from the public road. They were presented with a vast, blank expanse of creeper. There was no sign at all of the brick wall of the house, or of any windows set into it. Bottomley cupped his hands over the boy's ear, and whispered to him for about half a minute. Then he stood back, and Arthur Jones began to climb up the creeper.

Bottomley and Joe Bates watched the boy as he moved expertly upward, searching carefully for hand- and foot-holds in the branches of the mature creeper. After a while, the boy stopped, and began to tug at the bright red leaves. Presently, he had revealed part of a window, its small panes black with ancient dirt, its woodwork cracked and peeling. At a gesture from Bottomley, he arranged the creeper back across the window, so that it disappeared from view. Bottomley motioned to the boy to come down to the ground.

'Good lad,' said Sergeant Bottomley,

gravely. 'You've done well. I don't suppose you could see through that grimy window, could you?'

'No, sir. It was too dirty. But I could see a little through the creeper to the right, and I fancy there might be another window, further along the wall. Do you want me to take a look?'

'No, Arthur, you've done enough. As a matter of fact, I think there might be four or five windows running the whole length of that upper stretch of wall. But you've done your bit, now. Remember what I said, though: not a word to a soul.'

Bottomley delved into one of his pockets, and brought out a half-crown, which he gave to the delighted boy. He nodded to Joe Bates, who put an arm round Arthur Jones's shoulders, and led him back through the plantation towards the cobbled lane.

15
DEAD MAN'S CHEST

Inspector Jackson arrived back in England aboard the *Etruria* early on Friday morning, and by late afternoon he was back home in Warwick. Sarah Brown was waiting to greet him in his cottage in Meadow Cross Lane, and it was she who insisted that he had a meal followed by a rest at his fireside before giving his whole attention to the case in hand. After the two of them had dined off Irish stew followed by apple pie, he had retired to his old canebacked chair for forty winks.

When he awoke, cramped and cold, it was after ten o'clock, and as his eyes focused in the dim firelight, he saw that Sergeant Bottomley was sitting patiently in the chair opposite him.

'Sergeant,' said Jackson, 'where did you come from? I must have dozed off. Why didn't you light some candles?'

'I'll do that right away, sir,' said Bottomley. 'Mrs Brown washed everything up before she went. I arrived at nine, and she told me not to disturb you. Perhaps we can have a talk, now. Mr Mays sent that Australian cable up to me in London, where I was carrying out enquiries with the help of Dr Venner and Dr Altmann —'

'Were you, indeed? Well, Sergeant, you'd better tell me all about it, and then I'll tell you what I found out in America. For the moment, I'll resist the temptation to tell you what a wonderful place New York is, and what fascinating folk I met there. That'll all keep till later.'

'There's something else, sir,' said Bottomley. 'On Thursday, the twelfth, I discovered that Miss Ursula had taken fright at the general state of things, and fled, without telling her family where she was going. No one seems to know where she is. She's not with her old friend Mrs Wishart in London, and she's not at that lady's old family seat in Northamptonshire.'

'What does her uncle think? Really, Sergeant, they're very peculiar people, those Holts. Why don't they look for her? Or don't they want to?'

'They think she's gone to stay with a friend, sir, and I encouraged them in that belief. But I've a very shrewd idea where she actually is. I had a talk to George Potter, and he told me that Skeffington had another property out in the country, an old tumbledown place called Miller's Grange —'

'And you think she's there? I believe that Skeffington is very fond of Miss Ursula, Sergeant – that became very clear when I interviewed him at Providence House. She could well have turned to him for help, which he duly provided. So, yes, she could well be there. What do you propose to do?'

'I thought of finding this Miller's Grange tomorrow, sir, and taking a look round. If she's there, I won't alarm her, in case she does another flit. Let sleeping girls lie, as they say. But if she's there, she mustn't stay there for much longer. Skeffington's a triple murderer, and that girl knows more than is good for her. He may well be fond of her, but that wouldn't prevent him helping her out of this world if she stood between him and safety.'

Jackson remained silent for a while, staring at the embers of the dying fire. He felt tired, but curiously elated. He would allow himself five working days of the coming week to bring the whole evil business to its close. On the Saturday, the feast of St Simon and St Jude, he was to be married.

Somehow, the constraining lack of time added to the thrill of the chase.

'Sergeant,' he said at last, 'could you arrange for Dr Venner and Dr Karl Gustav Altmann to come with us to Charnley on Monday morning? You've worked closely with the two doctors in London, and I think we should have them both present when we put into action a little plan that I'm concocting. Doctor Venner will be particularly useful. We could travel in a reserved compartment. . . . Send a cable to Sergeant Potter at Ashborne Hill, and tell him to secure the services of two workmen with pickaxes – one had better be a bricklayer. They can all travel with us in the same train. It's time for us to act.'

'Ah! So that's your idea, is it, sir? Yes, it's time for us to act. I'm quite certain in my own mind that there are sealed-off chambers in that house. What about Skeffington? Isn't he going to smell a rat?'

'He won't be there, Sergeant! You recall how he lured poor Elijah Robinson to his death by means of a fake letter? Well, two can play at that kind of game. When we arrive at Charnley with our pickaxes, Jim Bolder, alias Mr Alexander Skeffington, will have received a summons elsewhere. He won't be there.'

The candles on the mantelpiece were beginning to gutter. Jackson treated himself to a luxurious stretch as he left his chair in order to light the oil lamp, suspended from the ceiling in its hoop of brass. For the next hour, the two men gave full accounts of their separate investigations, so that each knew every salient detail of the other's activity. Then Jackson stood up, and looked gravely at his sergeant.

'You've done excellent work during my absence, Sergeant,' he said. 'Quite outstanding, to my way of thinking, and I intend to inform Mr Mays to that effect. Well done!'

Herbert Bottomley blushed to the roots of his hair. Jackson was sparing with his praise, and Bottomley never looked for it. Jackson's words were all the more precious for that.

'Both doctors are anxious to see the thing through to the end, sir,' said Bottomley. 'I don't think there'll be the slightest difficulty in getting them to come with us to Charnley on Monday.'

'Excellent. You'd better stay the night, Sergeant: it's too late for you to be crossing Thornton Heath by starlight. There's a bed made up in the back room. I'll begin making arrangements about warrants and so forth first thing tomorrow. Meanwhile, the best of luck for your excursion to – what did you call the place? – Miller's Grange.'

Guy Fitzgerald walked slowly along the un-
named lane dividing one of his fine
ploughed fields from the overgrown wilderness of Miller's Grange. He was quite sure
that Alexander Skeffington would sell the
place to him, if only to rid himself of an
unwanted burden. Could he not see the
potential of the old Tudor house as a fine
dwelling? Certainly, Miss Ursula Holt
seemed to like Miller's Grange. She came
out daily to tinker about in the garden, and
yesterday, Susan Partridge's husband Bill
had accompanied her, turning the soil of
the sour flowerbeds with a massive spade.

Perhaps she was going to stay there? She
certainly looked well, as though country air
agreed with her. Why had Skeffington insisted on her calling herself Miss Bolton?
Even Susan called her that, although she
knew quite well who she was. Miss Ursula
Holt had been accused of vile crimes, and
sent to the asylum. Well, innocent folk had
been wrongly accused before this, and, no
doubt, would be in the future. He didn't
believe a word of it.

Who was that, moving surreptitiously
among the trees surrounding the old ruined
chapel? A burly, heavy-treading man in a

yellow overcoat and a battered brown hat. What was the fellow doing on Skeffington's land? It was only fifteen minutes or so since Miss Holt had left her daily stint in the garden to return to the house. She was in no state to cope with trespassers.

Guy hurried along the lane to a point where the ruinous wall had collapsed into the bordering grass and nettles, and climbed over into the demesne. He made no attempt to hide his presence, and pushed his way through the tangle of tree roots and fallen branches until he reached the clearing in front of the chapel.

The man in the yellow coat was sitting on a moss-covered log, smoking a thin cheroot. He glanced at Guy with shrewd grey eyes, and removed the cigar from his mouth.

'Good morning,' he said, 'Mr Guy Fitzgerald, isn't it?'

'It is. And who might you be?' asked Guy hotly. 'How do you know my name, and how the devil did you get in here? This is private land.'

'Sit down there, Mr Fitzgerald,' said the man. 'My name is Detective Sergeant Bottomley, of the Warwickshire Constabulary. Here's my warrant card. We're nice and private here, sir, so I can tell you all you need to know about Miss Ursula Holt.'

■ ■ ■ ■

'A murderer?' said Guy, when Bottomley had finished his tale. 'You are asking me to believe that Alexander Skeffington murdered that young American man, and then murdered Paul Staunton for good measure?'

'I am. This is neither the time nor the place for me to furnish you with all the proofs that we've acquired – the police, I mean. And there's one other murder, an ancient murder, committed by him, which remains unavenged. And now, Mr Fitzgerald, Mr Alexander Skeffington intends to commit murder yet again, and that very soon. Come with me down into the crypt beneath that chapel, and I'll show you how I know.'

Guy followed Sergeant Bottomley down the steps into the dismal resting-place of the Lemprière family. There, in the light filtering from the ruined nave pavement above, Guy saw the open grave, its mound of freshly turned earth, and the ready spade.

'This grave,' he whispered, 'who is it for?'

'Well, sir,' replied Bottomley, 'just supposing that there was a young lady who knew too much about you, and came too near to your undiscovered secrets, what better way of getting rid of her than telling her to assume a false name, Bolton, for instance, killing her, and burying her quietly down here?'

'What! Are you suggesting that Ursula – Miss Holt – is to be murdered by Skeffington, and —'

'I'm not suggesting it, Mr Fitzgerald, I'm telling it to you as a fact. After another week, the hue and cry for the missing Ursula Holt will be raised across the county. No one is going to look for an obscure Australian lady called Bolton, who stayed a little while at Miller's Grange.'

Guy Fitzgerald was quiet for a moment, absorbing the shocking tale that Bottomley had told him. Then he spoke.

'What do you want me to do?'

'Do you like this young lady, sir? Like her well enough to put yourself in danger for her sake?'

'I do. What you've told me, Sergeant, has concentrated my mind wonderfully. I think I'd do anything for her!'

'Then listen carefully, sir, while I tell you what I want you to do.'

On Monday morning, 23 October, the four colleagues caught an early train to Coventry, and then transferred to the branch line that would take them via Ashborne Hill to

Charnley. They occupied a first-class compartment, with stickers on the windows declaring that it was reserved and private.

'This man Bolder,' said Dr Venner, 'who exactly was he, Jackson? The sudden introduction of new names always confuses me.'

'James Bolder, sir, was born in 1826 at Port Jackson, New South Wales. He came from a decent and respectable background, but grew up to become a convicted confidence trickster and petty thief. That, Doctor, is the man now calling himself Alexander Skeffington, and living the life of a prosperous gentleman on a murdered man's money.'

Saul Jackson surveyed his audience as the train rattled and clattered its way out of Coventry and into the flat Warwickshire countryside. Herbert Bottomley sat beside him, his little notebook open on his knee. Facing them were the two doctors. Doctor Venner was as calm and urbane as ever. Doctor Karl Gustav Altmann, being a foreigner, allowed his excitement to show in a certain restlessness, and in the shining of his dark eyes.

'It is this man,' Jackson continued, 'Hawkeye Jim Bolder, alias Gentleman Jim, who slaughtered two young men, and drove a disturbed girl to the borderlands of insanity, in order to ensure the safety of his way of living – his wealth, his reputation for philanthropy, his standing as a former mayor of Charnley, and a pillar of society.'

'You said that this man Skeffington, or Bolder, is living off a dead man's money,' said Dr Altmann. 'What did you mean by that?'

'A *murdered* man's money, sir. There's a difference, as I think you know. Let me give you my reconstruction of what happened all those many years ago. Three young men, Alexander Skeffington of Pinnaroo, in Victoria, Jacob Robinson of New York, and Jim Bolder, a petty criminal, each of them aged twenty-five, formed a syndicate, and set out for the gold diggings in Bendigo. They stayed there for four years, and when they left, in 1855, Skeffington and Robinson had amassed fortunes. Bolder, though, had managed only to acquire a modest competence. He had, presumably, lacked the skills and application of his two companions. How he longed to be rich, like they were!

'Jacob Robinson returned to America. Alexander Skeffington – the real Skeffington, I mean – determined to go to England, and set himself up as a gentleman of substance. He was not the first colonial prospector to do so, and I don't suppose he'll be the last. Let me describe him to you. I've seen his portrait in New York, and he was a mild, round-faced man with a birthmark on his forehead, one of those men who wants to hide himself away whenever he can, because he's rather sensitive about what he regards as his "disfigurement".'

'And this Skeffington came to England?'

'He did, Doctor. He came here in 1855, to take possession of Providence House, at Charnley. He had been negotiating for its purchase through agents in Australia, and by the time he arrived in Charnley, the house was his. But he was accompanied by the hawkeyed, impressive James Bolder, who declared that he was going to return to Scotland —'

'Excuse me, Jackson,' said Dr Altmann, holding up a hand, 'but how do you know all this? Is it all surmise?'

'Oh, no, Dr Altmann, it's not surmise. I know all this because Jim Bolder told me! All he had to do was tell me the story of the three young prospectors, being careful first to show me a photograph of them, knowing that I would pick him out at once. But, of course, although it was the right photographic image, it was the wrong man. The self-effacing young fellow with the birthmark was the real Skeffington. So Jim

Bolder told me the whole story, quite openly and frankly, but with the identities of those two men – Bolder and Skeffington – exchanged.

'And so, as I said, the two men came to Charnley. Neither man was known to anyone in England, and it was while they were exploring the newly purchased Providence House that Jim Bolder conceived his evil plan to murder his companion, and pass himself off as Skeffington. That, of course, is surmise on my part, but I think you'll find that I'm right.'

'So what did Bolder do?' asked Dr Altmann.

'Well, as to that, sir,' said Jackson, smiling, 'I think you could provide us with the answer yourself. I gather that you've been very active in this business of Ursula Holt.'

'Well, Mr Jackson, you'll realize that I can talk only of probabilities, not actual facts. In their exploration of Providence House on some fatal day in 1855, the two men, fresh from Australia, find a room – a reception room, perhaps, or a little-used wing —'

'There is such a room, sir,' said Bottomley. 'I have only recently discovered it.'

'Excellent! So there is this room. Suddenly, and violently, this man Bolder strikes Skeffington down. There may have been no servants in the house at that time, making the murder easy to commit.

'Now, we may assume from Miss Ursula Holt's dreams that there was a wooden chest in that room. Bolder placed the body of his murdered companion in it – *and it is still there.* From that moment, he was able to call himself Skeffington, and to give all his attention to the business of refining on his imposture.'

'Well done, sir,' said Jackson. 'Your help has been quite invaluable in this business. Now, let me continue to reconstruct the false Skeffington's career. Everybody in Charnley would have been impressed by the sudden appearance of this distinguished-looking and wealthy Australian in their midst. Hadn't he come with a companion, a shadowy, retiring kind of fellow? Yes, but that man had returned to Scotland. That's how people would have talked.

'The years passed, and Mr Alexander Skeffington became a model citizen, while making shrewd purchases of land in the vicinity. A man whose information I can trust told me that Skeffington's land brings him in £12,000 a year, and that he has half a million pounds in gold on deposit. He's a rich man, sir, as rich as Croesus, and it was all done by the shrewd investment of his murdered victim's money.'

'And then —'

'And then, Dr Altmann, disaster struck, after forty years of security. Early this year, his old companion Jacob Robinson wrote to him, saying that he was coming to England on a visit. What was Jim Bolder to do? Robinson would recognize him immediately, and would denounce him as an impostor. If the police began an investigation, and conducted a thorough search of Providence House, then he would almost certainly be arrested for the real Skeffington's murder. Imagine his relief when he heard from New York that Jacob Robinson had died suddenly, on 8 February.'

'And then,' Dr Venner interposed, 'the son, Elijah, declared that he, too, was coming to England, bearing gifts. A legacy, no less. What a dilemma!'

'Indeed, Doctor. But the false Skeffington had already put in train the beginning of a plot to rid himself once and for all of this danger from America. It was, I think, one of the wickedest plots that I've ever encountered — Ah! We're drawing into Ashborne Hill. See, there's Sergeant Potter on the platform, and there are the two workman with him. They're getting into a carriage further along the train.'

'A wicked plot, you said?'

'Yes, Dr Venner, a wicked plot involving a young woman whose mind was not entirely settled, and who had been saddled with the curse of sleepwalking since childhood. Sergeant Bottomley, I think it would clear all our minds if you gave us an outline of Skeffington's plot.'

Herbert Bottomley closed his notebook and leaned forward in his seat.

'Gentlemen,' he said, 'the false Alexander Skeffington had known Miss Ursula Holt since she was quite a young girl. There's no doubt in my mind that he liked her, but his liking was a kind of sentimental affection, which wouldn't stand up to the test of reality. Skeffington – I'll call him that, for convenience – was the sort of man who'd poison his cat, and then stroke it to ease its passage from this world.'

Dr Altmann nodded. 'I've known men like that,' he said. 'And women, too.'

'I've a feeling,' Bottomley continued, 'that young Ursula once did something to make Skeffington wary of her. She mentions it in her journal, describing it as "an incident, ten years ago", in which she ventured through that door in the cloister, and found herself in a dark vestibule. Had Skeffington seen her?

'As soon as Jacob Robinson indicated that he was coming to England, Skeffington set about devising his plan to murder him. Then Jacob died, and the son, Elijah, declared that he, too, would visit these shores. By then, Skeffington's plan was taking shape.'

'And what was that plan?' asked Venner.

'His plan was to create an illusion, in which Miss Ursula Holt would be seen as a potentially dangerous lunatic, so that she would be committed to an asylum for the insane.'

'But why? Why do such a monstrous thing to an innocent girl?'

'Because, Dr Venner, a lunatic can't be hanged, so that Skeffington could later foist the murders of Elijah Robinson and Paul Staunton on to Ursula. If it could be shown that she could have committed those murders, she would be sent back to an asylum, but not to the gallows.'

Herbert Bottomley smiled sadly, and shook his head. Most people, he thought, were ultimately unfathomable.

'He was fond of Ursula, you see, Doctor, but he was even fonder of himself. He was also an amateur, with an amateur's arrogant certainty, planting clues wholesale, for the police to find – scalpels from Dr Holt's surgery, and later, after the doctor had locked his knives away at my behest, antique instruments, easily traced through your specialist knowledge.

'The wickedest of all the false clues was a pair of Ursula's long evening gloves, which he donned for the murder of Elijah Robinson. He stole them from her chest of drawers, and after the deed was done, he replaced them, dripping with blood. He did that, perhaps, to frighten that poor girl into believing that she had indeed murdered young Robinson. If she broke down and confessed, so much the better for him.'

'But his days of freedom are numbered, gentlemen,' said Jackson. 'By tomorrow evening, he will be in custody, preparing the pay the ultimate penalty for his crimes.'

'Doctor Holt, and you, Miss Kate,' said Saul Jackson, 'I have here a warrant to enter and search the space lying beyond the bricked-up door in the cloister, as I believe that it conceals material evidence connected with the murders of Elijah Robinson and Paul Staunton. You know Sergeant Bottomley. These two gentlemen accompanying us are police specialists.'

Doctor Matthew Holt was still clutching his copy of *The Times,* and cigarette ash clung to his waistcoat. Kate, as usual, was wearing her long white pinafore. They stood with the four investigators on the edge of the rear garden at Abbey Lodge, watching the two workmen wheeling their equipment, which included a bag of cement, along the path bordering the lawn.

'Well, Inspector,' said Dr Holt, 'you're welcome to do whatever you like, but everything beyond that cloister door is the property of my neighbour, Mr Skeffington. Won't he object?'

'Mr Skeffington isn't here today, sir. He went off early by train to Coventry, to consult his accountants.' And when he gets there, Jackson mused to himself, he'll find that he's the victim of a hoax, because I'm the one who's sent him off today on a wild goose chase.

'And what about my niece, Jackson? Have you found her yet? It's nearly a fortnight now, since she decided to go off without a word to either of us —'

'Miss Ursula is quite safe where she is, sir,' Jackson replied. 'When all this anxious business is over, she will come back to you unscathed. And now, if you please, we'll get on with the business in hand.'

As Jackson strode across the lawn with the two doctors, Herbert Bottomley drew

Kate aside.

'Miss Holt,' he said, 'when Miss Ursula was a young girl, she went through that cloister door. I know that, because she mentions it in her journal. Did she ever tell you about it?'

'Oh, yes. It was years ago – I don't think she was more than fourteen at the time. She opened the door, and to her embarrassment Mr Skeffington stepped out. He chaffed her a bit for her curiosity, and told her that all kinds of goblins lived behind that door.'

'Thank you, Miss Holt,' said Bottomley gravely. 'That was a little missing piece of the jigsaw. When all this business is over, I'll tell you what it was all about.'

The four investigators watched as the workmen wielded pickaxes in order to demolish the brick wall behind the cloister door. After a few minutes the flimsy construction collapsed of its own accord, sending a cloud of masonry dust out across the lawn. One of the men asserted that the wall could not have been built by a proper time-served tradesman. No, Jackson thought; Skeffington would have done the job himself.

They stepped over the threshold, and found themselves in a dim vestibule, warm and dry, but smelling of staleness and decay.

Bottomley lit a powerful lantern, and immediately they saw a flight of rough stone steps rising to an arch.

'This is what Ursula always saw when she entered her fantasy ballroom,' said Dr Altmann. 'It was gloomy, but unthreatening, so she saw the reality.'

They climbed the steps, and walked hesitantly under the arch. They were conscious of an immense dark cavern ahead of them, and it took a minute or more before their eyes adjusted to the light of the lantern. Jackson struck a match, and put it to the wick of a standard bull's eye reflector.

It was, indeed, a ballroom, but one that had been shut up and deserted for nigh on a hundred years. It was dry, but very cold. Thick festoons of cobwebs hung down from the dimly perceived ceiling. Along the wall to their left they saw an array of tall windows, all glowing a dim red from the foliage covering the outer wall.

Jackson stumbled over something, and saw that it was the deed box of Ursula's dreams. It came as a shock to find that it was still there, unretrieved. He picked it up, rubbed off a thick layer of dust with his sleeve, and read aloud some words written on its lid. 'Deeds to the English Properties of the Lemprière Family, Arranged AD 1850'. His voice echoed eerily from the ceiling of the darkened chamber.

Dr Altmann had commandeered Bottomley to light his way with the lantern. He uttered an excited cry, and pointed to something lying on the floor. It was a rusted iron bar, one end of which lay upon what appeared to be a handkerchief or scarf, heavily stained with a brown discoloration which they all knew to be dried blood. It was this brutal weapon that Ursula had mentally replaced by a substitute, the improbable silver flute with its incongruous red tassel attached.

They moved cautiously across the room. Suddenly, the light of Bottomley's lantern caught the figure of a man, tall and menacing. Unflinching blue eyes stared at them from a black face. His head was crowned with a stained and tattered silk turban. The four men jumped back in alarm, and then Dr Altmann laughed.

'An automaton!' he cried, and his voice rolled and echoed off the walls. 'It's made of iron, and got up to look like a Negro. They were in vogue as a kind of grown-up toy in the last century. There will be clockwork inside, and at the touch of a lever, the eyes will roll, and the limbs will move – though I expect it's all rusted together, now.

I've seen a number of these automata in Vienna.'

'So that was what Miss Ursula saw!' said Jackson. 'She interpreted it as being a servant in livery, and on another occasion as a young man – a guest of some sort. She expected the figure to speak, and so gave it words; but they were garbled words.'

'But the important point is,' said Altmann, 'that this figure proves that Ursula Holt had actually been in this room. Been in it physically, I mean, as a sleepwalker. With her eyes open, she saw all these things, but her sleeping mind interpreted them awry.'

'Yes, she was here,' said Jackson, 'which is, perhaps, why she tried to peep into the place when she was a child, and why, as an adult, she tried to tear the cloister door off its hinges. I'm beginning to think that Ursula penetrated into this place on an earlier occasion, before ever Alexander Skeffington found her on the threshold of the vestibule, and that he had seen her either going in or coming out, one night when she was sleepwalking. That would explain a lot.'

Their eyes had become more accustomed to the dimness, and they advanced now more confidently through the red gloom, past a cluster of chairs and tables, all thick with dust and cobwebs, past the corner of the great chamber, where a few old musical instruments lay abandoned on a dais, until they came to a wooden chest, six feet in length, and constructed of carved oak. Its coffered lid was adorned with carved images of a lion and unicorn upholding a star.

Saul Jackson threw back the lid.

Lying awkwardly and irreverently in the bare interior was the shrunken body of a young man. They could see that he was dressed in the fashion of the 1850s, but the clothes were stained and tattered, and the mummification of the body had twisted and torn them, so that they looked like a parody of vesture. The left hand, shrivelled and brown, protruded from a yellowed shirt cuff, and bore a gold signet ring on the fourth finger. It bore the initials A.S.

'Why did Bolder leave Skeffington's signet ring on his finger?' asked Jackson in a low voice. 'He could have used it to reinforce his deception.'

'He left it there,' Altmann replied, 'because he was afraid to touch the hand of a man whom he had just murdered. There are many deep-seated superstitions attached to the murdered dead.'

Doctor Venner moved forward, at the same time peeling off his gloves, and the others by tacit consent stood aside. Venner quickly examined the remains, his long fingers quietly probing those places that held special significance for him. Finally, he stood back, and carefully pulled his gloves on again.

'This is the body of a young man of thirty,' he said, 'which has been providentially preserved in what is virtually a sealed coffin, for a period of some forty years. The back of his skull has been crushed in with a violent blow or blows from a heavy object. There are signs of a birthmark on the brow. I will be able to tell you more after I have conducted a post-mortem examination, but I can tell you confidently that this young man – Alexander Skeffington, presumably – has been murdered.'

16

A WALK IN THE WOODS

That evening, Sergeant Bottomley sat in the bar parlour of the Goat and Compasses in Charnley, with a measure of gin on the table before him. He was reading a letter, which he had received in the first post that morning.

On Saturday, the twenty-first instant, I followed Alexander Skeffington to London. He visited the premises of an investment bank in Gresham Street, EC. From there, he took a cab to the Strand, where he lunched at Gatti's Café. In the afternoon he went to Marylebone Road, and visited the wax-work exhibition.

On leaving the wax-works he turned into Baker Street, and entered the premises of Curtis & Co., Chemists. When he left, I entered the shop and showed the proprietor my warrant card, upon which he made the poisons book available to me. Mr Skeffington had purchased a lethal quantity of cyanide of potassium. He had given his name as Dr Matthew Holt, of Abbey Lodge, Charnley. Warks.

James Edwards, Detective Constable,
Coventry Police.

Bottomley looked up as Miles, Alexander Skeffington's butler, entered the bar, looking nervous and ill-at-ease. He caught sight of Bottomley, and joined him at his table.

'You wished to see me?' he asked. 'I can't stay long, Mr Bottomley, because I've a lot to do before I serve dinner tonight. How can I help you?'

'I want you to arrange for me to be admitted secretly to Providence House this evening. Once I'm inside, you can forget about me, because you won't see me. Neither will anyone else. Now, before you start thinking up excuses, I want you to read this letter. After you've read it, I'll tell you what I want you to do.'

Bottomley watched the butler grow pale as he read. He's working things out for himself, he thought. It would be silly to talk about taking wasp's nests or rats under the floor. Why should his master buy deadly poison, and that under a false name, if not to make away with someone? Well, he, Bottomley, knew who that 'someone' was. In a few moments Miles, who looked like an intelligent man, would reach the same conclusion.

Alexander Skeffington left Providence House in his coach just as the day's dim light was yielding to the shadows of dusk. Beside him on the seat lay a leather-covered cylinder containing a dusty bottle of Craven's vintage 1880 port. His coachman would take him out the eight miles to the hamlet of Earl's Green, set him down at Miller's Grange, and then return to Charnley. He had told the man that he would stay the night at the grange.

Poor, doomed Ursula! Ten years ago, he had found her crossing the threshold of the closed-up wing of Providence House at the very moment when he was surveying the possibility of bricking up the doorway to the cloister. He had been amused at the young girl's embarrassment, and had made a joke of the matter. But later, he had wondered. . . .

Had Ursula Holt ventured into that place on an earlier occasion, during one of her bouts of sleepwalking? Had she seen what lay in the old wooden chest? He was enormously fond of her – loved her, even – but she was a threat to his security, and he would have to provide for any possible emergency.

The west yet glimmers with some streaks of day. Who was it who had said that? Shakespeare, probably, or Milton. It was almost dark, and he could see the carriage lanterns glowing more brightly now as they travelled along the country roads.

He had begun to watch Ursula Holt, and had, on a number of occasions, seen her walking in her sleep, arms stretched out in front of her, unseeing eyes wide open. From an upper floor of Providence House he had once observed her crossing the garden of Abbey Lodge, where she had stood uncertainly near the fatal cloister door. He had bricked it up himself the week after he had encountered her venturing into the dim vestibule. The entrance from the house he had concealed behind a panel soon after he had disposed of the real Alexander Skeffington in 1855.

One day in April, very early in the morning, he had seen the girl cross the garden in her sleeping trance, and leave the grounds of Abbey Lodge through a wicket gate into the lane. He had been sitting up late that night, and had not retired to bed. He had left Providence House and followed her, watching as she made her way across the cobbled lane and into the plantation. She had stumbled, and cried out in distress, and he had rushed to her assistance, only to find that she was still asleep.

He had gathered her up in his arms and walked with her through the trees, thinking to set her down in a safer, more open part of the woods. The sun, he remembered, was rising, and the glades were bathed in its silver light.

And then he had heard barking, and from his point of vantage beside a great oak tree, he had seen a young man belabouring a snarling dog. At the same time, Ursula had slipped from his arms, and had run out from the trees. By then, the young man had knocked the dog unconscious, and when he saw the wraithlike figure of Ursula gliding towards him, he had fled. It was at that moment that the means of deliverance from poor Ursula's threat, and the threat of a visit from Elijah Robinson, had come to him.

There had been a spate of mutilations in the fields around Charnley, and Skeffington had purloined some scalpels from his neighbour's consulting-room with a view to secreting them among Ursula's possessions. It was a vague plan at the best, and its intention was to ensure that the girl was found guilty but insane. There had been similar cases in the county over the years, and the sentence was inevitably from three to six months' incarceration in an asylum.

Any future killings, especially if they involved the use of scalpels, would be laid at Ursula's door, and if she were found guilty, then she would be returned to an asylum. That, perhaps, would happen when he had sent Elijah Robinson to his Maker. English law did not hang madwomen.

When the young man had fled, Ursula had sunk down beside the old wishing well, still asleep, but with her eyes wide open. Skeffington had removed a suitable scalpel from his pocket, and had slit the unconscious dog's throat. He had placed the bloody knife carefully in Ursula's hand, smeared her dress with blood, and then heaved the carcass of the dead dog down the well. As he had retreated into the woods, he had fancied that someone else was stirring among the trees. He had been enormously relieved to reach the security of Providence House unobserved.

It had seemed to him that no sooner had he crossed the threshold when Matthew Holt and Kate had come hammering at the door to tell him that Ursula was missing in the woods. He'd sent his two footmen to help in the search, but had not had the courage to accompany them. . . .

The coach slowed down to cross a narrow bridge, and Skeffington could hear the raging of a torrent of water falling over a weir. It was at this spot, he recalled, that the River Best narrowed, and fell some fifteen feet to its new channel below the cliff-like drop of great stones and boulders known as Haughton Weir. In another five minutes they would be in Earl's Green.

Everything would be well. Late on the previous evening, he had brought the bottle of port unobserved from the cellar. He had opened it, poured out some of its contents, and introduced a quantity of deadly and quick-acting poison, taking the precaution of winding a scarf around his mouth and nose to guard himself against the lethal fumes. He had been alone in the kitchen, and for a moment he had felt that he was being watched, that somebody not only saw him in the act, but knew what the act signified. Of course, there had been nobody there. He had kept the bottle, secure in its leather cylinder, in his study until that night. It was not a thing to be seen by the over-curious.

After tonight's dinner at Miller's Grange, Ursula would drink a glass of port, and die within seconds. She would feel nothing, and suffer nothing. He had always felt a tender regard for her. He could not bear to see her suffer. She had been destined, so it seemed, to be a sacrifice to the happiness of others, a consecrated soul. This day, Tuesday, 24 October, would be the day of his deliverance from fear.

Here they were, at the gates of Miller's Grange.

Skeffington entered the house through the vegetable garden, and knocked at the kitchen door. It was opened immediately by Susan Partridge, who was wiping her hands on a towel. He saw her glance at the cylinder containing the bottle of port. Her glance, he thought, bore no sinister meaning: he had written to tell her that he was bringing a special vintage with him to accompany his dinner with Ursula that evening. The kitchen was cheerfully lit with lamps and candles, and various savoury smells rose from the glowing range.

'How are you, Susan?' he asked. 'Is everything ready for dinner at seven?'

'It is indeed, sir. Miss Ursula is already in the dining-room. There's oxtail soup, roast saddle of lamb, fruit pie, and a jug of cream. The coffee's percolating nicely.'

Was there something odd about the woman's tone? A hint of nervous fear behind her cheerful words? Nonsense. He was imagining things.

'Excellent! Now, as I said to you in my note, I want you to serve the meal to us, and when it's done, bring in the coffee. You can go home, then, and clear things up in the morning. I've brought a special bottle of Craven's port – the 1880, you know. Put it out on a tray, will you, with two glasses. I'll come in to open that myself after we've had coffee at the table.'

He removed his overcoat and hat, and hung them on a stand beside the kitchen dresser. No doubt he would cut a more reassuring figure to Susan now that she saw him in evening dress. He felt in the inner pocket of his dress coat, and produced a small envelope.

'There you are, Susan,' he said, smiling. 'That's a little something extra for your trouble tonight. I'll go through now to the dining-room.'

It had proved to be a splendid dinner. Skeffington sipped his coffee, and then sat back in his chair. The old room had taken on a magical quality in the candlelight, and the fine china and silver had enhanced his gourmet's satisfaction with the food. Susan Partridge had always been a superb plain cook.

'So, when would you like to return to Abbey Lodge, Ursula?' he asked, watching her. She had been silent and thoughtful for most of the meal, occasionally glancing at him as he spoke, but giving most of her attention to the various courses of the meal as they were set before her.

'Next Monday, I think, Mr Skeffington,' she replied. 'I'll write to Uncle Matthew tomorrow, telling him where I am, and apologizing for causing him any anxiety. I'll send a line to Kate, too.'

'Very good. And you do realize, don't you, that you were totally innocent of all those charges? The police, I believe, have found the real culprit, and will soon arrest him. You did no harm to those animals. You had nothing to do with the deaths of those two young men. You were, in effect, wrongfully incarcerated in that asylum. When the time is right, I intend to move against those who were responsible for your predicament. I want you to go to your . . . your bed totally convinced of your own innocence.'

His eyes filled with tears. It was he who had driven this girl to the brink of madness. All he could do for her was to convince her of her own innocence, so that she could go to her grave in peace.

'An excellent meal,' he said, and stood up. 'I'm going now to fetch a very special bottle of port that I brought here tonight for the express intention of drinking a toast to your future!'

'You are very kind,' Ursula replied, and he sensed her watching him as he walked slowly from the room.

He threw open the kitchen door, and staggered on the threshold. Guy Fitzgerald sat at the long scrubbed table, the bottle of wine on the tray in front of him. The wine bottle had been opened, and Fitzgerald had poured out two glasses. Lying across the table, both accusing and menacing, was a single-bore shotgun.

'Fitzgerald! What are you doing here? What — ?'

'Good evening, Mr Skeffington,' said Guy. His right hand lay loosely across the trigger guard of the gun. He smiled pleasantly enough, picked up one of the glasses of wine, and slid it along the table-top.

'I was just passing – I'm a neighbour, as you know – and thought I'd call in to pass the time of night to Mrs Partridge. Alas! She wasn't here, so I've poured out a glass of wine for us both to drink a toast. To the health of Miss Ursula Holt!'

Skeffington looked at the young man. Behind every pleasant word he sensed an implacable nemesis lurking. What was he to do? Pretend to drink the toast, and see if his tormentor drank his glass first? He stretched out his hand across the table, but it trembled so violently that he failed to grasp the stem of the glass.

Guy sprang up from his chair, upsetting his own glass of wine in the process. His right hand seized the breech of the shotgun, and Skeffington saw his finger settle on the trigger.

'Drink it!' There was a taunting challenge in the young man's voice that chilled Skeffington to the marrow. 'Ursula Holt will not lie tonight in the grave that you have dug for her!'

Skeffington fled from the kitchen, and blundered into the dining-room. Ursula had gone. Then he heard heavy footsteps in the passage on the far side of the room, and Inspector Jackson entered. He was holding some kind of document in his hand.

'James Bolder —'

Skeffington ran back into the kitchen. There was no sign there now of Fitzgerald or his cursed gun. The wine bottle and glasses, too, had gone. He heard the clatter of Jackson's boots in the passage, and fled from the house into the darkness. Before the thick woods that almost encroached upon the demesne to the north had swallowed Skeffington up, Sergeant Bottomley, lying in wait in the grounds, had glimpsed his retreating figure, and had set off after him in relentless pursuit.

Alexander Skeffington walked along a woodland path, the foliage yielding before him. Was it still night, or had dawn broken? He could not tell. Presently, he came into a clearing, where a man was sitting on a log beside a dying camp-fire. Should he approach the man?

The man turned round and looked at him. His eyes held angry reproach. His throat gaped open beneath his chin, and his chest was soaked in blood.

'You shouldn't have done it, Jim Bolder,' said Elijah Robinson, and then turned back slowly to the fire.

Skeffington woke with a start. He was cramped and cold. How long had he slept there, hidden from searching eyes in the long grass? Odd, that he should dream about Elijah Robinson. . . . But then, all that blood in the churchyard grass had been rather unnerving. He'd used Ursula's long gloves to protect his sleeves from the splashing blood, and had later put them back in her chest of drawers. It had always been easy to come and go at Abbey Lodge.

He hauled himself to his feet, and staggered forward through the wood. He must have been asleep for hours, because the sun was certainly rising now. He'd make his way on foot to one or other of the main roads, and catch a lift into a town – any town would do. In a town, there were ways for a very rich man to make his escape.

Someone was coming! He flung himself to the ground and watched as a man emerged from the trees and looked about him. His face was blackened and bruised, but his eyes were keen and sharp. It was Paul Staunton, somehow risen from where he had flung him on the railway line at Ashborne Hill. Why were they all coming alive?

Providence had decreed that he should have been passing Halford's works when Staunton, looking pale and agitated, had hurried across the road to him. One of Halford's hands, he'd said, had seen something sinister in the churchyard – a man donning a woman's long, white gloves. Staunton had been another young man who was beginning to know too much. He had gone the way of Elijah Robinson.

He shook himself angrily, and when he looked across from where he lay, he saw that there was nobody there. So he was starting to see things. So be it. That was part of his burden. He made his way steadily north for a few hundred yards, and then stopped as he heard a sudden movement in the trees. Who would it be now? The real Alexander Skeffington, perhaps, risen from his oak chest at Providence House to reproach him?

He recalled his brief struggle with the real Skeffington a lifetime ago, a struggle to gain possession of the Lemprière deed box, and the sudden blind and jealous rage that had overwhelmed him. He had battered Skeffington to death, and used the old ballroom as his tomb.

Sergeant Bottomley emerged from the trees. This was no phantom, but the real man. Skeffington turned and fled, before the words, 'James Bolder, I arrest you for the murder of Elijah Robinson' could reach his pounding ears.

At length, as day had fully come, he heard the roaring of waters, and came out beside the bridge at Haughton Weir. A precarious progress across the wet stones near the foaming torrent would bring him safe on to the road. He stepped gingerly into the swirling margin of the River Best.

'James Bolder! I arrest you for the murder of Elijah Robinson!'

He glanced up in fear, and saw Jackson and Bottomley standing together on the opposite bank. At the same time, he heard the crashing of boots in the trees behind him, and the snarling of unleashed dogs. He shook his fist in impotent rage at the two policemen, lost his footing on the slippery stones, and fell headlong, shrieking, into the foaming waters of the weir.

'You were both very brave,' said Herbert Bottomley, 'you, Miss Ursula, for enduring that terrifying dinner with the man who'd come to murder you, and you, Mr Guy, for being prepared to confront him. As you see, our little plan was successful.'

'I'd have tackled him myself in the kitchen,' said Guy stoutly, 'if you'd have let me do so.'

'No, sir,' Bottomley replied. 'That's work for the police. By leaving the outer door open, Skeffington was lured away from yourself and Miss Ursula.'

'And there was cyanide in that wine?' asked Kate incredulously.

'There was, miss. I saw him pour it into the bottle myself. I was concealed in a little scullery leading off the kitchen at Providence House. He was afraid, you see, that Miss Ursula would suddenly recall with complete certainty what she had seen in that closed-up ballroom.'

'The dead body of the real Alexander Skeffington,' said Ursula faintly. 'That dream *was* becoming more distinct, you know. And so he decided to murder me. . . .'

Bottomley, Ursula and Guy, together with Kate Holt, were sitting in the old Tudor parlour of Miller's Grange on the morning after Skeffington's failed attempt at murder.

'Yes, he decided to murder you,' said Bottomley, 'and that's why, Miss Ursula, you must believe that you were, all along, completely innocent of any kind of wrongdoing. I tracked down the poor, mentally afflicted young man who mutilated those animals, and he's to be admitted to the County Lunatic Asylum at Coventry. As for Ben the sheepdog – well, I'm as certain as I ever can be that it was Bolder who cut his throat. He was very good at throats.'

'And my sleepwalking —'

'Your sleepwalking, miss, was used as a weapon against you by a man who valued his wealth and position more than your life or sanity.'

'I still can't believe it,' Ursula replied. 'He was always so kind to me, so attentive. . . .

He would protest my innocence to my face, with tears standing in his eyes. And yet —'

'People can be very complex, Miss Ursula. I've no doubt that he *did* like you, and had he remained an honest man with a small but decent income, I expect he would have shown more of that kindness. But Jim Bolder chose the way of murder, and had to live with the consequences.'

'Did he escape?' asked Guy. 'Or have we seen the last of him?'

'I don't think he escaped, Mr Guy,' Bottomley replied. 'He'll be somewhere in the River Best, and very soon, the river will cast him out. It's a bad end to a bad man.'

'Oh, can't we all forget him?' cried Kate vehemently. 'Are we to spend the rest of our lives talking about him and his wickedness? Poor Father was too shocked to come out here today. "I can't believe it, I can't believe it". That's all he said. I expect he'll be saying it until Kingdom come!'

Herbert Bottomley looked round the light, homely old room. You could do something with this old tumbledown grange if you wanted to, he thought.

'Mr Guy,' he said, 'I hope you'll persist in your determination to buy this old place. It's got a feeling to it – a good feeling. All Bolder's ill-gotten wealth and property will be administered by the Crown until any living heirs of the real Alexander Skeffington are found. I don't think you'll have any difficulty in purchasing Miller's Grange.' He added, glancing slyly at Guy and Ursula, 'It would make a fine family house.'

Ursula blushed, glanced briefly at Guy, and rose from her chair.

'Come, Mr Bottomley,' she said, 'let us take a little walk in the garden. There are some things that I want to talk to you about. I'm sure that Kate will want to ask Mr Fitzgerald a lot of questions about last night's adventure.'

It was a warm day for late October, and they walked slowly around the wild garden, glancing from time to time at the twisted old house that had waited patiently for decades for someone to rescue it from impending ruin.

'I love it here, Mr Bottomley,' said Ursula. 'I'm not bothered that Mr Skeffington chose to hold his horrible funeral dinner here, and had prepared a grave for me in the chapel ruins. I love this house, and would like to bring it back from decay to life. Maybe Guy feels the same.'

Bottomley stopped abruptly, and took Ursula's hand in his.

'Miss Ursula,' he said, 'I think that this

old country grange has been waiting for you for a very long time. You'll thrive here, if you determine to stay, and I think you'll find that Mr Guy will welcome that. I've seen the way he looks at you – and for that matter, I've seen the way you look at *him!*'

Ursula did not blush this time. Instead, she looked happily into Bottomley's eyes, and treated him to a brilliant smile. It seemed to him that all the anxieties and agonies of the last year were expunged in that sign of joy.

'But what about Abbey Lodge?' she asked. 'I spent so many happy years there.'

'Abbey Lodge became your prison, Miss Ursula. It contains too many painful memories for you, and if you'll take my advice, you'll go back there only to visit your uncle and Miss Kate. Get away from those two places, Abbey Lodge and its neighbour, Providence House, because if you don't, they'll stifle you.'

'I'll go and stay for a while with my friend Catherine in London,' said Ursula, half to herself. 'Maybe the two of us could visit Alderley Hall, and relive some of our girlish adventures. And then, if Guy really does want to marry me, we'll come here together, to Miller's Grange, and I'll learn to live all over again!'

Ursula suddenly threw her arms round Bottomley's neck, and kissed him on the cheek.

'You've been wonderful, Mr Bottomley, and I'll never forget you. You believed in me even when you saw me trying to bury those terrible gloves. Perhaps we'll meet again here, at Miller's Grange, and if we do, you'll be more than welcome.'

As Bottomley stepped out on to the public road a few minutes later, he saw Kate Holt emerge from the house and run across to her cousin. She linked her arm in Ursula's, and together the two girls walked back to the house.

Unless I'm very much mistaken, thought Bottomley, Miss Kate will stay with her old father. She's an intelligent and industrious young lady, and I shouldn't wonder if she goes on to be a successful novelist. Then, perhaps, she'll throw that pinny away, and realize that she's got a life of her own to live. Good luck to them both!

The Reverend Harry Goodheart, standing at the altar rail of St Lawrence's church in Ashgate, looked past the couple standing in front of him, and addressed the congregation.

'Forasmuch as Saul and Sarah have consented together in holy wedlock, and have witnessed the same before God and this company, and thereto have given and pledged their troth either to other, and have declared the same by giving and receiving of a ring, and by joining of hands; I pronounce that they be man and wife together. . . .'

Moments later, bride and groom were walking down the aisle, their progress accompanied by a cheerful outburst of martial music from the parish band in the gallery. Saul Jackson, stiff and stately in his best uniform, felt the pressure of his new wife's hand on his arm, but etiquette forbade him to look directly at the graceful figure in white dress and veil, walking at his side along the road to the new life that they had chosen together. His best man, Sergeant Bottomley, looked intensely miserable in uniform, despite being able to show off the splendour of his silver-embroidered sergeant's stripes.

Jackson glanced surreptitiously at the folk assembled in the pews. There was Superintendent Mays, wearing a civilian suit, and resembling more then ever a distinguished surgeon or physician. There was Dr Ambrose Phillips, and Mr and Mrs Dovercourt – how very kind of them to come! And – Dr

Venner, clad from head to foot in elegant pearl grey. The last time he'd seen Dr Venner in a church, he'd been dissecting an ancient corpse in the vestry.

Today was the feast of St Simon and St Jude. It was also a Saturday. How did the old rhyme run? *Monday for wealth, Tuesday for health, Wednesday the best day of all: Thursday for losses, Friday for crosses, Saturday for no luck at all.* Oh, well. . . .

They emerged from the church into the bright October day, to be met by a shower of rice and wheat-grains. Then they walked down a wide flight of steps to the parish hall, fashioned long ago from the parish tithe barn. A fine wedding breakfast awaited them, and a modest iced cake, which, in due course, they cut together. Herbert Bottomley made a curiously dignified speech, and followed this with an old Warwickshire wedding anthem, which he sang in his fine tenor voice, accompanied by the ubiquitous parish band.

After the anthem, the wedding couple and their guests gave themselves up to celebration, and as the wine and cider in the flagons diminished, so the conversations increased in volume. Saul Jackson and Sarah Jackson now had time to inspect the table, laden with presents, that stood beside the door. A box of table linen from Ellen, Sarah's sister, who was matron of honour; a Crown Derby tea set from Mr and Mrs Romanis of Copton Vale; a merrily ticking little silver clock from Harry Goodheart; a carving set from Mr Mays.

And what was this? A little parcel, done up in brown paper and tied with postman's string – 'For Mr Bottomley, with Love from Annie Jevons'. Brave little Annie – what a part she'd played in the business of the Dried-Up Man! Jackson beckoned to his sergeant, who came across to the table, and obligingly opened the parcel. It contained a quarter-pint bottle of Sherman's Gladiator Gin.

Just as Mr and Mrs Jackson were thinking of slipping quietly away to where Harry Goodheart's carriage was waiting for them, a uniformed constable came into the room rather bashfully. He removed his helmet, and then approached Jackson at the table.

'Very sorry, sir,' he whispered, 'but this came through from Charnley ten minutes ago. Most urgent, it says.'

Jackson glanced at Sarah, and made a wry face. This telegraph message could be an immediate summons to duty. Sarah smiled at him, and urged him to read the message.

Dead body of Jim Bolder, alias Alexander Skeffington, recovered from River Best at Yarnton Flats. George Potter, Sergeant.

'What is it, Saul?' Sarah asked.

'Nothing that won't keep, Mrs Jackson.' said Jackson.

In the early evening of their wedding day, before the declining sun had started to gild the tops of the great elm trees with faded gold, Saul and Sarah Jackson pushed open a wicket gate, and entered the quiet, closed graveyard of the hamlet of Coldeaton. Together they walked through the dew-soaked grass until they came to a modest headstone marking a grave upon which a faded swathe of spring flowers, placed there on the previous April, still lay.

This was the resting-place of Charlotte Anne Jackson, aged 29, and of her daughter Rebecca, aged two years and three months, both of whom had perished in a house fire on Thursday, 5 April, 1877.

Sarah Jackson, formerly Sarah Brown, stooped down, and placed her bridal bouquet upon her predecessor's grave.

ABOUT THE AUTHOR

Norman Russell was born in Lancashire but has lived most of his life in Liverpool. After graduating from Jesus College, Oxford, he served a term in the army and was later awarded the degree of Doctor of Philosophy. He now writes full time.

We hope you have enjoyed this Large Print book. Other Thorndike, Wheeler, and Chivers Press Large Print books are available at your library or directly from the publishers.

For information about current and upcoming titles, please call or write, without obligation, to:

Publisher
Thorndike Press
295 Kennedy Memorial Drive
Waterville, ME 04901
Tel. (800) 223-1244

or visit our Web site at:

www.gale.com/thorndike
www.gale.com/wheeler

OR

Chivers Large Print
published by BBC Audiobooks Ltd
St James House, The Square
Lower Bristol Road
Bath BA2 3SB
England
Tel. +44(0) 800 136919
email: bbcaudiobooks@bbc.co.uk
www.bbcaudiobooks.co.uk

All our Large Print titles are designed for easy reading, and all our books are made to last.